By mid-afte
manicure-pedicu
wrapped in pink a
in the jacuzzi, eye
"Why don't y
before your facial'

"Um, sure." Rebecca walked to the edge, remembered she was naked under her pink robe, and hoped the turban and sunglasses made her unrecognizable.

Tom looked up. "Rebecca, it's nice to see you again."

She nodded and tightened the belt of her robe. Poking one toe into the bubbling whirlpool, she said, "I think it's too warm."

"Sit for a minute. I wanted to ask if you are planning to come to my seminar."

"Do you think I'd like that kind of thing?" She sat down on the rim and slipped her feet into the bubbles, snugging the robe around her thighs.

"Maybe spirits are waiting to talk with you. I take messages." He grinned, shaded his eyes, and squinted. "Or, if you prefer, you could just watch."

She smiled. Tom was charming in a boyish way and she was beginning to forget that weird episode at the river. "George, my hotel concierge, said I need to do some very Sedona things. Would it be a very Sedona thing to do?"

"Absolutely. Very Sedona! Then, you'll come?"

"I'll think about it." The voice inside told her, *Say yes.*

"Please."

While he talked to her and kept eye contact, he moved around the circumference of the jacuzzi and now stood looking up at her. She looked down into the bubbling water. He wore no bathing suit. Now, she was really getting warm. Her sunglasses slid down her nose. She poked them back. Little Rebecca said, *Go ahead and look. Nothing we haven't seen before.*

# Romancing Rebecca

## by

## Amber Polo

Romancing Rebecca

Cover Art by *Tamra Westberry*

The Wild Rose Press
PO Box 708
Adams Basin, NY 14410-0706
Visit us at www.thewildrosepress.com

Publishing History
First Faery Rose Edition, 2007
Print ISBN 1-60154-126-0


Published in the United States of America

## Dedication

For Julie, who didn't laugh when I told her I was writing a romance novel and did when she read it.

Chapter 1

Rebecca turned the rental car off Interstate 17 and after fifteen miles saw the outline of Bell Rock: big, red, and bell-shaped, exactly as pictured in the glossy travel brochure. Unexpectedly her blood pumped in the same way it did every time she signed a celebrity client or won a big case.

Loud and clear, a voice in her head said, *He is close now.*

Rebecca didn't usually hear voices. Other people talked about paying attention to their consciences. One ex-shrink told her to get in touch with her inner child. Her mother reminded her to listen to her heart. She didn't have time. Activity and hard work quieted the voices in her head.

In a quirky vacation mood, she asked aloud, "Who?"

The reply popped into her mind just like an answer from someone in the back seat, *The one we have waited for.*

Rebecca laughed. She was talking to herself and getting answers! She turned on the radio and played with the stations, ignoring the lingering memory of that voice she hadn't heard since her twelfth birthday. The voice she had treated like an imaginary friend and had called Little Rebecca.

Rebecca followed the signs from Highway 179 past shops and condos, turned right on a gravel road, almost missed the arrow pointing to Rouge Mountain Hotel Registration, and with a squeal, braked and slid into the

Amber Polo

back end of a white van parked at the hotel entrance.

An auto accident had kicked off her first vacation since law school. Her palms slapped the steering wheel of the black Cherokee rental and she looked up through the windshield at the word "Beloved" in gold script painted across the back of the van.

She knew the drill. Call the police. Find the owner. Then came the yelling, screaming, and swearing. She fumbled in her bag for a cell phone and looked towards the cactus-flanked lobby entrance. Tree-shaded adobe-style cottages were spread out just like the brochure described. Every building she'd seen in this town was square and painted rusty red.

A tall man in white pajamas and a teenager in a baggy green jacket approached. She noted two potential witnesses.

Maybe she'd driven into a *Lord of the Rings* movie set by mistake. From what she'd seen so far, Sedona, Arizona had too many crystal shops to be a cowboy town or mountain biker paradise.

The closer the man in white came, the better he looked: tall, athletic build, smooth confident walk. She rolled down her window. Good, he was smiling. "Your van?" she asked. His nod confirmed he owned the Beloved-mobile. Whatever did he deliver?

A New Yorker would have already turned the air black with blue language. But the guy with the great smile didn't seem at all upset. He pushed back a clump of sandy blonde hair and focused his deep blue eyes on her.

She stepped from the air-conditioned vehicle into desert air the approximate temperature of a pizza oven. One stiletto heel sank into the crushed stone drive. Her body twisted, Armani sunglasses popped off, and she toppled drunkenly toward him.

He caught her and held on. The voice in her head sighed, *Oh yes.*

She'd get her balance in a minute. In the meantime, her cheek rested against his white silk shirt inches from a heavy gold medallion hanging in the middle of his chest, and ignored the edge that cut into her cheek. Despite the temperature, his body heat felt very, very good.

She inhaled the scent of cinnamon. "I just needed to

catch my breath." That smell, or the jolt of the impact, must have made her a little dizzy. "I'm sorry," she said, indicating his Beloved van.

"No problem." He steadied her, still holding her arm.

She pulled back. She knew that as he bent to retrieve her glasses, he was checking out her completely impractical shoes, black stockings, and shiny black skirt that stopped high above her knees. He probably noticed she wore no camisole beneath the fashionable suit jacket. Confident she looked good despite six hours on an airplane and a two-hour drive from Phoenix, her ringless left hand smoothed her severe black chignon.

When his inspection reached her face, their eyes locked.

The gawky kid, whose green elf jacket identified him as a hotel employee, examined the front of her vehicle and the back of the van. "Like, no damage, sir," he said, self-consciously pulling at the ring that pierced his left eyebrow. "Just some black paint on your bumper. Shall I call the police, Mr. Paxton?"

"Of course not. Thanks, Josch."

Josch moved Rebecca's well-traveled, black leather luggage from the SUV onto a wheeled cart. She automatically snapped, "Don't be so rough," and grabbed the computer case and briefcase to carry herself.

She turned back to the man in white. His shirt's loose sleeves billowed like a poet's. With the matching drawstring jogging pants, he looked like a role player in a Renaissance festival. "Thanks for overlooking the accident." She automatically handed him her business card. She considered offering to pay the dry cleaning charges to have her mascara removed from his pajamas. "Mr. Pax—"

"—Tom." He shook his head. "This was no accident."

His eyes held hers until she turned. She walked towards the lobby, absolutely sure he was watching her. The voice in her head said, *Oh yes, he is watching.*

An hour later Rebecca twisted open her liter bottle of Purely Sedona Artesian Spring Water, leaned toward the man sitting slumped against the tree trunk, and emptied the entire contents over his tousled blonde head. Water soaked his hair, cascaded over his face, and dripped down his white nylon tank top. His eyes opened. He did not move, but kept speaking, "Beloved Beloveds. I come to tell you how to find peace. Listen..."

She wished he'd stop talking in that scary monotone.

"Embrace life. Love one another," he droned. His blue eyes stared straight ahead and made the gorgeous man she'd met in front of the hotel look dull and—well—crazy. He'd seemed interested and interesting. On the way to her room she saw him again. Dressed for a run, his white running shorts left little to the imagination. He appeared to be the kind of guy who could make her Sedona vacation very interesting.

Hoping to meet him again, Rebecca hurried to her cottage, changed into running gear, and jogged down to the river. She found him. Leaning against a tall sycamore, babbling and definitely out to lunch, he looked more like a homeless loony than a prospective dinner date.

She leaned over and lightly slapped his face. "Tom..." No response. "Tom..." She slapped harder. Nothing. She smelled cinnamon again, sharp and strong like Wild Oats organic bulk spices, not like the kind that came in little Safeway jars.

Looking around for help—other guests, hotel staff, anyone—she called out, "Help! Down here!" The path couldn't have been more than fifty feet from the hotel lobby, but she was afraid if she left him, he'd stumble into the river, hit his head on a rock, and drown.

She picked up three sheets of wet paper from the muddy spill left by her expensive bottled water and spread them on a rock to dry.

His left hand reached toward her. She pulled away and unzipped her cell phone from her fanny pack. She punched 911 while he continued his gibberish, "Beloved. Listen to the future. I have the knowledge you seek..."

"Right. Just hold on," she told him. "Who made me Florence-what's-her-name?" She looked into his eyes and used what she hoped was a convincing tone, "Help...will...be...here...soon." He seemed physically OK, but in her opinion no one was home.

She gave the 911 operator the facts, "Rouge Mountain. It's a resort. 'Lush French ambiance in a desert oasis,'" she quoted the brochure. "You know it?"

She laughed. "Are you sure you're all right?"

"Just exhausted and hungry. I won't be good company 'til I get some rest. And...more water." He grinned. "See you later," he added hopefully and turned to walk up the path.

She watched the back of his white shorts, now covered with red dirt, until he was out of sight. She'd forgotten to return those muddy papers. She picked them up, saw they were an e-mail, and let curiosity overcome good sense. She read the message.

****

*From: ARIREBPaxton@STXEN.edu*
*To: TomPaxton@Beloved.com*
*Subject: First Entry*
*January 1, 1863*
*London.*

*(Illegible text) At usual parties, tea or sherry and a bit of something is served. Instead, we were directly ushered into the drawing room. Drapes were drawn and only one candle on the round table illuminated the eight chairs shadowed against brocade walls.*

*Let me say, I did most surely not want to come and did so only to please Uncle who wants me to get out with people my own age, which means he desires to find a suitable husband for dreadfully old, unwanted me.*

*At the table farthest from the entrance sat a pale young woman about my age wearing a black velvet dress, even more out of date than my conservative outfit. She did not smile nor acknowledge any of the party. Besides myself, there were three ladies and three gentlemen, and a rotund man who seemed to be in charge of the entertainment. He nodded for us to sit and as we settled ourselves the candle flickered. I almost giggled at the solemnity.*

****

Rebecca stopped, feeling a little guilty reading someone's e-mail. After all, there were laws. She decided to take the pages directly to the front desk and would have, but that niggling voice told her to keep reading.

This time she listened and read on.

****

>*The man began a sing-song mumbling to the girl. I was thinking it was all very silly. I do not believe in these things. When a loud gurgle issued forth from the young woman's throat, her head was pulled back as if by some unseen force. Her body shuddered, rose from the chair, then slumped forward. (Illegible text) When she lifted her head I would not have recognized her as the placid child of a few moments ago. Her skin was dark, her face quite lopsided. When she spoke from the side of her mouth, an extended Adam's apple moved up and down like a monkey on a stick.*

>*But her words shocked me even more than her appearance, when a low raspy voice croaked, "Rebecca, ey, ey, so you've come to see your old nursemaid. (Illegible text) I saw your parents die, I did. And cared for you until I, too, left this earth."*

>*I stood, mouth open while she continued. "I warn you. Your mother fears the dark man will harm you (Illegible text). Beware (Illegible text)."*

>*I ran from the room. (End of First Entry)*

>*So, dear brother, this is the first entry in the diary. I'll send further installments. The transcribing is slow going, wedged in between my other research and teaching commitments. The diary is in awful condition and the early entries almost illegible. More later.*

>*Love from your favorite sister,*

>*A*

****

No longer interested in exercise, Rebecca headed back up the path. The diary's writing style reminded her of second-rate historical romances by authors she'd rejected as clients. The temperature must have been ninety in the sun as she walked along the path back to her cottage, but the words in that e-mail brought goosebumps to her arms. These few paragraphs chilled her more than any novel she could remember. She waved the second page, which had soaked up more of the red mud. When it was dry, she'd leave them both at the front desk for the puzzling Mr. Paxton, regardless of what the voice in her opined.

****

Tom was sorry to leave the woman with the large chestnut eyes and delightful wide mouth, but he was too exhausted to talk. He couldn't have made a great impression babbling against that tree. Had he drooled?

He remembered her long legs sliding out of the black SUV as if it were a limo and discovering that the eyes behind those dark glasses were as enchanting as the rest of her.

She was so intense and shaken by a silly little bump, he knew before he read her business card that she was a New York lawyer. New Yorkers got upset about everything. Despite that protective black power suit and the aggressive attitude he disliked in women, he felt pulled toward her luminous personal energy. He was the expert on essential energy and this woman's essence fascinated and attracted him. He recognized that she was good and beautiful inside, despite the fact that her lacquered hairstyle reminded him of Princess Leia from *Star Wars*.

Seeing her in short running shorts and a skimpy top made it hard to concentrate on the inner woman. He imagined a little food and vacation relaxation would soften her thin, intense edge. She arrived with a lot of luggage, so she must be planning a long stay. Maybe the Sedona workshops wouldn't be so bad after all.

If only he could learn to control these trances.

Chapter 2

Rebecca snuggled back against the goose-down pillows to plan her vacation schedule. Her authentic French four-poster bed in her near-authentic French cottage was as elegant as the brochure promised.

Her cell phone rang and the LED screen identified super-efficient Heather—as if she'd ever tell her that. She flipped open the phone and without a greeting demanded, "Why are you calling me?" She had vowed this would be a real vacation. Angry that her mind was back on work, Rebecca took out her impatience on Heather.

She slid off the bed and hopped into the cottage living room. "This better be an emergency." One hand held the phone to her ear as the other wrestled the running shoes and socks off her sweaty feet.

Heather, as usual, ignored her boss's tone. "You know you're a workaholic. I'm doing the best I can here without you. I got the temp fired."

Rebecca waited for an explanation, but the phone stayed silent. Heather could be difficult. "That cute girl from Wellesley?"

"That cute girl from Wellesley's sister is president of Babs Hemingway's *Babs Brigade* fan club."

"Did she do much damage?" Rebecca held her breath. Fans infiltrating their favorite celeb's lawyer's office could be *beaucoup* trouble. No wonder Heather called them the fan-atics. They craved personal information. What kind of people wanted to know the name of their favorite author's orthodontist?

"I controlled that. But the serious problem is that Babs found out you're on vacation in Sedona at Rouge Mountain."

"So..."

"She wants to talk to you personally—immediately. Her latest book *Sweet Stacy* is—"

"Doing very well. I skimmed it on the plane. It's a rehash of *Sweet Sue,* not a sequel. If you tell anyone I said that, you're fired."

"The book's fine, but the audio version is defective. Factory error. A half million CDs and MP3 downloads have ten minutes of Cora Ayne's *Love Under the Banana Tree* mixed into Chapter 2."

Rebecca snickered. "You sure?" She walked to the cottage window, unaware of the vibrant red mountains, perfect green trees, and cloudless blue sky.

"I ran down to B & N and bought a copy. It's the funniest. Listen—" Rebecca heard Heather press the play button on her CD player. "...sweet Stacy patted Craig's cheek. No, no. I could never kiss you in front of my babies. Not until we are married...sure, babe, oral sex in the phone booth on Main Street is just..."

When Heather heard Rebecca gasp she turned it off. "You get the idea. The two books flip back and forth. I laughed so hard my Walkman flew out the office door and landed on the cappuccino cart."

"Funny, yes, but...oh, my God!" Rebecca's voice dropped to a whisper. "Babs is getting out of a limo with four kids and her nanny—at my hotel. They're all wearing Disneyland shirts and carrying huge mouse dolls. How did she get here so fast?"

"She was in L.A. when she got the news."

Rebecca dropped to her hands and knees, crouched beneath the window, and whispered into the phone, "Where do all those kids come from?"

"Rumor is that after one of her books becomes a bestseller the 'queen of secret baby plots' adopts another child and writes the next book about that kid."

Reaching up, Rebecca grasped the cord to close the draperies and pulled. In response to her too-sharp jerk, the curtain rod, drapes, authentic French dust, and tangled cords collapsed on top of her.

"Oh, and R.J.," Heather cooed. "Your mother stopped by."

Rebecca cringed, imaging Charlotte Dumaurier sweeping through Bankhead Blanding's stuffy office in fluttering pink ruffles and a garden party hat as big as a tourista's sombrero.

"She said to remind you of your siblings' birthday—the twins. Gee R.J., I didn't know your sister and brother were named Scarlet and Heathcliff?" Silence. "Rebecca Jane, are you there?"

Beneath the drapes Rebecca whispered, "No," and ended the call. She immediately called Babs' publisher and threatened to sue if all copies of the audio formats were not recalled and accounted for—regardless of cost—and then destroyed. When the publisher asked if she were calling from a broom closet, she clinically described what she would do if he allowed any hint of this manufacturing fiasco to get out to the press.

Suffocating, she crawled from under the drapes and poked her head up until her eyes peeked over the sill. No Babs. No children or nanny. She took a breath. The room phone rang. She unplugged it.

She had to lay low. Hiding from Babs was the only way to preserve her vacation. Using her cell phone, she asked the desk to send someone to re-hang the drapes. Then automatically, she checked her cell phone messages. Five from Heather. Two from her boss. And one "Unavailable." Wanting to avoid all business calls, on an uncharacteristic whim she pressed "Unavailable" and stopped in mid-breath. The recorded voice sounded like that guy by the river—after he stopped babbling like an idiot—when he talked with that cool Euro accent. The voice sounded smooth and very, very sexy.

"Miss Dumaurier, I am in serious need of an attorney and I understand you perform literary property work. I require representation in a contract dispute. Please agree to meet with me to discuss this matter tomorrow evening. I will be looking forward to the pleasure of your most esteemed and charming company."

She felt a tingle of excitement in her belly. The voice in her head said, *Pay no attention to him.* That damn voice from her childhood was definitely back in her head for the first time since her twelfth birthday. That was the day she'd decided she was too grown up for imaginary voices and had given up listening. She'd said, "Leave me alone," and proceeded to close her mind to the voice.

****

Rebecca stepped out of the shower. Instantly the desert air evaporated the moisture from her body. She immediately slathered thick dark gel on her wet hair, and combed and twisted every hair into her usual knot at the base of her head.

She shimmied into a pair of tight new jeans with a trendy pre-worn patina, added a white silk blouse with a tight cowgirl cut, and tucked her Sedona guidebook into a shoulder purse that resembled a saddlebag. She rejected the red cowboy hat that matched her red boots as too Annie Oakley.

Picking up the old-fashioned hotel key—no unauthentic plastic security cards—she headed for the hotel dining room. A call to the concierge had supplied the information that the Babs entourage had rented a van and was off to dine chez Pizza Hut.

No pizza here. This hotel restaurant rivaled the best in Paris. Eating expensive food must be rule one for a pampering vacation.

Reaching the faux-Western dining room with its authentic country French furnishings, she chose a small table by the window with a spectacular view of the creek and the red rocks above the treetops.

She sipped a glass of Chardonnay and ordered local trout encrusted with macadamia nuts, green beans with rosemary, and tiny red potatoes.

By the last bite of white chocolate truffle appliquéd with raspberry glace, she'd read through her guidebook. Vortexes? Crystal shops? Aliens? A massage? She smiled to herself; she hadn't thought of work for almost an hour. She *had* thought of the strangely interesting man in running shorts. And that phone call from the sexy voice. Was it really about business? He had left no name and no definite appointment. In town only a few hours, and two potentially interesting men had found her. Viva vacation!

The waiter refilled her cup with midnight dark coffee and she spooned sugar from a real bowl—no tacky pink and blue packets here. She glanced up and noticed the table across the dining room. An ethereal blonde with long, straight hair spoke loudly in a fake French accent. Her young anorexic body was covered with a white dress printed with gold astrological symbols.

"Why can't we eat at ze Enchantment? It is so much more, you know, sopheesticated? I love it there soooooo much."

"Aries, honey, please lower your voice and speak French, not baby talk," the man at the table told her.

Rebecca froze. She knew that voice. She'd estimated Tom Paxton's age as mid-thirties, close to hers. No wonder he hadn't asked her to dinner. He was staying here with that girl. She had been interested, then disinterested, but now switched him to the category of great-looking guys who made fools of themselves over younger women. Yet, he did have incredible blue eyes. What was that old phrase? If she fell into his eyes, it would take a ladder to crawl out. She certainly had no intention of falling anywhere. Still, there was something about him that reminded her of an English Lit professor she'd had in college. All the girls thought he was cute, but he never even noticed.

"*Vous* are just a sperm donor. I am going to ze room," the young woman he had called Aries said. She stood, arranged her filmy dress and turned, revealing an aries tattoo on her pale back. With a good imitation of the walk of a Paris model, she left the dining room.

The man watched her go, shook his head as he ran his fingers through his sun-colored hair. He looked self-conscientiously around to see if anyone in the dining room had noticed the scene. He caught Rebecca looking at him. She quickly dropped her eyes to her guidebook. But not fast enough. He knew she'd been watching. She knew he knew. She knew he had not looked away. He knew she wanted to look again and when she did, he grinned and shrugged his shoulders.

The voice she'd once called Little Rebecca sighed and said, *There he is!*

Rebecca commanded the voice to silence. Why was the voice from her childhood giving her so much trouble now? For the first time since she was a kid, her mind was not filled with law school, clients, and plans for making partner. As pure entertainment—what harm could it do?—she decided to let the voice share her vacation. However, if the voice was going to be her companion as it had been when she was young, Little Rebecca had better behave.

Embarrassed at eavesdropping on a lovers' spat, Rebecca lowered her head, pretending to read, this time vowing she would not look up. Though her eyes stared at the page, the man's image stayed with her. She could see thick sandy hair brushed back from a relaxed open face. The laced-front white shirt revealed his chest and a gold chain. She hated men who wore heavy jewelry, yet she remembered the feel of that silk shirt and the warmth of his chest.

She signaled the waiter, signed her check, and gathered her guidebook and saddlebag to leave. As she walked past his table, he stood.

"Please let me apologize for disturbing you again. You saved my life. Hydration is so important in the desert. My—" He grinned.

"It was nothing," she replied politely, ignoring his cute hopeful smile and those sweet blue eyes. "You were so kind to ignore our unfortunate accident. I hope you are feeling better."

"Perhaps you would let me make it up to you?"

Little Rebecca whispered, *Oh yes.*

Rebecca said, "I don't think so, but thank you." In her business travels, this type of restaurant scene was not unfamiliar. Men tried to pick her up, but she preferred to do the choosing, or more often, the not-choosing. With great effort she broke from his gaze and said, "Good night," nodded, and started to turn away.

He reached for her hand and stepped closer. His flowing white pants swished and his shoes made no noise. "I am so sorry my daughter disturbed your dinner." He gently took her hand.

She felt his firm, warm touch and soft squeeze, more apologetic than assertive. He immediately withdrew his hand. The way he tucked his chin made him look both introverted and apologetic. Rebecca was still absorbing the fact that the spoiled young woman was his daughter, when she realized he had left a card—too large for a business card—in her palm.

"A ticket to my seminar," he told her. "Please come tomorrow evening. The hours and location are printed on the back. Bring a guest, of course. I will leave your name—Rebecca Dumaurier—with the registration people." He looked like he was about to say more when Aries returned carrying her high heels. "Daaadd. You totally forgot! You promised you'd print out Aunt A's e-mail."

"I must have dropped it somewhere. I'll print it again." Tom lifted his eyebrows, in a kids-what-can-you-do gesture.

Rebecca smiled back. I'm having a conversation with a man wearing pajamas in a restaurant. I am jealous of his daughter. And I stole his e-mail.

A blonde, who looked like an older sister to the young woman—same clothes, same hair—rushed up. Ignoring Rebecca, she shrieked at Tom, "What the hell are you thinking letting Aries wander around alone?"

"Angie, lower your voice. This is Sedona, not New York. This is a safe hotel. You let her dress like a—"

"You're being difficult. Again. The opening session is tomorrow evening and we haven't done a walkthrough. Kevin's there, setting up the sound...I mean checking the harmonic seed attunement for the chi vibration experience. Damn it, this one's a sellout. The rent and advertising cost a fortune. Do you think if I call the local Sedona tribe I can get some Indian chief to do a sweat lodge at the last minute?"

Tom's expression did not change. "Sure, Angie."

"Angela! Call me Angela!" She turned and swept out. Tom followed her through the lobby herding their daughter in front of him.

Rebecca hurried to the concierge desk to ask about hiking maps. A matronly-shaped young woman, whose green paisley dress and supercilious manner reminded Rebecca of her law firm's librarian, watched the departing family.

"Do you know who that was?" The woman's tone was conspiratorial. "Tom and Angela! Together again." Her voice trailed off when she realized she was gossiping with

author.

She propped her new hiking boots on the dashboard and looked out the windshield at the brilliant red rocks. She poured a cup of that perfectly brewed French Roast coffee she'd enjoyed last night and sipped. When the first rush of pure caffeine reached her brain, she broke off the end of a flaky croissant. She found a real silver knife. No flimsy white plastic in this picnic basket. Spread with butter and a thick lump of strawberry jam, she dropped the first bite into her mouth and closed her eyes in contentment.

Noticing the morning desert smells, she brushed flakes of the most delicious breakfast she'd ever tasted off her green hiking shirt and shorts and unwrapped the second croissant. George, the concierge, had chosen her favorite breakfast.

Energized, she elbowed into her backpack, attached the canteen, and checked for her map, sunscreen, and digital Nikon. She pulled her floppy hat down over her helmet-like hairdo. No need to ruin her skin or hair for just a few days' vacation.

Rebecca was no exercise novice; besides jogging and Stairmaster workouts, she and Tristan hiked in upstate New York. They took day trips at New York State Bar meetings in the company of dozens of Manhattan lawyers turned out with enough gear to attack Everest.

Here she shared the trail with jackrabbits, a covey of quail, and roadrunners who reminded her of crazed city pedestrians. As the morning warmed, she slowed her pace and noticed flecks of gold in the powdered red dirt and scampering geckos. Bending to look more closely at a prickly pear cactus, a minute yellow wildflower entranced her.

The sun rose higher in the desert sky and her muscles stretched. Her obsessive determination to hike every trail in the environs melted in the warmth of the day. Encircled by spectacular cliffs of a box canyon, she stood at the spot her map identified as a vortex, but saw no sign or historical marker.

By noon she was back to the SUV for a crisp salad with blue cheese dressing and a crusty baguette stuffed with ham, avocado and Baby Swiss. White grape juice felt heavenly on her dry throat and for dessert, cookies—how did George know ginger cookies were her favorite?

The sun high and the temperature rising, she checked her map and drove to a shaded trail George had suggested along the creek where giant oak trees and fast water created a refreshing change from this morning's arid red setting.

She found a spot in the shelter of trees and bluffs next to the river looking out at the glorious rock formations in the sunlight. Water rushed across flat layers of exposed red strata and over rounded black and brown stones, then funneled into a fast stream. She removed her boots and socks and dangled her feet in the water. She hadn't thought of work all day and had almost forgotten the good-looking blonde guy, the strange phone message, and that London girl's diary. Her habit of carrying the day's major crises and cases on a calendar in her mind was hard to break.

She reveled in the feel of sun on her face and icy water around her toes until across the river, she saw Tom Paxton's tight jeans climbing a steep path—she'd know his backside anywhere. Her attraction to him brought out an uncharacteristic shyness. Maybe because he was so unlike the men that usually caught her eye. She leaned deeper into the shadow of a pine tree. She focused on him with half-closed eyes. Two men, not one, popped into her mind. Perhaps the Sedona air was making her imagination go wild.

The voice in her head confirmed without words that there were two men. That just showed why she could never trust Little Rebecca. That voice had always encouraged her to see things that were not there and now she was doing it again. Rebecca would not trust that voice. There was only one man—one very attractive man.

She was about to call out, when Angie rounded the rock outcropping and struggled up the hill after Tom. Near the river, Aries, their changeable teenager, settled into the shadow of a tree with a book. Not wanting to intrude on a family excursion, Rebecca pulled on her socks and boots and headed back to the trailhead.

****

"Stop! Damn you! I can't keep up!" Angie yelled up to

Tom. "Why..." she panted, "are you going so fast?"

"I wanted to get to a place where we can talk without Aries hearing." He stood coolly waiting on the top of the knoll. As much as he disliked Angie, he wouldn't hurt her with a reference to her age and lack of fitness.

"Aries knows everything." Angie reached his side and collapsed onto a mesquite-shaded rock.

"Because you have no sense. She's a child, not your confidant or girlfriend or..." his eyes narrowed, "...extension of your persona. What psychobabble!"

"You're just being cruel because I divorced you. You used to be such a wuss. Now for some selfish reason you want to fight for custody of my daughter."

"I wanted out. I let you divorce me. Besides, she is my child too, a talented, brilliant child. Don't mess her up the way you tried to ruin me. My God, Angie, letting a thirteen-year-old get tattooed!"

"So, my fair Thomas, I messed you up? Exactly where do you think you would be without me? Teaching Descartes in some third-rate community college, that's where. Married to a chubby kindergarten teacher and living in some prefab development in Kansas." Her face was red and hot from the climb. "Everyone called you the shyest man in the world. I made you a star. And still you continue to embarrass and humiliate me. You made me sleep in the room with Aries." She sighed and looked up at him through long lashes.

Tom knew at one time, that look would have melted his heart. "You booked a two-bedroom suite. We are no longer married, so we do not share a bedroom. Aries can figure that out." Turning his back to her, he looked up toward Cathedral Rock, remembering what he had been told about the powerful Sedona vortexes. Angie sure needed some energy balancing. Why couldn't she let him go?

"But people think we are back together—"

"That is not my problem. We are divorced. You are my manager, agent, and seminar facilitator—until our contract runs out. If you don't like it, get another room."

"Why won't you come to the day sessions? Everyone asks for you. What do I tell them?"

"Tell them my contract only requires me to be there

for evening trance sessions."

"I have to do it all alone. You are cruel," she whined.

"Your problem. Get Kevin, your new boy toy, to help you."

"Stop it, Tom." She tossed her head, forgetting her blonde hair was tied in a low ponytail. "Anyway, you were never that great. And now that fake trance stunt you've been pulling..." She rolled her eyes. "You can't fool me!"

"Fake? For ten years they *were* fake. *Now* they are real." He smiled at the irony. "You should be happy."

"I would be very happy if you would stick to the script." Ignoring his silly grin, she asked, "What do you do all day?"

"None of your business."

"Are you messing around with that skinny woman from the hotel with the big eyes and funny hair?" She saw his face tighten. She changed her tone again. "Please Tom, just take Wednesday morning."

"I can't. I have plans."

"With?"

"None of your business."

"Tom..." she cooed.

"An old friend and colleague."

"A woman? Did you have any women friends at Hick State?"

"You remember Steve, my friend since high school and the smartest person I ever met. He taught English when I was in the Philosophy Department. He's a successful novelist now."

"That geek. Successful? I never heard of anything he wrote. I never understood a word he said. He talked like a dictionary and was even duller than you—and so incredibly ugly. Keep him away from our fans. This Sedona Power Spot workshop is full of cosmic karma, I'm sure his looks will affect the energy flow. We're offering arcane neo-theosophical chromotherapy for the first time and I'm thinking of adding optional iridology-phrenology readings. And maybe a visionary prosperity session. If it works, I'll stretch that into an entire workshop week next year." She paused and softened her voice. "If you help me Wednesday morning, the geek can come to the workshop."

Tom waited for Angie to finish. He was used to

Angie's seesaw mood shifts and constant New Age jargon. "You're working Aries too hard. Give her every morning off. She's just a kid."

Angie's gaze shot daggers at him, but she nodded. He slid his fingers into the back pocket of his jeans. Rebecca's card was there with her firm's New York phone number. He definitely needed a new attorney.

\*\*\*\*

Back at the hotel, the front desk clerk, the one with his hair slicked back as flat as Rebecca's, handed her a bulky envelope. She ran her fingers over paper so thick it reminded her of an expensive wedding invitation. On the front, "Rebecca Jane, Cottage No. Two Hundred and One" had been written in elegant, formal script with a real fountain pen.

She ripped open the envelope and read:

\*\*\*\*

*Dear Rebecca Jane,*
*Please meet me tonight at ten on the bench at the river's edge in front of your cottage.*
*Until then,*
*My most sincere regards,*
*Max*

\*\*\*\*

This was very mysterious. The note was signed Max as if she was supposed to know who he was. Not at all the way business was usually conducted—even in the entertainment business. She had her share of odd clients and their peccadilloes. One woman would only hold meetings when she was immersed in a foamy pink bubble bath. Rebecca shivered, remembering the time the phone rang.

Returning to her cottage, Rebecca took a leisurely shower and enjoyed another calorific French dinner, via room service to avoid Babs. She expected Babs would soon tire of this game, take her children, and go home.

After the kid she thought looked like a overgrown elf with a pierced eyebrow cleared her dinner and served her coffee and dessert crepe, she powered up her laptop and read Heather's research.

\*\*\*\*

*From: rjd@bankheadfirm.com*

27

*To: heather@bankheadfirm.com*
*Subject: Dirt*
*Thomas Paxton graduated from the
University of New Hampshire. Psych Asst Prof at
Weatherton State. Met Angela Blessings summer
of 1989. Married September. Age difference 20
years (she is older!). Quit his teaching job and
published 4 books during the next three years.
Two trance channeled, one a sort of self-help, and
a historical bestselling novel "Master of the
Island," which became a TV series. Lots of sex,
violence, and voodoo.*

*One child, Aries (Arianna), age 13. Divorced
last year. He has ten books in print and is in
demand on the New Age lecture circuit. Angela
remains his manager and agent. Two years ago,
she launched her daughter's music career by
promoting her work as part of Tom's workshops.
His latest book includes a CD of Aries', "Heaven
and Love." That's all, so far. I'm looking for more
dirt.*

*H.*

\*\*\*\*

"He sounds weird," Rebecca told her computer. "Cute,
but weird."

The Little Rebecca voice said, *That's not the whole
story.*

\*\*\*\*

At eleven o'clock that night, as instructed, Rebecca
waited on the bench closest to the creek near the front of
her cottage, curious to meet the man with the great voice
and beautiful handwriting. Unfortunately, that particular
bench was the only one beyond the reach of the hotel
security lighting. She felt strange sitting in the dark in
her black business suit.

While she was getting dressed, Little Rebecca had
been especially difficult. First, she told Rebecca not to go
to the meeting. Then she made her stomach queasy just
like she used to do when Rebecca wouldn't do things her
way. When Rebecca continued to ignore her, she told her
that the mystery man was dangerous and not to be
trusted. Ha. Rebecca didn't believe her. She had told her

Tom Paxton was two men. The voice just spoke nonsense.

Finally Rebecca threatened Little Rebecca. She told her that if she wasn't perfectly quiet, she would put up that wall in her mind again. She had lots more control now than she had at twelve and not listening to one puny little voice would be a snap.

The two had come to an agreement that Little Rebecca would only talk when spoken to. Little Rebecca pouted while big Rebecca sat here at the river in the dark in her black business suit.

Above the flow of water over river stones, Rebecca heard noises from the hotel kitchen. She turned and in the dim light watched a man in a white coat approach. She sat straighter and was about to stand to greet him when she recognized the senior wine steward carrying a tray.

"Miss Dumaurier. A gentleman requested this for you," he said with a formal bow, but a knowing smile.

"What gentleman?"

"The gentleman said, 'If the lady asks, tell her an admirer.'" The waiter placed a delicate crystal wine glass and a linen napkin on the small wooden table next to the bench, announcing, "Champagne, 1988 Krug Clos du Mesnil." He added, "Our finest," to be sure she understood, then turned and retreated up the path.

Rebecca lifted the wafer-thin tulip glass to her nose and inhaled the distinctive smell of the legendary wine, allowing its bubbles to tickle her nose. A sip, just a sip. This was a business meeting. Yet, she couldn't deny herself a taste of the most expensive champagne ever imported.

"Excellent," she whispered.

"I am so happy that you like it," said a deep, very male, voice behind her.

Startled, she began to turn, but the voice she recognized from the phone message said, "No. Rebecca, please stay where you are. For now."

"Not turn around? Who are you?" she asked, trying to identify that spicy smell.

"Please call me Max. I left a telephone message for you."

"Yes, but why can't I see you? I'm not used to

business meetings in the dark."

He laughed. "Much business is conducted that way. My dear, you enjoy your champagne and I will tell you my story."

"This is so weird! I mean...irregular." For a moment she considered asking Little Rebecca more about this Max, but refused to give in to the bossy voice.

"Perhaps, a little romantic?" His voice, like warm honey, made her heart beat faster.

She ignored the heat, which felt a lot like desire. "Your message suggested a copyright dispute. Tell me the facts."

"Ah, of course, business first. Well then," he sighed. "I wrote a...let us say...a book. An unscrupulous editor obtained possession and after cutting, adding, and totally distorting my meaning and intent, published it."

"Did you have a contract?" Rebecca wished she had brought her laptop or at least a legal pad. All she had was a glass of champagne—the most expensive champagne she had ever drank. "What country? U.S. copyright law?" She was now positive his sexy accent was European.

"Oh yes, U.S., and sadly no, no ordinary contract. My words were tragically stolen and the copyright was applied for without my consent."

"There was no release form? Your name is on the book and you have no signed agreement?"

"Yes, that is correct."

"You may have a case. What do you want out of this? Money? Royalties? Do you understand that very few books sell well enough to make legal action worthwhile? Litigation is very expensive and time-consuming." She carefully repeated what she routinely told all prospective clients.

"I want what is mine."

"How many copies have been sold?"

"A million...maybe more. Fifty editions, counting translations and foreign rights. I am willing to forget about the TV series if they cease all rerunning of films immediately."

"Mr...Max, you are talking big money. Only a few authors ever have that kind of success. Who is this author?"

"I *am* the author. Will you take my case?" the velvety voice asked.

She felt breath warm on the back of her neck. She had to see him. She didn't think she could prevent herself from turning around one more minute. "Yes," she whispered.

"Good. The deal is made. I will deliver the documentation to you, soon. But now..."

Rebecca felt a hand rest on her shoulder, cool and strong. A shiver of excitement ran through her body. Unconsciously, she leaned toward his hand, deepening the touch.

He released her and brushed the back of his hand lightly against her neck and cheek. His voice trembled. "Enjoy your champagne, Rebecca, my dear."

She turned. Fine hairs stood away from the back of her neck. Trees rustled in the evening breeze and the creek bubbled past. That spicy sweet smell lingered in the air, but no one stood behind her. On the table beside the wine glass lay a perfect long-stemmed red rose.

Chapter 4

Rebecca returned to her cottage, sipping the last of the champagne and holding the rose. The thin young man with the pierced eyebrow waited on her steps with a huge vase containing twenty-three scarlet roses. Surprised by the late night delivery, she let him inside, remembered the kid's name was Josch, and pointed for him to place the roses on her table. She tipped him and snatched the card.

****

*To a wonderful business relationship and more...*

*With my fondest regards, Max*

****

Her brain told her this was a polite gesture from a client practiced in old-fashioned ways, but her heart beat faster as she breathed the heady scent of the roses. She'd been sent flowers by clients before. This meant nothing, she thought, as her finger brushed a velvet petal.

She needed to immediately notify her office of her new client. She and Max had a verbal agreement. But her boss would ask the client's name, address, the name of the property—stuff like that. She prided herself on always being precise with details. Now she felt stupid, yet savored the excitement of the mysterious man.

The next morning, Rebecca awoke stiff and sore from her hike. Every inch of her body ached. She took a warm bath and breakfasted in the hotel dining room on eggs benedict and pastries. The coffee was magnificent and the white china cup needed no plastic Starbucks lid.

Next, it was time to discover what all this massage hype was about. In the City, she'd never found time. One of her colleagues hired a personal masseuse for office visits twice a week, but Rebecca hadn't seen the big deal. One billable hour out of her day was a huge chunk.

George, the concierge, watched Rebecca limp up to her desk and immediately suggested a day package at the Pink Spa. Rebecca instructed George to book "The Works" in the name Rebecca, not R.J. That would make it harder for her clients to locate her since most had no idea her real name was Rebecca. Just for two weeks here in Sedona she'd be called Rebecca. What difference could it make? Maybe that voice from her childhood made her feel and act like a kid?

The exterior of The Pink Spa, a square Santa Fe-style adobe was, like most of Sedona, painted the colors of the red rocks. Minutes after checking in, she undressed and was wrapped in a luscious pink towel and whisked into a sauna with women in equally pink towels. Dehydrated despite the volume of fluids she'd been drinking, she lay flat on the hard cedar bench while her body absorbed clouds of steamy mist.

She became warm and opened the towel. It was so foggy she could barely see her own slim body. The other women were busy talking and Rebecca half dozed until the creak of the heavy wooden door opening startled her. She snatched up the ends of the towel and flapped them back around her torso.

A man in a pink tunic said, "Ms. Rebecca? I'm Eric, your massage therapist."

Rebecca followed him through the steam and out the door. Inside a pink treatment room, a picture window framed the distinctive shape of Bell Rock. After only two days, Sedona's skyline felt as familiar as Manhattan's.

She slid onto the massage table, making a note to buy the mystical flute CD that played as Eric slowly massaged her feet and legs with exotically fragrant oil he called ylang ylang. His powerful fingers, hands, and arms worked her calf muscles with firm, gentle strokes. Rebecca never imagined a man in pink could look so masculine.

Refusing to miss a moment, she forced herself to stay

awake and aware as he massaged her neck and arms, then asked her to turn over and worked her back methodically from her legs up her spine.

"You have the tightest trapezius I've ever seen," he said.

"Thank you," she sighed.

"The trapezius are those large muscles on the sides of your neck where you carry a lot of your stress."

"It's my job," she groaned as he worked deep into her shoulder blades. "I'm a lawyer."

He touched her hair. "What's that stuff on your hair? The sauna turned it gooey. I'll have Elise wash it out."

"A custom gel mixed with a temporary color my hairdresser makes especially for me to keep my hair flat and dark. You know, neat."

"Ugly," she heard Eric say under his breath as he added a wash and comb-out to her chart.

Her massage concluded with drops of warmed rose oil drizzled on her forehead. She got off the table enveloped in the scent of rose petals. Colors in the room glowed. The music in the room vibrated around her. All her senses were alive. Her body tingled, reminding her of the afterglow of sex with a skillful lover—although at the moment she couldn't quite recall when that had actually occurred.

In slow motion she slid back into the robe. The woman named Elise washed her hair and led her outside to a shaded patio table. Rebecca watched heat rise like waves and felt her hair drying. She imagined dreaded curls popping up from her skull and wrapped the pink towel tighter around her head. She slid the ends of her sunglasses behind her ears.

Elise brought iced chamomile tea flavored with lemon and a plate of tiny ripe bananas, kiwi, miniature grapes, and a bowl of gourmet trail mix with pecans, hazelnuts and balls of dates spiced with cinnamon and cardamom.

By mid-afternoon, as Elise led her from the manicure-pedicure area, Rebecca saw Angie and Aries wrapped in pink sheets on adjoining tables, while Tom sat in the jacuzzi, eyes closed, face turned to the sun.

"Why don't you spend a few minutes in the jacuzzi

before your facial?" Elise suggested.

"Um, sure." Rebecca walked to the edge, remembered she was naked under her pink robe, and hoped the turban and sunglasses made her unrecognizable.

Tom looked up. "Rebecca, it's nice to see you again."

She nodded and tightened the belt of her robe. Poking one toe into the bubbling whirlpool, she said, "I think it's too warm."

"Sit for a minute. I wanted to ask if you are planning to come to my seminar."

"Do you think I'd like that kind of thing?" She sat down on the rim and slipped her feet into the bubbles, snugging the robe around her thighs.

"Maybe spirits are waiting to talk with you. I take messages." He grinned, shaded his eyes, and squinted. "Or, if you prefer, you could just watch."

She smiled. Tom was charming in a boyish way and she was beginning to forget that weird episode at the river. "George, my hotel concierge, said I need to do some very Sedona things. Would it be a very Sedona thing to do?"

"Absolutely. Very Sedona! Then, you'll come?"

"I'll think about it." The voice inside told her, *Say yes.*

"Please."

While he talked to her and kept eye contact, he moved around the circumference of the jacuzzi and now stood looking up at her. She looked down into the bubbling water. He wore no bathing suit. Now, she was really getting warm. Her sunglasses slid down her nose. She poked them back. Little Rebecca said, *Go ahead and look. Nothing we haven't seen before.*

Elise came up behind her and asked, "Ready?" Rebecca jumped. "Or would you like more jacuzzi time?"

Nodding to Tom, Rebecca followed Elise back to the treatment room.

Elise closed the door and asked, "You like Tom Paxton?"

"He seems to be a nice guy."

"Nice guy? Tom Paxton? He's really big in the international guru community. Big mind, big intellect, big looks, and big...need I say more?"

Ignoring Elise's raised eyebrow, Rebecca asked about

Tom's books. After all, books were her business. Deepak must make a lot of money for some lucky attorney.

Elise pulled a book from the shelf that held her massage oils. "Here. This one's his first, *Loving in the Spiritual World*. And this," handing her another, "is his latest, *Love, Peace, and Passion*."

Rebecca read aloud, "'Channeled by Don Thomas, born 500 AD and died 1500 AD, transcribed by Tom Paxton and Angela Blessings Paxton.' What does channeled mean?"

"A spirit takes over your body and you say all kinds of things you could never know. Like being possessed."

Rebecca wondered if it was like having a little girl's voice in your head. Changing the subject, Rebecca asked, "What's a vortex?"

"High energy places. Some people think vortexes or vortices balance multiple aspects of your personality and help you find answers to your problems."

"That could save some people I know thousands of dollars in psychiatric bills."

Elise continued, "I personally believe vortexes are places where changes begin."

"If I find a vortex, what do I do?"

"You can meditate or just stand and notice if you feel energy spiraling up through your body. It may not knock your socks off, so just be open and see what happens. And be sure to try the food at New Frontiers, a health food store and a great spot for people-watching and shopping. Look on the bulletin board for notices of lectures by alien abductees or maybe a real alien."

Rebecca leaned back.

"Only kidding. Have you ever had a psychic reading?" Elise asked.

Rebecca shook her head.

"I know a great medium who can tell you about your future, your past, even your past lives. Dead spirits speak to her. Ask for Joy at the House of Crystals. She's young, but very talented. And go to a yoga class. I'll give you some names. Yoga is like giving yourself a massage."

"I doubt that anything could be that good." Rebecca twisted her arms and legs. "Do you think I can be turned into a pretzel?"

"Yoga isn't like that. You'll see."

"What about Tom Paxton's workshop?" Rebecca asked. "I have a ticket."

"I heard it's sold out. How'd you get a ticket?" Elise asked.

"He gave it to me."

"And I'm giving you advice!"

****

By late afternoon, mellow from her spa day, Rebecca floated along the path to her cottage, placed her foot on the first step, and felt her serenity evaporate.

"Babs, what are you doing here?" Rebecca asked, as if she didn't know and as if she hadn't been avoiding her angry client for the last two days. Babs Hemingway, queen of sweet romances and secret baby plots, sat on Rebecca's patio chair in a pink calico sundress, primly typing away on her portable word processor.

"Shush. I'm in the middle of a love scene," Babs' high-pitched voice squeaked from under the matching floppy hat.

"Your novels do not have love scenes."

"They do not have nasty *sex* scenes."

"Until the audio of *Sweet Stacy*."

Babs looked up and narrowed her eyes. "Yes, R.J., and that's what I am here to discuss." She turned off the keyboard-sized device and slipped it into her giant Minnie Mouse bag. She squinted at Rebecca. "Have you done something to your hair?"

"No." Rebecca pulled her hat lower. The thickest gel the spa stocked couldn't slick her hair down into her usual signature style. "Why are you here?"

"You need to stop those CDs from being sold. And protect me from ugly publicity. That is your job."

"There is no publicity. I took care of it."

Babs pulled a crumpled newspaper out of her bag and threw it at Rebecca. "Then...what is this?"

Rebecca caught the paper and flattened it on the table. "Oh, oh." The tabloid's headlines in large black letters read, "Romance Author Babs Hemingway in Sex Scandal."

"You've got to sue." Babs narrowed her eyes and stretched her neck towards Rebecca.

"Well, since the story is technically true, you can't win. Besides, a lawsuit would create more publicity—"

"I want them to stop, so I don't have to hide forever. I canceled my book tour. My agent is having a fit. The children are driving me crazy. They pick up on my state of mind, you know."

"I'm sure they do." Poor kids, Rebecca thought.

"Rebecca, don't be a puppy's mama. When I renewed my contract, we discussed my long term career goals. It's time my books were made into movies. You get Cora and Cleo movie deals. My books sell just as well. You also promised to pull strings to get me on the faculty of a literary writing workshop that would lead to a visiting professorship at a major university."

"Babs, one thing at a time." Rebecca almost said "in your dreams."

"I am related to Ernest Hemingway, you know."

"Yes, you told me a few times." As if *Truly Triplets* and the *Little Booties* series are classics like *Farewell to Arms* and *The Sun Also Rises*. Then she added quickly before Babs noticed her sarcasm, "Go to your room. I'll make a few calls and get back to you. I'll try for a retraction, but other papers may have picked up the story by now."

Babs arched her goosey neck, gathered up her bags, and stomped down the stairs.

****

That evening Rebecca didn't see the Paxtons in the hotel dining room. She supposed, if the Beloved Seminar began tonight, they would be there. Bored, she asked for her coffee and dessert to be sent to her cottage.

When she got back and opened the door, the smell of roses greeted her. Every time she left her room, another dozen arrived. There were pink ones now to bring the total to four dozen. She was getting used to roses.

When that same Josch kid brought her coffee and napoleon, Rebecca tried to tip him but he wouldn't take the money or move out of the doorway.

She glared at him. She wanted to be alone.

He mumbled, "Mrs. Du..du..."

She glared.

"Miss..."

She glared.

"I mean Mzzz."

She signed. "What do you want?"

"Um...I heard someone at the front desk say you were a lawyer."

"Yes."

"I have a problem. I work at this outdoor produce market during the day."

"Your day job?"

"My morning job. I fix computers in the afternoon and work here at night. I'm...I'm..."

"Go on. The fruit stand..."

"Well, it's supposed to be all organic and lots of Sedona people buy the produce. You know how health-conscious Sedona people are. Some have allergies and sensitivities..." He stepped closer and she tried not to wince at his pierced eyebrow.

"That's nice. But—"

"—in the morning I unload produce from the trucks. The driver brings the stuff in from a big food warehouse in Phoenix. The same place all the supermarkets get theirs."

"Where is this going, young man?" Rebecca couldn't understand how he could talk so much and say nothing.

He withered and began talking very fast. "Uh...uh...they hire little kids to pick sticky labels off the bananas, apples, oranges, pomegranates, peaches, kiwis, eggplant..."

"Enough! I get it. So, you are saying they are misrepresenting..."

"Yes. Misrepresenting. Fooling nice ladies who think they're buying healthier stuff. And you wouldn't believe the prices."

"I'm an intellectual property attorney, not licensed to practice law in Arizona."

"But the signs say Organic, Pesticide Free. Non-Eradiated. Some even say Local."

"That's too bad, but I can't help you."

Josch's face fell. Rebecca stepped closer. He moved back and tripped on her Oriental rug. She backed him out the door, closed it in his disappointed face, and turned back to her room. She noticed the gorgeous complementary fruit basket on the table and wondered where the fruit came from.

She took out Tom Paxton's first book and settled herself onto the velvet lounge chair. By eleven o'clock, she had finished it. No wonder he got attention. He explained spiritual concepts in simple, easy-to-understand language with lots of humorous anecdotes. As happened so often when she read books by authors she knew personally, she heard the author's voice in her head. So tonight when she tried to sleep, she was not surprised when Tom's voice continued to talk to her.

Finally she got up and checked her e-mail. The most interesting message came from Heather, who had intercepted an office memo stating that Tristan, Rebecca's former fiancé, had quit the firm that morning. Rebecca knew that she'd get the official word tomorrow, but this again proved Heather was the best assistant she'd ever had for providing her with fast, accurate gossip.

She was relieved that when she got back to the office Tris wouldn't be there to fuel the gossips and flaunt his new relationships. Little Rebecca asked, *Do you want my advice?*

"No. I am doing just fine by myself."

*Well, you really made a mess of your love life by yourself, didn't you?*

"It's not my fault Tristan was a jerk."

*It was your fault you picked a jerk. I could have helped.*

"I don't need a fairy godmother."

*That's not what I am.*

"What are you?" She had always wondered where this voice came from. It was her, but not her. Sometimes the voice seemed lots older and knew things she did not know. Other times Little Rebecca seemed not to know ordinary things like how to use a phone and about cars.

Now the voice was silent.

"What are you?" Rebecca repeated.

*You are not ready for that answer.*

Rebecca closed down the conversation, poured the last of the after-dinner coffee from the carafe and went back to reading. By 3 a.m. she finished Tom's second book and fell asleep hearing his voice.

## Chapter 5

The next morning Rebecca arrived at the hotel dining room precisely as it opened. With three hours of sleep she felt a little buzzy, but determined. A bowl of yogurt and granola, fruit and coffee woke her up.

She carried a pastry to the lobby and was waiting when the concierge arrived. "Good morning, George. Could you tell me where to find the best alternative bookstore and crystal shop? And where can I buy clothes?" she asked with a self-conscious laugh. "All I brought were hiking and cowgirl outfits. Where can I find long dresses like everyone here wears?"

George beamed. "Shopping advice? I am here to help."

A few minutes later, the front desk clerk waved her over as she walked towards the lobby exit. Rebecca considered asking him where he bought his hair products. He handed her a brown paper-wrapped package. Ripping it open, inside she found a worn leather-bound volume entitled *World's Greatest Love Poems*. The inside front cover was inscribed in broad script:

\*\*\*\*

*To Rebecca Jane, with my deep affection,*
Max.

\*\*\*\*

She asked the clerk to send the book to her room. These gifts from the mysterious Max were kind of hokey. Yet she had to admit that roses, champagne, and now a book of love poetry made her feel good—special—

feminine? Did she like the attention? Or did this stuff always happen on vacations? *Why don't you ask me?* the little voice nagged.

Because I don't want your opinion. You are no fun, Rebecca told her silently, but the wall that kept Little Rebecca quiet didn't feel very strong right now.

Rebecca shopped the great Sedona stores until her rented SUV was loaded with crystals and clothes. In the last shop she changed from jeans into a soft red dress and strappy sandals. Little Rebecca sighed. *I love this dress. You have to buy it. I haven't felt this good—*

"What do you mean? I don't have to do anything. It's my body and my credit card. I'll buy it because I like it, not because you say so."

Little Rebecca was silent, but Rebecca sensed she was happy with their purchase.

The long, flowing dress felt soft and sexy on her bare legs and she checked her reflection in the mirror, convinced the bodice made her breasts look fuller. Hiking, massages, and healthy food had removed the city pallor from her skin. A rose quartz crystal sparkled on a gold chain around her neck. Chakra bracelets and a moonstone ring finished what the clerk had described as the "Sedona goddess" look.

She purchased all of Tom's books and a CD version of the first one. On Little Rebecca's urging, she added a copy of the Beloved Diary with a Tom Paxton quote for every day of the year. Little Rebecca teased, *A diary! Just what you need. Tell the truth for once in your life. It'll do you good.*

By the time she pulled into Tlaquepaque, the upscale mall built like a traditional Mexican courtyard, she'd listened to him narrate the first half of disc 1.

In a shady outdoor café, she selected a taco salad and ordered iced tea instead of her usual espresso. She examined the books and carefully read the bios on each of the back covers, wondering why she was so interested in this guru guy. Perhaps it was merely her professional interest in successful authors. She didn't care about gurus, though he was cute in or out of those pajamas.

A woman at the next table stared and twisted until she made eye contact. "Are you attending the Beloved

Workshop?" the woman asked in that too-friendly way
people on vacation talk to strangers. This would never
happen in New York.

"Workshop? Oh, Tom Paxton's?" Rebecca noticed the
woman wore a purple dress identical to her red one. "No.
I'm not." She began packing the books back into her bag.

"I am, but I snuck out for lunch. Couldn't stand
brown rice and sprouts or whatever the menu for those
pure-of-body vegans is today. Tomorrow there is an extra
charge for a entire day of raw food. Can you imagine,
paying people to not cook your food?" She lifted her glass
and swirled her double margarita around the heavily
salted rim.

"Are you enjoying the program?" Rebecca asked with
genuine curiosity.

"Oh yes." The woman lowered her eyelids halfway.
"Tom Paxton is scrumptious. Most gurus are short and
dark. He is so tall and, well, my type..."

Rebecca felt a little heat, which she was sure was not
jealousy, and asked, "What about the lectures?"

The woman leaned closer and in a conspiratorial tone
said, "So far, it's just stuff from his last book. During the
day sessions Angela plays old tapes of Don Thomas'
lectures about life, life after life, and life before life. We
meditate and do cutesy exercises. That sort of boring
stuff."

"Why come here if you can buy the book?" Rebecca
asked, tempted to ask what a vegan was and about the
cutesy exercises. She wondered how authors attracted
groupies like this. Loyal readers she understood, but the
workshop circuit mentality was beyond her.

"Just being around him feels so awesome and Angela
looks like such an angel. The part I like best is hearing
the new material before his next book comes out. Stuff I
can tell my friends back in Santa Monica. Actually, most
people pay the big bucks mainly for the evening
channeling sessions."

Rebecca perked up. "Channeling?" This woman, who
talked as fast as any New Yorker, was easy to talk to.

"That's when other spirits come to talk to the old
Spanish guy Tom is when he's not himself. You have to
see it to believe it. This is my third. I did New York and

Chicago, but Sedona is spiritually special. I expect tonight will absolutely blow me away. I'm signed up for a private phone session and video for a $10 per minute donation."

"Before you know what will happen or even how long the session will be?"

"That's Angela's policy. Besides, this week is so romantic. Tom and Angela are back together. You know he's much younger. Gives us older gals hope." She winked. "If you're not here for Tom, what did bring you to Sedona?" The margarita woman finally took a breath.

"I heard about Sedona, I wanted to see it," Rebecca told her, then grinned. "Oh, hell. I'll never see you again. The truth is, it wasn't my idea. My fiancé booked a week at Rouge Mountain for what he called our engagement honeymoon." Little Rebecca laughed. *Remember what I said about telling the truth once in a while.*

"How romantic!"

"That's what he said when he accused me for the zillionth time of being unromantic. This trip was supposed to be a test to prove I could be as romantic as anyone. I ordered enough Western wear and hiking gear from L.L. Bean and Cabalas to turn myself into a cross between Annie Oakley and Indie Jones."

"What about lingerie—little nothings?"

"I expected Sedona to be a big dude ranch, not filled with crystal and angel doodads. Well anyway, we work for the same firm and it wasn't easy for us to take so much time off together."

"What do you two do?" Uninvited, the woman pulled her chair to Rebecca's table.

"Intellectual property law at a mid-sized boutique firm."

"Movie stars?" The margarita lady leaned closer.

"Mostly bestselling authors. Tristan, my now ex-fiancé, handles the N.A."

"Native Americans?" The woman scooted her chair even closer.

"What we used to call New Age. Now it's pretty much mainstream—complementary health practices and spirituality without churches. Sales make up a significant market share. Tristan is good. He pretends to meditate and knows how to talk the spiritual lingo. He wears his hair long enough to put the woo-woo people at ease. I guess I'd call him the sensitive, but masculine, type."

"Cute? I bet he's a real stud muffin? You're such a beautiful young woman and, I'm sure when you aren't depressed, have gorgeous hair."

"He's cute, in a shallow way." As Rebecca said it, she knew it was true. She ignored the hair crack. Non-New Yorkers never understood her fashion acumen. "I caught Tristan coming out of his private bathroom with Carmel de Amore, author of *Goddess Sex and You*. If you ask me, that wasn't a very romantic or spiritual location. Anyway, we broke off our engagement and I came here alone. And it's all charged to him," she added with a satisfied grin.

"That would make the beginning of a great romance novel. All you have to do is meet the great love of your life here." The margarita woman swallowed the last of her drink. "I should get back for at least part of the afternoon session. I'm having my iris reading."

Rebecca watched the woman walk away. "Fat chance I'll meet anyone, much less the love of my life." What bothered her most was that she really didn't feel that bad not being engaged to Tristan. She did fear returning to the office. Relieved that Tristan quit the firm, with any luck at all, she expected newer gossip to emerge before her vacation ended. She didn't care if she ever saw the jerk again.

****

Back in her cottage, she checked her cell phone messages and returned Heather's call.

"R.J., you sound different," Heather said as soon as she heard Rebecca's voice.

"Must be the thin air. Don't they say lack of oxygen can make you giddy?"

"Like the vortex stuff."

"You know about vortexes?" Amazing what was common knowledge these days. The little voice probably knew all about vortexes, or was it properly called vortices? Lucky she was a lawyer and not an editor. "So, what else did you find out for me about Tom Paxton?"

"Well, he's brilliant. You got the facts in my e-mail—nerd philosopher historian extraordinaire. Brightest student, etc., etc. Boring, boring, boring."

"And?"

"His fortune changed when he met Angela Blessing at a spiritual retreat in New Hampshire and became her toy boy—"

"What?"

"Altitude affecting your hearing? She was forty-two and wanted a kid. He had the looks, the brains, and could even write books. He became her entrée into the growing New Age craze."

"She used him?"

"Absolutely. They became famous and she gave birth to the perfect child. Have you noticed the kid's blonde looks and talent? The file photo makes her look eighteen, not thirteen. Mature for her age. Angie picked a great sperm donor—"

"Who said that?" Rebecca remembered Aries had called Tom that last night.

"Angie Baby said it herself in an interview after their divorce, when she wanted custody of the kid."

"She sounds crass and mean."

"A tough businesswoman who gets what she wants— your kind of chick, R.J."

Rebecca ignored Heather. She put up with her assistant's disrespect in exchange for the young woman's super-efficient work. "So, why the divorce?"

"That, Ms. Perry Mason, you'll have to ask Mr. Paxton."

"Me?"

"Sounds like you've got a thing going with him."

"No...no. Absolutely not." Heather was definitely over the line today. Should she tell Heather about the auto accident? That would explain her interest in Tom.

"No? But if you want to know more...he wrote a novel that Angie edited and promoted into a major network mini-series. After the sex, violence, and commercials, there wasn't much spirituality left. Pulling in a few favors in the office—remember Angie was one of Tristan's clients and I am friends with his former P.A.—the scuttlebutt is that he was major pissed."

"Tom seems so nice. Tell me more."

"That's all, so far. How's your vacation going?"

"Great. Best in years."

"You haven't taken a vacation in years. You can thank Tristan for this trip."

"Right." Rebecca snapped the phone shut.

Rebecca wasn't interested in talking spirits, but she was intrigued by Tom Paxton. So, if there was nothing else to do *après* dinner, she might wander over to the workshop. "What else was there to do?" she said aloud. Little Rebecca was silent, but she could feel her satisfaction.

She finished her shopping in the elegant Tlaquepaque shops, picking up a few more pieces of jewelry and sending a woodcarving of an eagle as a peace offering to her boss. He collected sharks, but she couldn't find any in Sedona. She bought gifts for her mother and Heather. Traveling without a business agenda was kind of fun. She stopped at the post office to mail postcards, then went shopping for more sunblock, water, and a yoga outfit.

\*\*\*\*

The yoga class Elise recommended ended with meditation. Rebecca left feeling stretched and peaceful, "blissed" in Sedona-speak. Returning to her cottage, she blissfully climbed the steps, blissfully opened the door, and screamed, "What in hell are *you* doing here?"

Tristan, her ex-fiancé, sat in her lounge chair next to a dozen newly-delivered pastel-colored roses, paging through her copy of *World's Greatest Love Poems*.

"What kind of a greeting is that? You sound like the old R.J., not the new woman who reads love poetry in bed. Or does the guy who sends you roses read the poems? 'Fess up," Tristan teased, with that edge in his voice that drove her crazy.

"None of your business. Just get out of my room. And out of my life. I'll have whoever let you in here fired. This is a violation of my privacy. Why are you here?"

"R.J., or is it Rebecca Jane..." He referred to the flyleaf of the poetry book and read, "My dearest Rebecca Jane..."

She snatched the book from his hands.

"The hotel gave me a key to *my* own room. Remember it's on my credit card. I agreed to pay out of a temporary case of remorse. The deal was room, meals, car rental—

but not roses. Wonder where they came from? Who is Max?"

Rebecca ignored him and repeated, "Why are you here?"

"You sound like a broken record. Business came up in Sedona and I realized I already had a very nice hotel room. So I moved in."

"You quit the firm."

"My, my, gossip travels fast. However, that doesn't mean I have no business." He gave her that I-am-so-cute look that swayed women judges and jurors and turned female clients to mush.

That look no longer held power over her and Little Rebecca cheered.

"What fascinates me, R.J., is how fast you've changed. Look at you. A long, low-cut *dress* and your hair...what happened to the black Cinnabon?" He walked closer, reached out, and patted her head. "The petrified effect is gone. Almost feels like hair." He looked closer. "What color is it, anyway? It looks a shade lighter than death-black."

She batted his hand away. "Don't make me create a scene. I'll call Security."

He held up his hands, palms facing her. "Truce. Let's have dinner on my tab. You can tell me what you've been up to and then we'll come back to our room." He looked at her with that sexy leer—like old times.

"No to dinner and you can sleep on the sofa...and find another room tomorrow."

Chapter 6

While Tristan showered, Rebecca locked the book of poetry and Max's notes in her glove compartment. Tom's books were still safe in the SUV. She had no intention of having dinner or anything else with Tristan. She was sure he was here to see Angie and he'd find out soon enough she knew Tom and Angie—if you called having Angie hate her, knowing her.

She drove to New Frontiers and filled up on deli food. She checked out the posted flyers and noticed one for an Autumnal Equinox Meditation and Wiccan Potluck. In the Arizona heat, she had trouble remembering it was almost Fall. Wiccan did mean witches, didn't it? Back in New York, her colleagues would be planning foliage weekends, not pagan potlucks.

Proud of her healthy choices—even one vegan dish— she left the health food store with a tube of cruelty-free hair lotion and a bottle of all-natural organic hair cream. Instead of returning directly to her hotel—she was in no rush to spend time with Tristan—she decided to drive past Tom's seminar site. She'd just take a drive on a beautiful moonlit night. She followed the concierge's directions and drove down a dusty road and through a gate to a stucco building.

She looked up at the building, domed like an old mission church, and considered getting back in the SUV and finding other entertainment for the evening. Reluctantly she checked in with Little Rebecca. *Thought you'd never call*, Little Rebecca's girlish voice replied immediately.

"Don't be smart. I just want your opinion on this endeavor. It seems creepy."

*Don't you remember all the fun, creepy stuff we did when you were a kid?*

Rebecca said, "This is different!" Right. I'm a grown woman talking to voices in a public parking lot.

*OK, I say you go in. It's not dangerous, but it is your destiny. Our destiny.*

"Enough." Rebecca closed her mind and opened the SUV's door. "Be quiet."

She parked and walked past about fifty empty vehicles to the main entrance. Using her shoulder, she slowly pushed open the massive wooden door and entered a dark foyer. The air felt thick, like a church. A high window allowed in enough moonlight to illuminate a long table stacked with books, CDs, t-shirts, guru action figures, and then another set of double doors.

She pushed against the left-hand door. It swung open more easily than she'd expected. Rebecca regained her balance and let her eyes adjust to the darkness. She'd stumbled into the central domed hall. Candles illuminated rows of chairs and two inner circles of cushions. She estimated that over a hundred people sat in the dark room. Considering the exorbitant price printed on the ticket for the ten-day workshop, the Paxtons were doing very well.

Tom sat on a platform higher than the others. His white silk outfit reflected the candlelight. Angie, with a beatific smile, sat on his right in a white robe and Aries, on his left, wore pink and played a harp.

No one turned. The music had masked Rebecca's entrance, but a thick-bodied man next to the door blocked her way. She showed him the pass Tom had given her. The guard nodded and placed a cushion on the floor in the first row. She guessed that this was her seat and she settled awkwardly tucking the red dress around her, grateful the afternoon yoga class had stretched out her floor-sitting muscles.

When Aries' music trailed off and she'd set down the harp, Angie extinguished the candles and the room became totally dark.

From somewhere, Rebecca wasn't sure if it was in front, or behind her, a deep voice echoed through the room. "Beloved ones. Beloved ones." The repetitious chant wasn't Tom's voice, but some old guy with a bad Spanish accent.

"I have a spirit here to speak with Mona," the echo voice announced.

A woman yelled, "That's me!"

The voice told her that her mother on the other side was fine. "All is love and happiness here."

Rebecca wondered to what other side this woman's mother had gone.

More ridiculous emotional scenes followed. She was positive neither Tom's lips nor throat moved.

Her legs ached and her back was sore. She was considering walking out, when she heard a loud groan and another voice echoed through the room overpowering the first. The second had an Asian accent, like that student from Katmandu she'd known in law school. "Rebecca. Do not leave," the Asian said. "You are here for a purpose." The old Spanish voice was still intoning in the background about a teddy bear named Bobby, then cut out in mid-word, as if a tape was switched off.

The second voice was definitely coming from Tom, though it did not sound like him. Tom's lips moved and he rocked back and forth. "Rebecca. This is the time for change. The Equinox approaches. This is the time for love. Rebecca. You must warn him. You are more powerful than those whom folly leads."

Rebecca really wanted to get out. She guessed—hoped—there were three or four Rebeccas in the crowd. She began to crawl towards the door, trying not to rip her long dress. Her inner voice was sure wrong about coming in here. She didn't care if this was her destiny. This was weird.

The voice coming from Tom continued, "Rebecca Jane. Do not leave." She stopped.

Angie shook Tom's shoulder. He ignored her. She grabbed Aries' harp and banged his knee. He kept talking.

Angela stood and relit the candles. "Beloveds," she said loudly, "this evening's channeling session is ended. Don Thomas is very tired. Continental breakfast at 8 a.m.

51

No CD or book sales or signings this evening. If you registered for early morning Optional Re-Birthing sessions, meet at the hotel pool at 5 a.m."

"Stay where you are!" The candlelight threw Tom's seated shadow across the room. "There is no Don Thomas—I am the entity Ku."

Angie jumped. The margarita woman Rebecca had met at Tlaquepaque sat behind Aries, mouth open. The muscular doorman had sidled around to a position behind Tom. But as he moved forward to grab Tom and pull him backwards he stumbled against Angie and fell into her lap. Angie screamed. Tom looked across into Rebecca's eyes and smiled. "Are you ready?"

"Ah! Ah!" Rebecca sputtered.

Tom looked different. His face was softer. His eyes now slanted in an almost Asian manner. His hair was darker and shorter and his mouth smaller. Rebecca knew it was probably just the candlelight, but Tom's face had a yellow cast.

He spoke, "There is nothing to fear. The harvest approaches. Those of us with pure hearts are all love."

She stood. Her aching legs cramped and she did a little hopping dance. Everyone stared at her.

Tom was Tom, but not Tom. She looked into his eyes. They were kind and gentle, but not Tom.

"Rebecca, I am here to tell you of your destiny," he said.

"My what?"

"This man whose body I wear needs you."

Rebecca's knees began to bend. The lights went on.

Tom's peaceful face tightened. A violent spasm passed through his body, his eyes flew open, and he became Tom again. He stood, rubbed his knee, and as if awaking and seeing Rebecca for the first time, smiled sheepishly. "Hi."

Rebecca stepped back. "Hi? What the hell *is* going on?"

Angie called loudly, "Good night, Beloveds! Remember the Hundred Monkeys! Be careful driving to your hotels. Wasn't tonight's session enlightening?"

The doorman guided people out the door. No one really wanted to leave now that things were getting good.

Angie grimaced, obviously furious, and Aries pressed her lips together trying not to laugh.

When the last of the attendees was gone, Angie screamed, "Kevin, lock the damn door. Tom! What the hell is going on? I told you I wouldn't stand for another one of your scenes."

Ignoring Tom, Angie pointed at Rebecca. She was twitching. Her eyes flashed. "You! I know who you are! Leave!"

Rebecca stood her ground. Up close Angie didn't look so good. The eyes that stared out of her too-tight face were not young. "I will not leave until you tell me what is going on."

Angie shook her head. "It's not your business."

"Yes, it is," said Tom and Rebecca together.

"You are ruining everything," Angie screamed at Tom. "After all I've done for you. I created you...a celebrity...a god."

"You're crazy," Rebecca told Angie as Kevin tried to take her arm. She pulled away. "Take your hands off me."

"Take your hands off her!" Tom stepped between Rebecca and Kevin, put his arm around Rebecca and led her to the door, out through the foyer, and into the cooling evening.

The few people remaining stood talking next to their cars.

"Do you have a car?" Tom asked Rebecca. "We need to get out of here."

Rebecca pointed to her black SUV. He took the keys and helped her in. Ignoring gaping onlookers, he drove out the gate as the Beloved Workshop attendees turned their attention to Angie screaming, "Come back, you bastard. Come back."

****

Tom drove to 89A and found a coffee shop. As soon as they were seated, he ordered eggs, fries, toast, juice, and pie.

"Sorry," he apologized, "but after these things I'm tired and can't get enough food."

"After what things?" Rebecca had waited for answers, but her patience had run out. This had been a pretty peculiar evening and she wanted answers.

"Let me explain." Taking a bite of toast loaded with butter and jam, Tom looked around to see if anyone was listening. Satisfied, he reached across the table, took her hand and began. "One night when I was in grad school my hand started to write words that were not coming out of my brain. At least that's what I thought. By dawn when I stopped writing, I was no longer tired. I felt as if I'd awakened from a very restful night's sleep. That continued for months. I thought I was going crazy. I never told anyone."

The waitress brought the rest of Tom's order and he went back to eating.

"What kind of writing?" Rebecca tried to focus her mind on the literary aspect of his preposterous story.

"It's called automatic writing. Another being, spirit, entity, takes over a body." Tom watched Rebecca lean away from him. "Really, I'm not crazy."

"I know a lot of writers and not one ever said writing was like that." Rebecca, to keep her hands busy, dipped a fry in ketchup. "And some are pretty unconscious most of the time."

"Automatic writing isn't common. If you ever used a Ouija board, your hand movements were not conscious. In my case, the writings were not answers to questions, but a description of a unique philosophical view of life. The philosophy part intrigued me because that was my field, and the spirituality explored a new view of the human condition I was sure I was meant to share. I had no clue how to publish the material. It wasn't academic writing and I didn't even believe I wrote it. I did know that if I even talked about it, I could lose my teaching job. I was confused and scared. I packed the notebooks away and taught Philosophy 101 to freshmen. But at night I dreamed of telling people about the wonderful ideas in the notebooks and began to work the concepts into my doctoral thesis."

Rebecca was quiet.

"Do you believe me?"

"Yes," she said slowly. She did. "But it's a pretty wild story." She didn't think she would have believed anyone else, but she couldn't imagine this man telling a lie. She wondered if having an entity write with your hand was at all like having a voice that was someone else babbling in your head. She didn't want Tom to think she knew anything about what he was talking about because she certainly did not.

He took a breath. "Thank you. You seem like a feet-on-the-ground kind of girl." Rebecca nodded, not really sure at this moment that she was.

He reached for her hand. "Please tell me what I said tonight. Angie and Kevin never let me hear the tapes when I really go into a trance."

"You don't know what you said? Is it like that writing thing?"

"Tonight was a *real* unconscious trance. I'm not there at all. Angie won't believe me. These authentic trances began after our divorce, so she thinks I'm faking to force her to let me stop doing these gigs. I do want to quit. She won't let me break my contract. There's a lot of money in the books and the TV call-in show. She thinks the TV exposure will help Aries break into the music business as a spiritual music diva. I think she's too young."

"You're her father."

"That never counted. You should see the pre-nup."

Rebecca strained to recall what she knew about celebrity pre-nuptials.

"Remember that argument you overheard, when Aries called me a sperm donor?" He watched red-faced as Rebecca nodded. "Angela wanted a child. She checked her biological clock and went looking."

"You expect me to believe that?" His words validated Heather's research, but she wanted him to deny it.

"It's true. After my first year teaching, I spent the summer trying to understand the stuff in those notebooks. I met Angie at a camp where I was studying with a spiritual teacher."

"Angie was a spiritual student?"

"She believed the New Age craze would grow and wanted to cash in on it. She was a psychologist who'd published one book on getting in touch with your inner shrink and was trying to get on the lecture circuit. I was flattered by her attention and to impress her told her about my notebooks. She read them and convinced me we could sell the ideas through channeling gigs."

"You were part of a scam?" She couldn't believe Tom was a charlatan.

He shook his head. "It didn't start out that way. We got married and she turned the writings into saleable books. I began lecturing and gradually she added more and more guru paraphernalia. We divorced after eleven years. She got custody of Aries and remains my agent and manager. When I told her I wanted to go back to teaching, she went ballistic. Then, ironically, I started really channeling. Like tonight. Not scripted. No background check on registrants to create the tapes, only the spirit who wrote in my old notebooks speaking through me. Angie claims I'm ruining her."

"What can you do?" Rebecca was already mentally planning a legal case to win back Tom's daughter.

"I'd fight her in court, but lawyers don't want weird cases like who gets custody of the ghosts." He laughed. "I'm used to this talk, but it must be blowing your mind?"

"Actually, yes."

During their conversation, he'd finished the eggs and toast and three cups of coffee. Handing her a fork, he said, "Help me finish the berry pie. Then I'll need some fresh air to keep me awake."

Ten minutes later, he drove south. Moonlight faceted Sedona's red rock formations into fantastical sculptures.

"I love this place," Rebecca told him. "I don't think I'd ever seen stars before. Night here is as beautiful as day."

"Of course, everyone knows cities don't have stars." He smiled at her excitement. "You don't seem as interested in Sedona's spiritual stuff as its natural beauty."

"I'm happy when I look at mountains. I've spent my life in cities, but being here feels good. Sedona must be affecting me. I'm more relaxed than I've ever been, even before law school. But I still don't buy the vortex hocus pocus."

"Hasn't anyone told you that spiritual stuff is about feeling good?" He turned into the Bell Rock parking lot. "Let's take a little walk and you can test my theory."

She jumped out of the SUV. The sky was dark except for the moon and a million or so stars.

Little Rebecca said, *Isn't this heavenly? Tom is*

*wonderful and so handsome and caring. He has a daughter,* she babbled. *Take his hand. This is so romantic.*

No! Be quiet, Rebecca told her silently. You promised to be quiet when I didn't want you. Little Rebecca said, *OK, but don't mess this up* and then was silent.

"Here." Tom reached out for her hand.

"Thanks, I'm fine. I've been scampering over these rocks."

He seemed disappointed, but noticed that even in places where the trail was wide, far from the cacti or spiny mesquite, she walked close to his side.

"Some people say Bell Rock is a doorway to another dimension," Tom told her.

"I thought this was going to be a nature hike."

"If you want, but this spot is also a vortex." They had reached a flat area near the formation's base. "Stand still and see what happens."

Rebecca stood, closed her eyes, and waited. She shifted her weight from one foot to the other. "Nothing. Nada. Am I supposed to see aliens or spaceships?"

"Actually, aliens come here because Sedona is such a great vacation spot."

"Good choice." Rebecca laughed.

"They like the people-watching here, but when they go home no one believes them."

"I've seen some."

"I don't believe you. Can we climb to the top now?"

"Sure." Tom took her hand, and led her up to the next level. "Being with you makes me happy," he told her. "I don't have to play guru."

"I like being with you, too," Rebecca told him and realized she was having a very good time.

57

Chapter 7

Rebecca pushed Tristan out the door and, stiff from sleeping on the couch, set the last piece of his luggage on the deck. "A taxi is on its way. I found you a suite at Poco Diablo." She slammed the door in his handsome face. She wanted her ex-fiancé and Angie's attorney far away from here. Out of Sedona would be best.

She'd enjoyed her evening with Tom. He was a very nice man and Angie was, as Babs would say, a puppy's mama.

She remembered she hadn't checked her voicemail since yesterday. The first one demanded, "R.J. Call me! Now!" She noted the number, but already knew it was her boss Donald Bankhead, Managing Partner of Bankhead, Blanding and Gillimesh. She took a deep breath and pressed callback.

"'Bout time." Don's raspy New York voice always sounded impatient.

"I'm on vacation."

"Have a good time. Now that the small talk's out of the way, I set you up with a prospective client. I've given him your cell number. Talk today and close the deal."

"What deal?" The word "deal" erased any lingering vision of an uninterrupted vacation and made her heart beat faster.

"Tom Paxton needs a lawyer. Know who he is, don't you?"

She took a breath. "Donald, I handle the romantics and a few chick lits. Remember, Tristan is your guy for woo-woos." Rebecca pretended she didn't know Tris had quit. She had to protect her gossip-mongering assistant.

"Tristan's flown. Took Angela Paxton's contract with him. Tom Paxton is looking for separate representation. Angie and Tom are both working in Sedona as we speak. I want you to sew him up before he calls Gefflinger in L.A. Those California firms get all the good gurus. Tris brought in Angie and Tom. If we lose them both, we're dead. You can do it. You're the best in the business."

"You want me to screw my ex-fiancé for the firm?" She looked down at her long dress and the sparkling crystal dangling between her breasts. "Donald, I'm not a New Age kind of girl."

"I know you, R.J. Revenge is good medicine."

Rebecca considered this for about two seconds. Now her heart was definitely beating faster. "Fine. Have Heather get the files to me."

****

In an hour Rebecca got the secure file attachment from Heather, read it, and immediately wanted to talk to Tom. But if she called his room, Angie might answer and she couldn't chance that. She had to do some fast work to keep Angie from taking Aries back to California. Rebecca wandered through the lobby and was casually checking the dining room for the sixth time when her cell phone rang. She flipped it open and heard Tom's soft voice in stereo on the phone and behind her.

"So you're Bankhead's new woo-woo girl? You told me you didn't know anything about this spiritual stuff."

"I thought you were the psychic?" She felt her face flush, turned, and countered with a smile. "How do you know about the term 'woo-woo'?"

"I know you lawyers call us 'spiritual properties' woo-woos! I may be a trance channeler, not a psychic, but I know a lot. For me, all the interesting stuff happens when I'm not in my body. At least lately." He flashed her a playful grin. "That's pretty woo-woo, don't you think?"

"I try not to think about it. Talking about bodies being taken over still makes me squeamish." She ignored the lately comment. "Will you let me take yours to breakfast?"

"Sure. I'll let you woo the woo-woo."

59

"Don't tease. This is serious business." But Rebecca relaxed. Knowing Tom personally made her more interested in working with him. He actually seemed nice and definitely not crazy like most of her romance clients. She already knew he liked her, which should make closing the deal a piece of cake. He hadn't done any sexual numbers—though she had no doubt he was attracted to her—so their relationship would just be business, as long as she ignored his interest in deep eye contact and hand-holding. She'd never had a client she wanted to help more. "Let's go to the Enchantment. I hear it's the only place in Sedona more exclusive than Rouge Mountain."

A half hour later, they were settled at the best table in a dining room with a 180-degree panorama of Boynton Canyon spread out before them like a Cinerama screen.

As soon as the waiter poured their coffee, Rebecca got down to business. "Let's take care of the details and then we can have a great meal on my expense account." She reached into her briefcase and extracted a contract. "This is standard. You know the drill. Bankhead is the best. We'll defend you in court professionally and personally, give advance advice when we can to keep you out of trouble, and post bail when it's too late. Our retainers are reasonable and," she grinned, "you know I never take a vacation. And when I do, I keep working."

Tom leaned forward and stirred his coffee, slowly adding a packet of stevia he took from his pocket. "I know your firm worked hard for Angie and me when there was an Angie and me. Angie handled that part of the business. The firm was great. Tristan Morris was a little obsequious, but a competent lawyer." He paused. "Was it true you and Tristan were engaged?"

She nodded. Had Tom been waiting for an opportunity to ask that question? "Tris can be a pain in the butt, but he's a good attorney. We may have to—" Rebecca stopped. Tom was staring behind her. She turned to see Tristan and Angie at a table on the far side of the dining room. She grinned. "I got the better table. Besides, if we get into litigation, I know all his tricks. All of them." She pushed the contract an inch closer to Tom and laid a pen near his right hand.

"There is one problem I would like to discuss first."

Rebecca took a breath. Here it comes. Negotiation wasn't her strongest suit, but she was confident she could settle this before their omelets arrived.

"I'm trying to spend quality time with my daughter. Angie is fighting me. Aries is a bright, talented teenager and Angie's turning her into a drama queen. I want to encourage her music, but still let her be a kid."

Rebecca noticed that for the first time Tom seemed agitated. His fingers drummed the table and his lips tightened. "I understand. You're her father. You should have a say. You shouldn't have to ruin your life to protect your daughter. We can take care of this." She heard herself sound as if she had a plan. She was not a family practice attorney. What did she know about kids? Yet she'd been a teenage girl once—with a divorced mother who was a drama queen. She *could* understand.

"You saw that scene in the restaurant. Sometimes Aries can be an Angie double. But other times she's sweet—"

"—like you."

He grinned shyly. "I like to think she's like me before I met Angie and like the me I want to be again. Angie thinks she did a lot for me. I think she got me into a world I don't like, where entertainment is more important than truth."

"Why did you do it?" Rebecca had a firm rule of never asking clients why they got into the particular mess she was supposed to get them out of, but she wanted to know more about Tom. She had no idea how this sweet guy could have gotten hooked up with insensitive Angie and her berserk moods.

"I'm a philosopher. I know that sounds nerdy, but that's what I am. I was given ideas that needed to be put out in the world. If I could have found a publisher for my dissertation, about twenty-two people would have read the first page. Angie showed me a way to reach millions."

"But people think the books contain your ideas."

"I never told them that." He looked into her eyes. "Do you ever hear voices?"

She stopped. "What do you mean?"

Little Rebecca said, *Tell him about me.*

"No, never...I...um...never...ever hear voices."

"I just wondered. Lots of people do, but would rather not talk about it. Some children have imaginary friends and others hear voices in their heads. It's more common than you might think." He paused, waiting to give Rebecca an opportunity to say more.

She dropped a sugar cube she didn't want into her coffee cup. "So why did you publish your books?"

I wanted to help people and Angie knew how to market. She edited the notebooks and distorted Ku's teachings, but a lot is still good and true. Channels are sometimes called seers or visionaries. I desperately wanted people to know Ku's words. As far as why I married Angie and stayed with her..."

Rebecca shook her head indicating he didn't have to tell her.

He continued, "At first I was flattered. Later, I think I really loved her and got caught up in her obsession. By the time I woke up to the realization that our dreams were completely different, we had Aries and I didn't think I could ever leave her with Angie."

For the first time in her career Rebecca was touched by a client's story. Her eyes actually felt damp, but she told herself that would be the restaurant's air conditioning. Little Rebecca said, *No way.*

Tom smiled. "Now, let's be honest with each other. I know your boss wants a contract today."

"Well. Yes. I'd like—"

"I'll sign—"

"Great." Rebecca let out a sigh. "Sign here."

He nodded. "—if you'll help me out." He took the contract and held his pen poised above the signature line. "Let Aries hang out with you every morning."

"What? She's a kid. I'm not good with kids."

"She's pretty mature. Just let her stay around you. Do whatever you would do. Shop. Hike. You'd be saving my life. Again."

"What does she like to do?"

"She reads a lot. Talks about clothes. Thank God, she hasn't discovered boys. Lately, she's become interested in history. My sister Arianna is a historian and is deciphering an old diary."

Rebecca wasn't listening. She could taste success.

"Sure. Sure, Tom." She watched him sign his name.

\*\*\*\*

Tom walked Rebecca back to her cottage. His head dipped a few inches forward toward her cheek and she sensed he might kiss her and ask her to dinner, a chance for more personal conversation. She stuck out her hand.

He reluctantly took it and held on.

"Thanks, Tom." She had been attracted to him. Although he didn't have Tristan's devilish charisma, he was great looking and she felt that warm buzz when he took her hand or touched her back guiding her into a room. But now he was her client. Clients were off limits. She stepped back.

"Rebecca." He leaned towards her.

A green-coated hotel steward wheeled a metal cart past them and screeched to a halt. He climbed the steps and opened Rebecca's cabin door with his passkey, then carried in a TV.

Rebecca followed the steward, noting it was Josch. "Wrong room. No media during my vacation," she told him. Besides, with all the roses there wasn't room for a TV.

Josch consulted his clipboard. "You're Ms. Dumaurier, Room 201?" She nodded. "One TV and," he handed her a brown envelope, "one DVD."

"I didn't order—"

"No, ma'am. The concierge rented the movie from a local video place. The TV is complements of the hotel."

Rebecca watched Josch retreat. Confused, preoccupied, and curious about this latest delivery, she said a quick, polite goodbye to Tom and closed the door in his face.

She ripped open the envelope. A plastic DVD case slid out containing *Somewhere in Time,* her mother's favorite movie. According to Charlotte, Christopher Reeve was dreamy and Jane Seymour was exquisitely beautiful. Rebecca never watched movies her mother liked.

After a long shower, she wrapped herself in the thick hotel robe. Another knock at her door brought Josch back with a tray holding a bottle of wine, a large gold box of Godiva chocolates, and a package of microwave popcorn with butter.

She tipped him, ignored his grin, and closed the door. "Oh hell," she said to the TV. "Who needs dinner?"

Two hours later, tears streaming down her face, Rebecca groped into the Godiva box and pushed a Raspberry Cordial into her mouth, letting the tart sweetness melt on her tongue before she washed it down with red wine. She never realized how hard it was to cry and eat at the same time. She pointed the remote at the TV, clicked, and sadly watched the center dot vanish. Swallowing, she took a deep breath.

Her room phone rang and she picked it up, scattering popcorn from her robe all over the floor. "This is Rebecca," she gulped.

"Rebecca Jane? Are you all right?" asked the concerned voice of her mother, Charlotte Dumaurier.

"Mom? I'm fine. I was watching a movie."

"A movie? That doesn't sound like you. Do you have a cold? What movie?"

"*Somewhere...Somewhere in Time*," Rebecca sniffed.

"I've seen it at least fifteen times. I didn't think romantic movies were your cup of tea. What *are* you eating?"

"Um, chocolates..."

"Godiva?"

"The Signature Ballotin box, like the one I gave you for your birthday, so I know how much it costs."

"*Tres cher!* Four pounds of heaven!"

"And Madeira." Rebecca pushed aside the Marzipan Almond and chose a Chocolate Cream Heart and a Scallop Shell to try tandem flavors.

"Sounds very decadent for my super-serious lawyer daughter."

"But the movie was so sad."

"Yes. So sad and so very romantic." Charlotte sounded pleased Rebecca was relaxing on her vacation, but concerned about such uncharacteristic emotional behavior.

Rebecca could hear in her mother's voice how high her eyebrows were raised.

"I was worried that the breakup of your engagement would be difficult for you. Tristan was so handsome. I never thought you would hold on to him."

"Mother, mind your own business," Rebecca snapped, though she knew Charlotte never would. Her mother could be as irritating as Little Rebecca. At least Charlotte wasn't privy to every thought that went on in her daughter's head. Wouldn't that be something? Her mother at least pretended her thoughts were her own business.

"You are my daughter and that makes you my business. Actually dear, I was more worried that the breakup would not faze you. But this sobbing at a movie is quite unexpected. Though I'd always held out hope you'd find time to experience the emotional side of life."

Tonight her mother's criticism didn't bother her the way it usually did. Instead of hanging up the phone, she began talking. The wine must have loosened her tongue. "Mother, I dumped Tris. I came to Sedona and sort of ran into this cute guy. Then I find out he's a famous guru and his ex-wife is the bitch from hell. And now—he's my client!"

By the time they finished talking, Rebecca had stopped sobbing and told her mother an abbreviated version of her Sedona vacation so far, omitting any reference to the mysterious Max. She had not had that much wine.

This was not the way she normally behaved. She'd just told her mother a lot more than Charlotte needed to know.

When she hung up Little Rebecca said, *That was nice. Confiding in your mother that way. I wished I'd had a mother to confide in. Maybe then...*

Rebecca wondered if Little Rebecca was feeling the effects of the wine, too. She'd also cried throughout the movie but for once offered no advice on how Rebecca could improve her life. She did say that she'd never tasted chocolate so wonderful.

The room phone rang and she searched through sheets and pillows to find it. Immediately, Max's smooth voice asked, "Did you enjoy the movie, my dear?"

"Oh yes. Wonderful, but sad."

"Great loves often are, but not always."

"Thank you for sending it...and the chocolates...and the wine."

"You are so welcome. I called to wish you a good

night and to tell you how much I miss seeing you."

Before Rebecca could respond, the connection clicked off and she held the phone, dial tone buzzing in her ear.

Chapter 8

Rebecca looked up from her laptop and found Tom's daughter Aries staring at her. The kid looked so adolescent in pink shorts and a ruffled top. "What are you doing here?" She'd assumed that her cottage patio would be a perfect place to catch up on e-mail without interruption. Her head felt like a large exercise ball and her stomach was still queasy from last night's chocolate and wine. Pulling on shorts and a t-shirt had taken great effort. Now her space was invaded by this perky pink child.

"It's eight o'clock." The teenager stuck out one hip and tossed her the grownups-are-so-stupid look.

"So...oh, God, I promised your father I would babysit for you."

"I'm, totally, not a baby." Aries turned and put one pink sandal on the lower step.

"No. Don't go. I promised. I'll do it." Rebecca rubbed the top of her head where pain throbbed and told herself she would not jeopardize her client even if she was dying of last evening's excess.

"Don't put yourself out," Aries said over her shoulder.

Rebecca grimaced. What had she gotten herself into? "Honey—"

"Don't call me honey! Like I don't know the deal you made with my dad." But she climbed back up the stairs.

"Fine, but stay. I know you don't want to be here. Give me a few minutes to finish a couple of e-mails. I have a slight headache."

"I saw the Godiva on its way to your room last night. Did you eat the whole box?" Aries walked inside.

"No." Rebecca watched Aries' tight, thin thighs. She worked hard to stay fit and watched her diet—depriving herself—but her thighs never, ever looked like that. "You'll spoil your...your lunch." She heard a parent voice coming from her lips.

Aries walked across the popcorn-strewn floor and found the gold box on the bed partially hidden under a quilt. "Totally empty." She came back outside, sat on the top step, pulled a book from her pink messenger bag and started reading.

By the time Rebecca closed her laptop, she saw Aries engrossed in the book. Craning her neck, she tried to see what the girl was reading. Aries snapped her book shut and pushed it back into her bag.

"What are you reading?" Rebecca attempted a polite conversational tone. Was that possible with a child?

"None of your business." Aries indicated the book sticking out of the side of Rebecca's briefcase. "What are *you* reading?"

"Totally, none of your...well, fine, if you show me yours?" She exposed the cover of Claude Festerman's latest novel *Urban Chaos & Tragedy*.

Aries held up the same book. "We have the same taste."

Rebecca was impressed. Claude's book was seriously brilliant, the kind always reviewed in *The New York Times Book Review,* even though no one could understand half the reviewer's words without a dictionary.

"Actually not." Aries slipped off the dust jacket and with a devilish grin showed Rebecca that the book inside was Cora Ayne George's *Love Under the Banana Tree.*

Rebecca slid the jacket off her book to reveal the same title. "I put my *War and Peace* cover on Babs Hemingway's latest. I read in airports and other public places." She saw surprise in Aries' eyes. "They're my clients. I have to read their books...for work."

"It's for school. I need five book reports," the thirteen-year-old countered and grabbed Rebecca's book. "We're on the same page. How totally gross!" She grinned in triumph.

Rebecca felt the first layer of tension lift. "Fine, kid, since you know so much about books, what else do you like to read?" She decided to use Aries as a market research subject. "And what do your friends read?"

"Some read series romances and think their lives will be all wrapped up with a happy ending when they grow up. We all read sex scenes for research. Cora—not Babs. I don't think Babs ever had sex. What do you think?"

Rebecca laughed. Aries was really smart.

"And those secret baby plots make no sense."

Very smart.

"I'm also reading a nineteenth century diary. My aunt Arianna is a famous historian and it's her research. It's like a very cool true confessions Jane Austin novel." Aries realized she'd fallen into a grownup conversation with Rebecca and changed her tone. "So, you're Dad's attorney."

Rebecca nodded.

"Then I think you'd better come to this evening's workshop session."

"I've been to one."

"I think you should come tonight. I overheard Mom talking to Kevin. She was pissed about last night's trance and called Dad's Ku-Ku act a ploy to get out of doing workshops. I told Dad she had a plan to hurt him, but he won't listen. He said she couldn't make him do anything he didn't want to do. He said that's why you were his attorney."

Rebecca noticed how worried Aries looked. This kid really loved her dad. "I'll do my best."

"Mom's getting totally crazy. More than usual."

Rebecca wondered about a girl who thought her mother was acting crazy when her father went into trances and let short Tibetan men use his body. "She can't hurt anyone."

"What do you know?" Aries glared at Rebecca. "You don't know anything about this business. She's planning a fire-walking gig tonight. That can be dangerous."

"Tom told me he's done those before."

"Please. Just come about nine o'clock, before the final ceremony."

Rebecca agreed and started reading a contract,

signaling that she was working and the conversation was over. Aries took out a copy of *Teen People*. In a few minutes Aries interrupted. "Dad says you are an awesome lawyer."

Rebecca smiled, pleased, then realized the girl wanted something. "Is that a compliment or a bribe?"

Aries smiled. "Dad says lots of things about you that make my mom mad."

Blatant flattery got Rebecca's attention. "Fine. What do you want?"

"I have a friend who works at a produce market. He..."

"He?"

"Josch says he needs a lawyer because the owners are doing illegal stuff. Since you are the best lawyer I know—"

"You don't know many lawyers."

"I know Tristan. He's around with Mom a lot."

"I am a better lawyer than Tris any day."

"So, you will help?"

Rebecca knew she had been tricked. "How do you know Josch?"

"Oh, we kind of hang out together."

Rebecca's eyebrows shot up. "How old is he?"

"Um...sixteen, but totally smart. He's been home-schooled and is starting college in January. He's working three jobs to save money."

"Tell me about the hanging out?"

"I meet him behind the kitchen when he takes his break. We talk." She looked up into Rebecca's anxious face. "Just talk. Don't you trust me?"

"No. You're too smart."

"Like you." Aries grinned. "That's what Dad says. He also says you are totally smart and the absolute best at fixing legal problems."

"I'm not getting involved with the fruit problem. Tell that ringed Romeo to talk to someone with an office here. Someone who likes cantaloupes."

\*\*\*\*

Tom loaded his old friend's luggage into the Beloved van just as the Sky Harbor security guard approached.

"You didn't have to drive all the way to Phoenix to

pick me up." The man on the curb stopped ogling a passing flight attendant and told Tom, "I could've rented a car or taken a limo."

When they were both in the van, Tom maneuvered out of terminal traffic and onto Interstate 10. "Hey, Steve, I was anxious to see you. For two years all I've heard from you were devastating funny e-mails and blogs. Missed your ugly face." Tom turned and looked again at the startlingly handsome man next to him. He was still miffed that Steve had not given him a heads-up on the physical changes that he'd gone through. He found it hard not to stare at his friend.

A red Corvette pulled into a minute space between Tom's van and a Winnebago and Tom turned his attention back to Phoenix traffic.

"Sorry if I discombobulated you," Steve said, not sounding sorry at all. "If I hadn't held up that sign with your name, you'd have walked right past me."

"Well, you do look like a completely different person. Is any part of your body the same?"

"My brain, Tom. My mind and my quiddity, or as you gurus say, spirit. My spirit wished to turn my body into an analogue of what my mind wanted it to be...a chick magnet, like you."

"Seriously."

"I commenced with a little love handle liposuction..." he patted his perfectly flat belly, "...and kept going. Eyelids, nose job, chin and cheekbone implants and then some tucking and Botox. A year with a personal trainer was torture, but it was worth it."

Tom knew women did stuff like that. Angie's addiction to "cosmetic improvements" made sure she looked great for her age, if anyone could figure out that number. He didn't think it was honest to spend all that time, money, and pain to become someone else. "When do you have time to write?"

"Writing is the most effortless thing I do. You know I'm an insomniac. I crank out thousands of words a day— on each book. And when I work at it, I can be really fecund." Steve smiled and leaned back, watching the Arizona landscape roll by as they left the Phoenix metro area. "I have to say, I do so enjoy it when women take cognizance of the new me. Like the redhead I met on the plane. I know she was seriously interested in me. I am so unversed at this kind of thing, I neglected to ask her name or get her number. Great legs—looked like a movie star and she came on to me. She could be the one!"

"Great, Steve." Tom laughed. If a little surgery could make his old buddy so happy, what was the harm?

"In the old days when we'd go out, the babes would drool over you while you were too petrified to make a move. I called you the shyest man in the world."

"It wasn't that bad." Tom shook his head.

Steve nodded. "It was. They only tolerated me to get your phone number. Until Angie snatched you. Speaking of She-Who-Commands, how is life without the blessed Angela? I never understood a word that woman said. She always spouted psych gibberish or spiritual balderdash."

"Life is much better. I wish I'd gotten out sooner." Tom's eyes stayed on the road but he knew his friend was smiling. Steve had never liked Angie, and Tom suspected that a crazed psycho killer named Angelica in one of his novels was based on Angie. "She still controls my life and Aries', but I just found a terrific lawyer. I know she can help."

"She? Is that a lilt in your voice, old buddy?"

"Rebecca's great. Smart and funny and beautiful, but I can't get her attention except for business. At best she treats me like a friend."

"Now you fathom how I felt."

****

Rebecca returned from lunch and found her cottage door covered with notecards decorated with bunnies—all from Babs. She ignored them and went inside. As usual Heather had left a dozen call-me-now messages.

She called Heather. "I can't believe we're talking again. Are all my clients in crisis simultaneously?"

"Before I fired the temp, she leaked your vacation location to Claude."

"Claude's fine. Everyone knows Cleo and Claude are the two most reclusive authors in the business. He doesn't travel."

"Not anymore. He's decided to do interviews and a book tour."

"That's impossible. Cleo St. Cloud isn't real. Cleo is only a pen name. Only real people do book tours. Besides, Claude looks like a mole. His sister's picture has been on his book jackets for ten years and she's not that good-looking."

"He's lost eighty pounds and has had some procedures—"

"—Impressive. Sounds just like Cora. Don't worry. I'll talk him out of those idiotic ideas."

"Rumors say he's the author of a hot new military action series under the name Bullet Shotman. He has another attorney for that *nom de plume*. You only handle his Cleo and Claude books."

"He's writing three bestsellers a year?" Even for a prolific hack, this was hard to believe.

"Barbara Cortland wrote seven hundred romance and historical novels," Heather reminded her.

"She wasn't my client." Rebecca, angry that Claude bypassed her for another lawyer, continued, "If he announces that sweet old-fashioned Cleo St. Cloud, author of ladylike romances, is a guy, his book sales will fall faster than that writer who killed the cat. Some things readers do not tolerate. I'll call the traitor right now." Through the window Rebecca saw Josch bringing another package. "Got to go." She'd been disappointed there were no new roses today, as if there was room in her cottage for one more vase.

Josch set the heavy package on her table and Rebecca tipped him without making eye contact. She had no interest in another conversation about produce.

Rebecca ripped open the box and found books. She unpacked copies of *Wuthering Heights*, *Jane Eyre*, *Wide Sargasso Sea*, *The Outlander* and naturally, *Rebecca*. Of course, *Rebecca* by Daphne du Maurier—the more French spelling, no relation—was the one novel she'd always refused to read, no matter how many copies her mother gave her. *The Outlander* was thick, but its cover didn't look like a dreaded romance. Also, the copy of *Wide Sargasso Sea* seemed safe.

An hour later she was engrossed in *The Outlander*. The book was not at all what she expected. The bright, self-sufficient heroine's time travel adventure was absorbing.

She ordered room service, turned off both her cell phone and the room phone and continued her reading at her usual rapid speed. The sex scenes between this woman who traveled to another time and the young Scott were amazing. She skipped ahead and read the final chapters. The heroine gets pregnant and returns to her own time to save their child. Babs could never write a secret baby story this exciting. A foreign lover from another time sure made things steamy.

She read the *Wide Sargasso Sea*'s dust jacket. She'd always thought of taking a vacation in the Caribbean. Looking at her watch, she realized it was time to leave for Tom's workshop. She wanted to keep reading, but she'd promised Aries she'd be there by nine.

Little Rebecca had enjoyed the books and now her excited voice wanted to offer advice on what to wear. The long red dress seemed to be her choice and since Rebecca was getting used to the swishy feel of long skirts she gave in.

The little voice was getting very chatty and the company felt good. Little Rebecca babbled on, *The book is so sad. Aries is so sweet. Thomas is a wonderful father. I knew he would be. Aries is worried. We can't be late.*

"Do you think I'd like the Caribbean?"

Little Rebecca was quiet before answering. *We would love to go back to the islands. Swim and listen to the birds. It is so beautiful.*

"You've taken a cruise? Is that what you've been doing the last twenty years while I've been working?"

*It's not like that. And it wasn't exactly a cruise. I can't explain.*

"If you won't tell me more, be quiet."

Little Rebecca was silent and let Rebecca drive.

Rebecca arrived at the seminar site just in time to interrupt a group meditation. Angie glared at her. Rebecca expected Angie to give a "buy more tapes, t-shirts, and mouse pads" speech but instead Angie began, "Gods and goddesses, tonight's closing ceremony is a special exciting treat for you!"

Kevin, Angie's Beloved bouncer, opened the side door and the attendees filed out into a walled cactus garden lit by flickering torches. Aries waited for Rebecca near the door.

"What's going on?" Rebecca whispered.

"A POF. Old-fashioned hot coals take too long. Mom insists Dad do his fire-walking thing tonight on a gas Path of Fire."

"He told me he'd done it before." Rebecca stopped, realizing the group had become silent.

Angie swept into the center of the informal circle, holding Tom's hand so tight it appeared she was dragging him. "Gods and goddesses. Beloveds." Her voice crescendoed. "Tom will attempt to walk the infamous Path of Fire." She pointed her free hand with a flourish to the edge of the garden. A three-by-ten foot patch glowed and ignited into flame. The attendees oohed and ahed. "Behold, a perfect example of Meta-Karma Convergence."

Rebecca watched Angie raise Tom's left arm like he was a winning prizefighter. What next? A drum roll?

A recorded drum roll exploded from a speaker near the door, followed by a flute solo.

Angie continued, "Yes, there is danger." She paused for effect. The margarita woman gasped. "But Tom is magnificently prepared with the clarity of mind and steadiness of purpose he learned from the teachings of our beloved Don Thomas. And...during the 'Winter Bliss and Love Retreat' in Colorado, January 12th through 18th we will all do it. Yes! We will all learn to walk through fire." More gasps.

Tom's eyes flashed in the light. He nodded toward Rebecca and Aries.

"Did that mean he's OK?" Rebecca asked Aries in a whisper.

Aries grimaced. "I hope so. Dad's such a trusting guy. I hope he checked it out."

Tom smiled at the group, slipped off his sandals, turned, and walked across the cooling terra cotta pavers towards the glowing metal pallet. He looked like he was going for a peaceful walk.

Rebecca stared at the rectangle of low flames. "Where do you get stuff like that?"

"New Age warehouses rent them, along with pyramids, giant crystals, and backjacks by the dozen."

With a whoosh, the flames blazed two feet above the bed, then settled back into a six-inch-high carpet of fire.

"Is it safe?" Rebecca wondered aloud.

"Yes," Aries whispered, not taking her eyes off her father. "I guess. So far it looks totally cool. I mean, OK. The fire has to be really hot. Then, right before Dad steps onto the coals, Kevin turns off the gas down the center."

Rebecca relaxed. This was a trick. A show. No real danger. Tom couldn't get hurt.

Little Rebecca said, *Stop him. This is not safe.*

"Be quiet," Rebecca whispered.

Aries said, "Shush."

Tom's eyes were closed. He appeared to have quickly gone into a meditative state. He stood fifteen feet from one end of the Path of Fire and began to move forward in small slow steps, shifting his weight from the ball of one foot to the heel of the other while a tape played *Chariots of Fire*. He moved towards the flames at a smooth snail's pace.

The workshop attendees, who at first had crowded closer, now backed away, giving him space. He walked towards the glowing path. His pace quickened but remained steady. His eyes stared ahead, oblivious to anything of this world. He walked to the glowing edge and without hesitation stepped onto the coals. Nothing changed. His face stayed peaceful. Flames sizzled around his bare feet.

Rebecca couldn't help herself. She cried out, "Tom. No."

Aries whimpered. "The flames didn't go down."

"Stop him!" Rebecca took a step forward.

"It's too late!" Aries grabbed her arm and pulled her back.

"Shush," Angie hissed. "If you distract him, he will get hurt."

Aries squeezed Rebecca's hand. "Mom's right."

Step by step, Tom walked steadily on, chin high, eyes straight ahead.

At last, after what seemed to Rebecca and Aries as hours, he stepped out of the fire back onto the tiles.

The group applauded. Aries and Rebecca let out their breaths. Aries ran to Tom and hugged him. Rebecca heard

Angie say under her breath, "Damn. He did it."

Kevin hurried the attendees out of the garden until only Tom, Angie, Aries, and Rebecca remained.

Tom wiped sweat from his forehead. "Where was the water?" His eyes shot daggers at Angie. "The pan of water I walk through first!" His voice was low and steady, but his tone was angry. "This is the last straw. I'll never work with you again."

"I guess Kevin forgot." Angie rolled her eyes.

"No way," Aries stood at the edge of the garden holding a flat pan. "Someone moved it. And Kevin did not lower the flames."

"I guess he forgot that, too." Angie looked at Tom's feet. "You're fine. No problem." She turned and followed the attendees back to the concession area.

"How did you do that?" Rebecca asked Tom. Her face was pinched, imaging the pain of walking through those flames. His face appeared cool and calm despite the sweat dripping from his face.

"I think Ku stepped in," Tom told her.

Rebecca looked down at the smoldering charred hems of Tom's pant legs. "You people are crazy!" She turned and ran to her car. How could she protect him if he did things like this? It was her job to keep her clients out of the fire.

Chapter 9

At six o'clock, the phone next to Rebecca's bed rang. Last night after the fire walk she'd been unable to sleep and she read until three, expecting to sleep in. Little Rebecca had been in a frenzy. She claimed she'd warned Rebecca that Tom was in trouble and Rebecca had ignored her. She asked what good it did to have a voice in your head if you refused to take advantage of it? She hadn't exactly said voice in her head, she'd used the term "personal seeress," whatever that meant?

Automatically she answered the phone. A shrill wail, like a horror film scream, assailed her ears. Rebecca was about to hang up when the shriek-moan stopped.

"Don't you dare hang up," the voice on the line panted. "It's me, Babs. I bribed the desk clerk to ring your room. I told him it was an emergency."

"Babs, stop hyperventilating." Rebecca let out a sigh. Staying in the same hotel as a client was like living with a nightmare. "What's wrong?"

"Wa...Wal...Wal-Mart banned my books!" Babs whined.

"How do you know?"

"It's in USA Today!" Babs wailed. "And on CNN!"

"Good sources."

"Rebeccaaaa! What can I do? Lots of fans buy my books at W-W-Wal-M-Mart."

"You think it's because of the audio—" Rebecca began, still half asleep.

"Of course, it's because of the audio. *You* didn't stop

it."

"No one could have put a lid on that."

"It's your fault," Babs blubbered.

"Stop crying." Rebecca was now wide awake. "Listen to me. Call George. Have her send the nanny and the kids off on that Grand Canyon bus tour. Then have her call the Pink Spa and book 'The Works.' Go there by cab and stay until dark. Then come directly back to the hotel and call me."

"You'll fix everything?" Babs sniffed. "Promise."

"Just do what I say." Rebecca hung up. Dealing with Babs felt more like babysitting than being with Aries. She called room service and ordered croissants and coffee.

Later in the morning, Rebecca reviewed Tom's new contract while Aries sorted through Rebecca's books.

"Where'd you get these?"

"From a friend." Rebecca didn't look up from her laptop.

"*The Outlander* is one totally cool book. Have you read the whole series?"

Rebecca shook her head.

"The heroine goes back to save the Scotsman and after her husband dies she takes their red-haired daughter back. Totally romantic."

"She's not a dimwit."

"No way. She becomes a doctor and knows all about stuff people in olden times didn't know, like how to make penicillin."

"Um, a romance heroine who's a doctor, has a secret baby, is a damsel in peril, has great sex, and attempts to change history."

"Don't forget the marriage of convenience, lovers from different worlds, and adventures."

"I bet her publisher went crazy with a book so much longer than the usual romance. My clients are careful about the length of their books."

"Is Cora Ayne George one of your clients?" Rebecca nodded. "I'd like to meet her."

"I bet your mother would like her."

Aries grinned. "I don't think so."

"Too much alike," they said together.

"Cora is beautiful," Rebecca admitted. "Heather's

rumor source says she's had a procedure done after each book."

"She dates Hollywood stars."

"That's because her books make good movies. Each one gets more sexy."

"Have you something against sex?"

"I have something against formulaic sex." Rebecca was beginning to realize Aries really listened to her. She'd have to be careful what she said. The more she liked Aries and was comfortable with the young girl, the more complicated this babysitting deal became.

"You saved my dad."

"I did not. I poured water over him and called 911. He didn't even need rescuing."

Aries smiled. "He's a lot happier since you rescued him."

"Tell me about the novel your dad wrote."

"He didn't exactly write a novel. That book was channeled, too. He kept it secret for a long time. Mom found it, edited it and added more sex and violence." She grinned. "When she published it, Dad insisted that it was channeled by someone named M. Winter, Esq., not dopey Don Thomas. Some historian thinks the guy was a real person and could have been Dad's ancestor."

"What does Tom think about that?"

"He said that if that disgusting guy was real, he didn't want to know if he were the guy's descendant. Dad turned down movie deals twice. Finally Tristan brought Mom a miniseries contract behind Dad's back and Mom signed. After that, Mom and Dad didn't get along at all. Now Mom's pissed—I mean upset—that Dad won't sleep with her."

Rebecca said nothing. She did not want to discuss relations between Tom and Angie with their kid. She'd hoped silence would help change the subject.

"Dad's friend, Steve, writes books that become movies. He writes under more than one name. He's really smart, but it's confusing."

"Writers do that for many reasons. I am sure he has his."

There was a knock at the door and Aries dashed to answer. Josch stood in the doorway without roses, packages, or food.

Rebecca looked at him. "What do you want?"

He said nothing. Aries whispered, "Ask her about the fruit stand."

Rebecca looked at Aries, who gave her a pleading look and mouthed, "Please."

"Fine. I give up." Rebecca watched Aries' face open into big a grin. She was as good as her father at getting her way.

Josch pumped his arm in victory. "Thank you, ma'am...uh...Miz."

"I need the name of that fruit stand. And an address..."

Josch took a crumpled piece of paper from his baggy pants. "Here."

Rebecca scanned it. "Good. Now, this is what I am going to do. This is all. You hear me? I will write one letter telling them to cease misrepresenting the fruits."

"And veggies," Aries added.

"Will that work?" Josch looked doubtful.

"Young man, my letters work. A few of my words on New York law firm stationery bring large corporations to their knees. One papaya purveyor doesn't stand a chance."

Aries took Josch's hand. "I told you she was totally great."

Luckily Josch had returned to work before Tom arrived. Rebecca decided not to tell him about his daughter and the busboy.

Tom asked Rebecca to come along when he dropped Aries at the seminar site and suggested a walk along Oak Creek to fill her in on things she needed to know to handle his case. What could she do? Her boss had ordered her to keep Tom happy.

****

Tom drove Rebecca to a trail where they could walk in the afternoon shade. He looked great, but more ordinary in jeans and a t-shirt than the flowing white outfit. Rebecca resolved to keep the conversation strictly business. "Tell me more about these trance things that you do?"

Tom smiled. "What do you know about trance

channeling?"

"Not much. I've seen gypsies with crystal balls and TV guys that talk to dead grandmothers. Stuff like that."

"Channeling is like that, but different from fortunetelling or being a shaman—a witch doctor. I, personally, have no psychic talent at all."

"You can't read my mind?" He shook his head. "Thank goodness." She laughed as if it were a joke, but she was relieved. She'd had thoughts she'd rather not share, like how good holding his hand felt and how warm parts of her body became when he looked at her. She reminded herself again that Tom was her client.

"Some people channel an historical dead person like Socrates or Shakespeare, if they were actually real historical figures. Others channel entities from the astral plane who may never have lived in what we call a body," Tom explained.

"That's hard to grasp. Lawyers have a different definition of entity."

"Imagine a spirit who knows many things that people who live on this earth don't know. Someone like that, looking at us from above, could be a great teacher."

"Like a god?"

"We would think so. Ku is an entity who takes over my body and teaches wonderful things. A long time ago he had a body for a while, so that's why he appears to be Asian. He, or it, which is closer to the truth, started speaking through me about six months ago. I was so excited, I asked friends in California to audiotape one of his teachings, but when they tried to transcribe, the tape was completely blank."

"You don't know what you said?"

"No. When Ku takes over, I am what is known as an unconscious channel. Conscious channels are aware what the entity or spirit is saying. Some can even carry on a dialogue or ask questions."

"Like talking to yourself and getting answers?" Rebecca laughed. She didn't understand what he was trying so hard to explain, but Tom was so serious, she didn't want to hurt his feelings. "What about automatic writing? I thought that's what you did."

"When I began to write, my hand felt as if it belonged

to someone else. The handwriting was not mine and the thoughts were not mine. The only way to stop my hand was to throw the pen against the wall."

"Sounds weird."

"After a while, all I had to do was pick up a pen and the writing would start. In one hour a night, pages and pages were written. I felt comfortable with the spirit who was doing the writing. Sounds silly, but Ku—that's how he signed the papers—thanked me for helping him record his words. I wanted to help him."

Tom checked to see that Rebecca was still following his story and continued, "To shorten a long story, when I started grad school, I tried to talk to my professors about my spirit writing. They made it clear they thought I was weird, so I stopped talking. Since the content of Ku's writing gave me the ideas for my dissertation, I thought I could publish that and share the great things I had learned from him."

"Is your spirit like a personal seeress...uh, seer?"

Tom looked puzzled. "Where did you hear that term?"

"Just around. What does it mean?"

"A seeress is a female seer, like a prophetess. It can mean a powerful spirit who is taking care of you for some karmic reason."

"Are these spirits like ancestors?" Rebecca asked, remembering what Aries told her and wanting to end any talk of her own inner voice which she was sure was just imagination. Just imagination.

"Sometimes." Tom looked uncomfortable. "Once a spirit I thought was my ancestor demanded to take over my body. He wasn't like gentle Ku and seemed to have a very different agenda. I felt sick when he wrote. The next time, I said no. That was the first time I realized I had some choice. He returned stronger and forced me to write down what became the *Voodoo Island* story Angie published."

"So you published the work of this bad guy who moved your hand." Rebecca was trying to understand how the process worked. Sometimes she wondered where her authors got the bizarre stuff they wrote. Did many other writers do it this way?

"I was trying to get my dissertation published when I

met Angie. She read it and said she liked my ideas and asked if I had more. I showed her my six years of notebooks. She said they were publishable—if we set me up as a medium."

"That's what you were."

"I never thought of myself that way. Besides..." he looked down, "...after I met Angie, Ku never wrote through me again. When I tried to contact Ku, the nasty spirit took over and wrote about 1800s West Indies plantation life filled with sex, violence, and cruelty. Angie liked it. By then I was already making a name with workshops and the first Ku books."

This talk made Rebecca's head spin.

"But, now you go into *real* trances."

"Right. Now Ku is speaking—not writing—through me. I know he's come back to get those words right—the ones my hand wrote all those years ago. I never should have let Angie distort his teachings."

"Can you go into a trance, so I can see?" Rebecca wanted Tom to stop being so down on himself. Normally, when one of her clients began negative talk like that, she'd recommend a shrink and medication before writer's block impacted her firm's bottom line.

"I don't know. I'm like an old-fashioned party line telephone. Sometimes you can't know who is going to call or when. Now my trances are happening when I'm playing that fake Don Thomas. I think because I'm more open then." He saw disappointment in Rebecca's eyes. "I can try. Like the time at the river. When you found me." He winked. "Promise you won't pour water on me?"

She rolled her eyes. "I am sorry about that."

They walked on until Tom found a bench under a large sycamore. He settled himself and Rebecca sat next to him.

"Don't worry," he told her. "Nothing bad is going to happen. If you're uncomfortable at all, shake my arm gently until I come out of it. Call my name. No yelling or water. Promise?"

She smiled and nodded. He was joking and acting as if having someone else in his body was the most ordinary thing in the world.

He sat back on the bench, closed his eyes, and slowed

his breathing. In a few minutes his breath accelerated and his hands, which had lain motionless in his lap, twitched.

Rebecca jumped. She stood and moved in front of him to watch him more carefully.

The changes began, faster than the other time. His face contorted and his head snapped back. He moaned. Already she wanted to call for help. Now that she knew Tom, seeing him this way was much more frightening. She forced herself to stay still, though she held her cell phone tight in case she needed to call for help. She already wanted to shake him awake.

His clothes seemed looser. He shook and settled again. A voice—the gentle voice from that night in the lecture hall—began, "Beloveds. I speak through this good man to teach. I mean him no harm. I mean no harm to any human in body. I seek to tell of joy and happiness for all who become one in spirit."

"Tom. Can you hear me?" Rebecca whispered.

"Tom," the voice answered, "as you call him, cannot hear you or me. But you, Rebecca, can hear me." The spirit thing was talking to her. "Tell Tom there is another powerful spirit who comes through his body. I feel his residue in Tom's cells. His motives are not peaceful. At this moment he is fighting with me to come through."

Tom's face tightened and he shivered. His face regained firmness, but did not return to looking like Tom. Instead his chin broadened and his eyes became larger and less Asian. His skin seemed to weather before her eyes.

Rebecca saw a rakish smirk contort Tom's gentle lips. A deep voice rasped, "I won and I will win again."

Tom's body was now twitching all over. Little Rebecca cried, *Wake him up, now!* Rebecca couldn't stand it any longer. She grabbed his arm, "Tom. Tom. Wake up." Then louder, "Wake up. Now!"

He shook his head and morphed back to Tom.

"You scared me." She reached forward and took his hands. One was icy and the other very warm. "Please don't do that again." She released his hands.

"No need to do that," he said, squeezing her hands before they slipped from his grasp. "You can hold my hands any time."

Rebecca laughed self-consciously, but squeezed back. "I was just worried about my client spacing out."

"Remember, I space out a lot. This time I did it because you requested a trance. Tell me what happened?"

"There were two people or whatevers. One, Ku I think, said to tell you there is a not-so-good-guy who comes through your body."

"I had that feeling. I think that's why I get so tired. I've known for a long time there is something about me that allows spirits to pop in. I've always been a pushover."

"Who's that second guy? My God, now I'm talking as if having two extra guys in your body is normal." She covered her face with her hands. "This is crazy."

He smiled and looked into her eyes. "You're doing fine. You know what I really want?"

"Food and rest," she answered. "I can take you out to eat. That I do very well."

He sighed. "You're getting to be a great woo-woo lawyer after all." He pulled her to her feet and led her up the path.

She moved along at his side. Law school had not prepared her for days like these.
****

Back in her cottage, Rebecca opened her laptop and clicked to her e-mail. The messages took longer than usual to load. When the inbox came up, it was filled with 42 new messages: two from Heather, a note from her mother, and 39 messages from...Max. She opened the first. Blank. So were the next fifteen. Then one contained merely "Dear Rebe..." She scrolled down to the last one and opened it.
****

*From: maxwinter@yahoo.net*
*To: rjd@bankheadfirm.com*
*Subject:*
*Dear Rebecca,*
*I am struggling with your style of communication. I have been told it is instant, but I have spent hours to send even one message. The young person who is helping me told me I was pressing the "Send" button instead of the space*

*button. I will send documentation soon to you, but not yet. I will learn scanning and attachments when my tutor can get off duty. Are you sure this is the way everyone communicates now?*

*Your frustrated Max*

## Chapter 10

The next morning, Rebecca woke from a fiery dream and couldn't concentrate because she kept remembering Tom's scary trance. Aries opted for shopping at outlet mall stores near Bell Rock, so now Rebecca watched the young teen zigzag through the Gap. Why the kid wanted to come to national chains when there were delightful unique shops all over Sedona, Rebecca didn't know.

Aries picked up and discarded tiny tops and shorts from sale tables. Both hands flicked hanging garments as if she were flipping through a magazine. When she touched something that caught her interest, she'd stop, rifle for a size tag and throw the item over her arm until she called, "Rebecca, ready for the dressing room?"

"Sure." Rebecca took the black skirt and jacket she'd found and followed. At first Little Rebecca had been shocked, then fascinated, by the fashions and lingerie in the shops. She'd told Rebecca she liked Tom's daughter Aries but thought she acted much older than any young girl she'd met.

Aries stripped to her bra and panties and began trying on the tangle of clothing. She was already tossing rejects on a chair, while Rebecca took off her long dress and slid the black skirt over her hips. It was tight. Usually a six was a perfect fit. This one must be mis-sized. That was one of the reasons she hated outlet shopping.

Aries stopped. "Where are you going to wear that?"

"Casual business stuff...dates." This kid constantly

put her on the defensive. She had great fashion sense and a fabulous wardrobe.

"You said you didn't date."

"I date. When Tristan and I were engaged, we went out all the time. Business dinners, parties, that kind of thing."

"Cool parties? My mom goes to parties with lots of famous people."

"Well, sometimes I meet movie people—Brad Pitt once—and authors, but mostly other lawyers, at Bar Association lectures—I mean galas."

"You have no social life because you have totally no wardrobe."

"My wardrobe is fine for my life."

"Then you need to get a life. I saw that suit you wore when you got here. You're too old to wear black." She pulled a skirt from her pile, slipped it over nonexistent hips, tied a fringed scarf around her waist, and shimmied into a tiny rainbow top. She added black glass earrings and plopped a gold lamé baseball hat on her head.

"If you showed up dressed like this for one of your little parties, you'd be dating those movie stars. Rebecca, you really are an attractive woman."

"I'm old enough to be your mother. I don't need a thirteen-year-old fashion consultant."

Aries untied the scarf and wrapped it around Rebecca's hips, arranged the fringe, and added the earrings. "Put on the hat," she ordered.

Rebecca did as she was told. The hat looked surprisingly stylish, though it covered most of her hair.

Aries nodded. "Good. Let's pay for this stuff and get some shoes."

They dressed. Aries scooped up the keepers and Rebecca hurried after her. At the sales counter, Aries paid for her purchases with her own charge card. Rebecca bought the skirt in a size eight, as well as red glass earrings and the gold hat. The black skirt was a good buy, despite the label with the wrong size. What the hell, it didn't mean she'd ever wear the other stuff.

At the shoe store, Aries found two pairs of sandals that were perfect for Rebecca, then dragged her through the lingerie outlet. Aries bought three thongs and two padded bras. Rebecca announced she didn't see anything she needed. Aries carefully explained that you never really needed underwear, at least not sexy, romantic lingerie.

"Then why buy it?" Rebecca asked.

"Because you never know."

"Know what?"

"You know."

"Oh." Rebecca blushed. What else did this kid know? "So, it's like wearing clean underwear just in case you have to go to the hospital?"

"Exactly."

Rebecca shook her head. During her unexpected sexual encounters—she'd had a few—underwear had never seemed all that important. Getting it off had been the issue. Anyway, what did a kid know? "Aries, do you have a boyfriend?" she asked, trying to determine her level of experience.

"Sort of...well, not anymore..." Now Aries blushed. "Well, I totally liked this cute guy in my class, but—since Mom's divorce I've traveled with her—I'm not in regular school any more. My girlfriend, Korika, told me Damon was going out with Pandora. How can I have a normal life if I'm never home? There are never, ever any guys at these retreats. One time there was a fifteen-year-old with his mother, but he was a total weirdo."

"What about Josch?"

"He's cute and totally smart." Aries smiled. "Dad would go ballistic if he knew such an old guy was my friend. I'll be a virgin forever if I have to stay with Mom all the time."

"Would you rather live with your dad?" Rebecca made a mental note to bill this shopping trip to Tom's account as an interview for the custody hearing.

"Yeah, that would be cool. He's tough and, well, geeky, but he'd let me go to a real school and have friends." She sighed. "The end of unlimited charges and lots of freedom would be bad, but I'd get a life."

They checked out two more shops and ended up in the bookstore. Aries surprised Rebecca by buying the latest Jennifer Crusie and Julie Kenner novels and ignoring the remainder tables, filled with cheap literary mistakes in all genres mixed with brilliant first novel authors.

Rebecca, as usual, scanned the remainders for books by her clients, and happily found none. Bad sales or overprinting of a hardback edition could be a sign that an author's career was slipping. Once she saw one of Claude's books on a remainder table three months after publication, the result of a postponed movie deal and his refusal to do late night talk show interviews.

Rebecca bought the sequel to *The Outlander* and they walked to an outdoor café for lunch. When Rebecca came back from paying for their lunches, Aries was reading, but not one of her new purchases. "What's that? Those pages look like part of a manuscript."

"My aunt's e-mailing me one chapter at a time. Remember the diary I told you about?"

"Is it good?" Rebecca felt remorse for never returning the borrowed pages.

"An old gothic novel with a brave heroine. Very English."

"Read a little to me. Maybe I could get her an agent."

Aries began to read:

****

*January 12, 1863*
*London*
*My dear Uncle thinks he is getting old and wants to find me a husband, yet since that awful séance party I have refused all social invitations. He has been my guardian after my parents' death, and both mother and father after his barren wife passed on.*

*I am a girl of marriageable age in a household without a woman, but I fear many men will never consider me, for I am excessively bold and busy myself with ledgers and contracts, which is quite unseemly. I pull my pale hair back quite tightly and wear plain dark dresses. I have grown tall with eyes and mouth too large to be considered a beauty.*

*Although I am dreadfully old for marriage, I am not unaccomplished. I am mistress of my Uncle's home and help him in his business. He often says no son of his could have a mind half as quick as mine. But he cautions me to be not proud.*

*If I were his son, I would have my own ship and sail the world—perhaps to the West Indies for real adventures.*

\*\*\*\*

"Totally like you, Rebecca," Aries teased.

Little Rebecca said, *She's right. What a bright young girl. She sees the resemblance.* Rebecca ignored her.

"No way. What's this heroine's name?"

"Arianna. That's also my aunt's name."

"Were you named for her?"

"Sort of. Mom was in a weakened condition. She agreed to name me Arianna, if I could be called Aries like my astrological sign. Dad likes that it's a family name."

"I like the diary. Read some more."

\*\*\*\*

*January 20, 1863*
*London*

*Today as I worked on accounts, a tall, dark man came to do business with Uncle. The man saw me and was dumbstruck. I felt like an iced teacake spied by a young boy who then began to plot how to have the cake before his companion.*

*Uncle thinks well of this man whom he calls The Major and agreed when the gentleman asked to call on me. I am used to the company of men because of my association with Uncle's shipyard, but the looming man does not put me at ease. This evening he came to dinner and brought small trinkets. I feel him arrogant and do not believe his tales of military life, seafaring, and the rich lands he owns in the West Indies.*

\*\*\*\*

*January 28, 1863*
*London*

*This dark man fawns and sends gifts and wheedles into the graces of my Uncle who is impressed by this man's fine manners and vows of eternal love, but his eyes shift when I look into them. I trust him not. I am no longer a silly girl.*

*Uncle's business ventures are extensive and I am his only heir.*

\*\*\*\*

*February 4, 1863*
*London*
*Last evening Uncle and this Major were closeted in the study of our townhouse. This morning Uncle came to me and told me the gentleman asked for my hand in marriage. My heart turned cold. I told Uncle I would never marry him.*

*Tonight the Major returned to present his suit to me. My ears were deaf as we walked in the garden. The Major took me in his arms and performed a great liberty. My body felt as if encased with rough oily wool. I broke away and ran to Uncle. I stomped my foot and told him I would never see this despicable person again. Oh, if Uncle knew all, he would have thrown the not-gentleman out on his oh-so-fine-black-suit.*

\*\*\*\*

Rebecca nodded. "Feels historically authentic. Little Rebecca added, *I'd say so. Life was very different. You modern women have no idea the limitations women in the past suffered. That woman could have become a lawyer like you.* She sounded so sad, Rebecca wondered how her imaginary voice could know. "Pretty feisty lady for her day. Let me know when you have more."

"So, you're hooked, too."

\*\*\*\*

After lunch Rebecca dropped Aries at the seminar site and Tom got into her SUV. She realized she'd begun to look forward to spending afternoons with him.

"I have a job for my new attorney," he told her with a smug grin.

Rebecca was curious. Tom usually was pretty straightforward, which helped her forget his peculiar career choice. At least he didn't want to hear about her plan for the custody suit—because she didn't have one.

"I've rented a sound studio in town with audio and video facilities. I want you to help tape a trance. I'd rather not have outside techies. This will not be for prime time."

Rebecca liked the plan immediately. "We could document it like a deposition."

"Good idea. An hour should be enough time. Can you help set it up and then run the equipment?" He tapped the steering wheel in anticipation.

"Sure." Rebecca laughed. "You look very happy."

"This is so great. I've never seen what happens to me during a trance. Even when I did automatic writing I was not there. I wondered how I looked. A little Asian?"

"Actually, when I found you along the river I thought your eyes were a bit slanty."

Tom smiled. "As Aries would say, totally cool."

They turned left onto one of Sedona's few commercial side streets and found that the studio was an ordinary boxy warehouse in a town where McDonald's had a southwestern façade and no arches.

Jim, the studio's owner and manager, showed them around while a rock band packed up and carried gear to a VW bus.

"I didn't think there were any left," Tom commented.

"Musicians or VW buses?" Jim raised his eyebrows. "We get all types here. Lots of new New Age musicians performing their meditation, environmental, and healing music with sound effects. We also produce CDs and videos for resale. Lots of Sedona woo-woos have their own distribution channels...sorry," he said when Tom and Rebecca began laughing.

"We're familiar with the term," Tom told him. "Technical, right?"

"Of course. Some days I think I'm still a woo-woo roadie." Jim relaxed and led them to the main studio. "I learned sound work on the road with gurus in the 60s and lived to tell about it, so I can laugh at them now." When the last of the band's gear was off the sound stage, he said, "So, what will you need? I have lots of props."

"A chair, a plain white backdrop, and good lighting," Rebecca requested. "I need two cameras set with date and time, continuous filming, and a copy of today's newspaper, so there can be no question of tampering."

"That is a problem with digitally produced film. Any teenager with a computer and a little software can alter digital records. You should see the alien abduction films that are coming out of New Mexico. Even old grainy flying saucer clips can be doctored to look as real as the latest sci-fi flick at Harkins."

Jim set up the two cameras. Rebecca specified one front view and one for a continuous side shot. He started to clip a mike to Tom's shirt.

"No. That'll get in the way." Rebecca removed the mike. "Jim, do you have a boom mike?"

Jim went to find an old boom and Rebecca began arranging the set. She chose a simple folding chair and a white sheet backdrop from the prop room. Then she sent Tom to change. "Don't forget. No sandals or watch. And lose that necklace."

"You don't like the chain?" He'd noticed her little grimace. "I wear it for public appearances. Angie says it goes with the guru garb and hides the wireless mike. We sell replicas." He pulled it over his head. "I never liked it. Too heavy and fake."

Jim came back with the last of the equipment and asked Rebecca, "Are you sure you don't want me to hang around?"

"I'll be fine. I've taken video depositions all over the country."

"I know it's none of my business, but this looks a lot more interesting than wedding videos and educational lectures. That stuff pays the rent, along with rock bands that all sound alike and New Age music that's mostly flutes, waterfalls, and weird electronics. The rest of my work is radio ads for used car dealers and palm readers."

"Sorry Jim..." Rebecca began to dismiss his offer. "You seem like a solid kind of guy. What's your take on Sedona spiritual stuff?"

"I keep my opinions to myself. The guru trade helps pay my bills." He gestured toward the restroom. "Your client is Tom Paxton, isn't he?" Rebecca nodded. "I'd love to do work for him and break into the big time, but..."

"But..."

"Personally, I think most of it is crap. Guess I've seen too much."

"Perfect." Rebecca nodded. "Please stay. We could use you. Another pair of eyes would help and another camera. Then I'd like to interview you. You'll get paid for the interview."

"Sounds great, Ms. Dumaurier. But you don't have to pay me extra and I won't charge for Camera Three. I'll use film instead of digital on that one. Just for the record." He began setting up the third camera and loading film.

Tom came out barefoot in a white tank top and running shorts. "How's this?" he asked.

"Good. The fewer clothes to get in the way, the better." He looked better than good. Nicely muscled body, but not that gym rat ripped look some men go for.

Tom gave her a sexy look. "That's what I say."

She ignored him and began checking camera angles. "Please, sit down and say a few words for the sound check."

"One Beloved...two Beloved..." Tom droned in a gravelly imitation guru voice.

"Stop kidding around. The clock is running. The hourly rate here is not as high as L.A. or New York, but it's expensive." She tried to sound tough, but she really liked how Tom could be funny, even at serious times. She sensed he was worried about what happened during his trances.

"Can you turn off the lights? I need to relax. Give me a few minutes, then slowly bring them up. You do the intro and then I'll try to go into a trance. If it's going to work, it shouldn't take long."

"*If* it works? I thought..."

"Spirits aren't always on call. Ku could be out to lunch with Gandhi or Seth."

Rebecca and Jim looked confused.

"Sorry, it's an inside joke," said Tom.

When Tom looked ready, Rebecca signaled Jim to turn up the lights and she stepped in front of the camera. "My name is R.J. Dumaurier. I represent the law firm of Bankhead Blanding of New York City. This is Wednesday, September 30, 2006. I am here at Video Productions Studio in Sedona, Arizona. With me is Jim Kinney, owner and manager, and Tom Paxton. We will film Mr. Paxton as he attempts to go into a trance. Three cameras are recording this test." She turned to Tom. "Mr. Paxton, will you read the prepared statement, so we can record your natural speaking voice and facial mannerisms."

Tom smiled boyishly, looked directly at the camera in front of him, and began reading. Rebecca stood to one side and nodded. So far, so good. She'd been around Tom long enough to know he was a good lecturer with a warm, kind manner, but not a polished actor. She wanted to be sure everyone viewing this video knew it too.

When Tom finished, she took the paper from his hand, stepped back, and waited. He closed his eyes and began slow, deep breathing.

Rebecca held her breath. Nothing happened. She looked at Jim, who'd pulled up a chair behind the main camera and was monitoring sound levels. He looked bored, but she'd pay him well for an hour of Tom sitting in a chair and breathing.

When she saw Jim's eyes open wide, she snapped her attention back to Tom.

Tom's torso jerked and he gasped for breath. His head fell back like it was not attached to his neck. His entire body jumped like a man jolted with the first surge from an electric chair, then jerked all over in epileptic movements.

Little Rebecca just kept repeating, *Thomas, Thomas,* over and over.

Rebecca wanted to go to him and prevent him from falling off the chair, but as she shifted to move forward, he stopped. He stretched and contorted the muscles of his face, then relaxed and began swaying back and forth. His fingers twitched and his bare toes wiggled. All expression was absent from his face. He appeared younger, softer, and paler. The skin below his eyes was smooth, the fold over each eye was definitely Asian, and his forehead looked higher.

She hoped the cameras were getting all this. She couldn't wait to depose Jim and get his impressions on tape.

Tom became still. His eyes opened. He took a deep breath and spoke. "Beloveds. I am honored you want to talk with me. I am Ku Wan Ku. My old friend, Tom, has welcomed me into his body to speak with you. He tells me there are cameras. Today that is fine with me, for it is important to Tom."

Rebecca stood motionless. Tom was no longer Tom. His eyes curved up at the edges. His voice was higher pitched and sounded much older. His shoulders looked less muscular and more relaxed and—she wanted to say—peaceful. His whole being now appeared non-threatening and wise in a way that made her feel warm and calm inside. What was she thinking? This was Tom, not some Asian alien.

"Rebecca," the kind voice said, "don't be afraid. Tom is not afraid. He has graciously loaned me his body as he has done many times before."

Jim whispered to Rebecca, "Talk to him."

She looked Ku in the eye and stepped to a position where her profile would be filmed by the left camera. With more confidence than she felt, she began, "Ku, sir, I am Rebecca. I am honored to meet you. Can you raise your hands, please?"

Ku slowly raised one arm, then the other a little more surely, as if he were manipulating a puppet. "How interesting. I have not had a body of my own for thousands of years. I remember now." He shifted his weight and pushed himself off the seat and stood. His movements were creaky, like a very old man, not a healthy young runner. He did a slow shuffle in a circle around the chair, keeping one hand on the chair back for support. She saw a shy smile and was pleased for the old man. She saw Tom's body, but the muscles and joints appeared to belong to someone else. Not Tom at all, but Tom's friend, Ku.

Whoa...what was she thinking? Until this moment she'd convinced herself that it didn't matter if Tom really became a different person, but now her breath came short and quick. He was actually letting someone use his body. A shiver went all through her at the thought, but yet she was drawn to the gentle Ku.

Ku finished circling the chair and sank back to sitting. "So, was that good?" he asked.

"Yes Ku, that was excellent." Then louder to be certain the mike picked it up, she added, "Thank you."

"My friend, Tom, feels I need to prove who I am. I am considering how to do that..." Ku's voice faded.

For a few minutes nothing happened. Then Ku began to sing. The song was meaningless syllables to Rebecca, but Jim nodded and began to sing along. When Ku finished, Jim took the mike, "Thank you, Ku. My wife is an ethnomusicologist and she taught me that very ancient song, passed down to the people she studied in Tibet."

Ku nodded and said, first in English, "Beloveds, I bring words of peace and love..." Then he seemed to be repeating the same words over and over, each time in a different language.

When Ku finished, he bowed stiffly to Rebecca and Jim. "Goodbye Beloveds," he said sweetly and closed his eyes.

Rebecca watched as the transformation changed the ancient Asian back into the young, vigorous Tom Paxton.

Tom opened his eyes, gasped and shook his head. Rebecca stepped up and touched his shoulder. "Are you all right?" she asked. Tom nodded. Then she faced the camera. "Mr. Paxton, can you tell us about your experience? How did you feel?"

"Ms. Dumaurier, all I can say is, I had a nice nap. Did I miss anything interesting?" he said with a very American grin.

## Chapter 11

Still reviewing that afternoon taping session, Rebecca cracked the door, expecting the young pierced waiter to be coming to retrieve her dinner tray. Instead Babs Hemingway squinted out at her from under a big floppy hat. Opening the door wider, she told Babs, "Come on in."

Babs slipped in, turning her long neck clandestinely over her shoulder to see if anyone had seen her.

"How was your spa day?" Rebecca noticed Babs' less gooselike posture.

"Fine," Babs said. "The day will be much better if you have made my publicity crisis go away. After my massage, I realized that all the retractions in the world would not make the problem vanish."

"Good. You're starting to understand the way the world works."

"Don't be snide, R.J., I can fire you any time. I am a major American literary figure. I can take my business elsewhere."

For a gleeful moment Rebecca considered taking Babs up on her offer. But Babs' books did sell well and she was not usually a nasty client. This was a difficult time for her. So, in her best barrister's voice Rebecca asked, "Ms. Hemingway, would you fire the person responsible for booking you on *Oprah*?"

Babs' mouth dropped open. "You..." she sputtered.

"You can talk about whatever you like."

"I can talk about my books and raise money for my

orphans' home?" Babs' head bobbled up and down.

"Yes, and you have just two days to prepare." Rebecca took a breath. Babs was out of her hair.

Babs turned. "Only two days. I have to get back home. I'll take all the children. Oprah will love them. We'll wear..." Halfway out the door, she twisted her neck. "Oh, R.J., I knew you'd think of something."

Rebecca couldn't wait to tell Heather that Mother Goose was flying home. But when she called, Heather ignored her news. "Check out the latest issue of *Publishers' Weekly*. An article claims our Claude is from Venus."

"Heather. Talk sense," Rebecca demanded.

"There's this new computer program that can tell if a book is written by a man or a woman."

"The programs I am familiar with have not been proven that good."

"The developers of this one claim eighty to ninety percent accuracy. There are lots of jokes about the mistakes, but the theory is causing quite a stir. Some English professor in Ohio claims Queen Elizabeth wrote Hamlet."

"What does this have to do with Claude?"

"Well, someone took the latest Cleo St. Cloud book, the one about the Borgia countess and the Chinese warlord, and ran passages through that program. The writing came up Male-Masculine, a category only a man could have written—theoretically."

"Romance novels are written about women for women." Rebecca stopped. "But...Cleo is Claude. And Claude is a guy."

"Bingo. And now Claude is using the publicity as an excuse to come out of the ladies' closet."

"I need to talk him out of it. Give him my number here." Rebecca looked around at her room. Besides the laptop and printer on the antique desk, piles of books and papers made the room look more like an office than a vacation retreat. "Tell me again how that program works."

"The basic theory claims women use more personal pronouns and guys are more comfortable with things— nouns. This particular program utilizes a higher level of artificial intelligence to analyze text than the older versions."

"So, they are saying Cleo's book is about things?"

"No. That the writing talks about women's stuff like a man."

"That's silly. E-mail me all the research on this program."

"One more tidbit. Tristan—remember your old flame—left a message. He said, 'Tell Rebecca not to try to take Angie away from me.'"

"As if Angie Baby would even talk to me."

"Because you're in love with her ex?"

Heather was in trouble now. "Tom and I are friends. He's my client."

"R.J., you never had a guy friend. Especially not a client." Heather paused. "I don't think you ever had a girl friend."

"Enough. You have crossed the line—again! And send me the latest legal stuff on plagiarism."

"Why plagiarism?"

"Because I asked for it." Rebecca clicked off before Heather could ask more questions. She still wasn't ready to talk about Max.

As she finished responding to the day's batch of e-mails, she heard a knock. She opened the door and Josch handed her a large flat white box tied with a pink satin ribbon.

She carried the box to her bed. Opening the box—she knew it was from Max—she began separating layers of tissuey paper until her fingertips brushed fabric. She stroked cotton so soft it felt like fine silk. With care she lifted a garment free from the wrappings and held up a nightgown. No. Calling this a nightgown would be like calling a vintage touring auto a used car. This piece of lingerie made Victoria's Secret panties look like nylon flea market bloomers. Looking closely, the antique linen looked handmade with exquisite stitches so tiny she couldn't see where one ended and the next began.

She examined the linguini-thin straps and bits of silk embroidered into an intricate design of roses at the bodice and hem. Matching rosebuds framed the low-cut neckline. The dress was revealing, but, she told herself, no more than many designer evening gowns.

Little Rebecca said, *That is lovely. Don't you just love gorgeous night dresses? But it doesn't feel quite right. Where did it come from?*

Rebecca picked up the note, that in her rush to open the package, had fallen on the floor.

\*\*\*\*

> *Dearest,*
> *I cannot wait to see you wearing this.*
> *Until tomorrow evening,*
> *Love, Max*

\*\*\*\*

Rebecca was afraid to try it on. She held it up and stood before the mirror inside the armoire's doors.

"Oh," she told the mirror. "This is the most beautiful thing I have ever seen." Little Rebecca's voice quivered. *Send the dress back.*

"No! It's a great dress."

*You can buy lots of great dresses. You said your plastic money is good all over the world.*

"But I like this dress. No one ever gave me a gift like this. And if you don't like it, be quiet. I won't let you spoil my vacation."

The phone rang. She cried, "Max!" Still holding the dress, she rushed to the phone, snatched it up, and gushed, "I love it. Absolutely love it. Thank you so much."

The voice on the other end sounded miffed. "Rebecca? It's Tom."

"Oh. Tom. Sure. Sorry. I thought you were someone else." Earlier Tom said he wanted her to meet an old friend of his. She'd been rude to brush him off, but in the evenings, her mind was consumed with thoughts of Max and his gifts.

She stroked the dress. This gift could mean only one thing. More than roses or poems, this was very, very personal.

"Rebecca, I'm worried about you." Tom sounded concerned. "I thought you might reconsider and join me and let me introduce you to my old friend Steve."

"I'm fine. Have a nice dinner." She hung up.

\*\*\*\*

Tom put down the phone and turned to Steve, who

was doing one-armed pushups on the rug in Tom's cottage. "Rebecca turned me down. I wanted her to meet you. I'm not doing so well with her." He yawned just watching Steve work out. Where did his friend get all the energy? After their five-mile run this morning, Steve did laps in the hotel pool. Then after he'd rested by writing a couple of chapters for his Bullet sequel, he started this intense workout.

"Advice on romance? I can't help. I'm still pretty new to that game, but I do like those hotels that leave a blue Viagra pill on your pillow instead of a mint."

Steve's humor didn't make Tom smile.

"Got to take care of the old bod. Sure went through a lot to get it." Steve grunted. "Let's make reservations for dinner at that steak place again." He pulled the phone book out of the desk along with a CD of the Gideon Bible. "I'll make reservations."

"I might as well deal with my e-mail." Tom opened the new laptop he'd bought for this trip and punched keys for a while. "Someone's been messing with my computer. I want to get my e-mail and now this infernal thing won't take my password." Until their divorce, Angie had done all their correspondence and financial work that required a computer. Tom was convinced anything electronic hated him. Files would disappear overnight. Floppy disks demagnetized if he came close. Cell phones refused to work, but now he needed to handle his own business and computers were mandatory.

Steve said, "Let me take a look. What's your password?"

Tom told him, "Rebecca."

Steve raised his eyebrows, typed it in, and waited. "Access Denied."

"That's what I get."

Steve's fingers flew over the keys. "I see several giant e-mail files, but without passwords I can't touch them. Some guru—computer guru—set this up. I can't figure it out. If it were mine, I'd wipe everything and start over. How do you live without being computer literate?"

"I have a typewriter and send pages to a typist. People think I'm old fashioned using phones with wires, but it's the only way for me. One time Angie asked if I could do automatic writing with a computer. What a joke. My sister Arianna gave up sending me e-mails and now she's e-mailing segments of that diary directly to Aries' laptop."

"I always liked your big sister. She was nice to me when I was an ugly kid. We had some great conversations, but she wouldn't date me." Steve ran his fingers over his abdomen. "She should see my new six-pack."

"She was a lot older than you."

"She told me that when you were a kid, you weren't shy—before you started having the imaginary friends."

Tom looked down. "That was before my mother left. I was twelve, Arianna was already in college. After that Dad wouldn't talk about my special extrasensory talents."

"Tough age for a boy. Why did...I mean...I never asked..."

"That's OK. I've been thinking about what happened. Mom left after the summer the whole family went hiking in Arizona. I fell climbing in Sycamore Canyon and clunked my head pretty bad. Mom sat up with me all night. Now I think that might have been the first time I went into a trance. She was always complaining of Dad's dreams or sleepwalking, or what she called crazy talk."

Steve nodded encouragement and Tom continued. "I found a note she wrote to my dad. She said she'd put up with his nightmares for twenty years, but she couldn't bear to see her son go crazy the same way. From then on I worried that if I was alone with someone I could accidentally go into a trance and they'd tell everyone I was crazy. I got pretty shy."

"That's bad."

"I suppressed all ESP stuff till the automatic writing. When I married Angie, that stopped. When she got me to do the fake guru stuff, I almost forgot the real thing. I guess I'm still the weak channel again. I'm like a telephone that gets everyone's calls."

"What about your dad?"

"He refused to talk to me about it. Dad was disappointed I studied philosophy. He hoped I'd join his law practice."

"Parents try to do the best for their kids. Would you

want Aries to be a medium?"

"No. And I definitely don't want her to marry one."

## Chapter 12

Aries arrived at Rebecca's cottage at the usual time to find Rebecca still in her robe sorting through bottles of lotions, oils, and powders. Aries sniffed. "This room smells like an aromatherapy testing laboratory."

Rebecca didn't raise her turbaned head from reading cosmetic labels. "Elise from the spa is coming to give me a massage and facial. I could go there to get wrapped in seaweed. Or mud. Which do you think would be better?" Rebecca jumped up and phoned the spa and added a manicure and pedicure to her order. "So much to do." She paced back and forth between the bed and bathroom.

"What is going on? You are totally frantic." Aries sounded like a grownup talking to an ADD child.

"Nothing. I've got a...a date tonight—that's all. I want to look my best."

"A massage isn't the answer," Aries said, examining the assortment of hair products.

"What does that mean?" Rebecca heard herself sound like an insecure child looking for approval.

"Your hair." Aries sat on the bed and pulled the towel off Rebecca's head.

"Don't touch my hair. I had my hairdresser in New York FedEx a bottle of my regular stuff." She held up a clear plastic bottle containing a black substance. "I always use this."

Aries took the bottle and squeezed a dollop into her palm. She smelled, wrinkled her nose, and rubbed the substance, the consistency of black toothpaste, around with the index finger of her other hand. "Ugh! Totally ugh!" She walked to the bathroom and started squirting the contents into the toilet.

"Stop. You brat. That cost a fortune."

"I know a lot about hair. I do all my friends' hair."

"What color? Blue? Green?" Rebecca grabbed the half empty bottle.

"*If* they look good with blue or green hair. You..." she squinted, "would not look so good in green hair."

"Give it up. Get out."

"Let me fix your hair. If you absolutely hate it, I'll help you spread this ca-ca on your head for your date with my dad."

"I'm not going out with your dad. He's my client. I don't date..." Her voice trailed off, realizing Max was also her client.

"Dad really likes you. You'd be good for each other. Do you remember the book where Babs had this thirteen-year-old girl find her dad a new wife?"

"That was just a story. Your father and I are friends, just friends."

Aries snapped back, "No guy, except Popeye, wants to date a woman with Olive Oyl hair."

Rebecca thumbed her nose. "You're just a kid. What do you know?" Little Rebecca whispered, *Give the kid a chance. She's right. How much worse could your hair look?*

Aries washed Rebecca's hair over the bathroom sink. She finished and sat the squirming woman in front of the desk. "You need a distraction while I finish the styling." Aries pulled pages from her messenger bag. "Here. This just came. Read it out loud."

Rebecca eagerly took the pages and read.
\*\*\*\*

*March 8, 1863*
*London*
*This glorious day a sweet gentle man named Thomas came to Uncle to arrange a shipping contract for the West Indies plantation he has inherited from his father. I saw that he was still sad over his loss and to be leaving his education to take over the running of the plantation called St. Albans Moon. To ease his sadness, I smiled*

108

*boldly at him and he lost the words from his mouth. My heart is light. I do hope he is not too shy, but returns soon.*

****

*March 12, 1863*
*London*
*Thomas has come to the office every day this week and we amended his contract many times. Tonight he came to call upon Uncle at our home and Uncle told me sweet Thomas asked for my hand. I immediately said yes, I would be this wonderful man's wife. I feel like one of my roses opening to greet the dawn of a new life.*

*Because Thomas needs to reach St. Albans Island by the pineapple harvest, we will be speedily wed and travel to the West Indies in the Captain's Quarters of his ship, The Windswept.*

****

"Now comes the good part," Aries said, brushing the still-damp back of Rebecca's hair.

"I doubt if your aunt would send you anything too racy."

"You don't know my Aunt Arianna!"

****

*June 20, 1863,*
*The Windswept*
*Modesty forbids I comment on the joys of the journey. I am sure it would have been quite tedious, save for my sweet Thomas. In the long hours at sea he teaches me about plantation accounts and educates me in the ways of plantation life.*

****

Rebecca laughed, "I bet he did."

Aries looked disappointed. "I hoped for more details."

There was a knock on Rebecca's door.

"Aries, honey," Tom called, "are you ready?"

"Come on in, Dad. I'm finishing Rebecca's hair."

Tom opened the door. Rebecca stood next to Aries. His mouth dropped open. He stared. "You're a..."

"Yes." Aries grinned. "Who could have guessed? Her dark comic book look was totally a cover-up. Rebecca may be a blonde with beautiful wavy hair. More than one washing will be necessary to remove all the dark tint, but this is a start. I made her beautiful."

"You didn't make her beautiful." Tom stepped closer. "But you really changed her hair." He reached out. "So soft, like dark amber."

"No. No. Leave it alone," Aries warned. "It's still damp."

Rebecca grimaced. "Your daughter is pretty stubborn when she sets her mind to something."

"I know. But in this case, she was absolutely right. You're beautiful."

"Thanks," Rebecca said.

Aries hugged her. "Have a great time and tell me all the details in the morning."

"About what?" Tom asked.

"Totally girl talk." Aries pulled her reluctant father through the door.

"Where is she going tonight?" Tom asked as he carried Aries' gear to the van.

"I can't tell you." She tossed her head in the way women learned to exclude men from their world.

****

Tom left Aries with Angela. Then, still mulling over his clear-headed attorney's strange behavior, drove back to Rouge Mountain to pick up Steve. First, Rebecca had been hard to deal with because she was only interested in work. He'd urged her to relax and have fun. Now she was acting like a skittish teenager going to her first prom—and not with him.

"Where's your girlfriend?" Steve asked when he climbed in the van.

"Women! At least I don't have some female spook using my hands to write shopping lists or taking my body to the spa for a manicure." He pulled into the parking lot of a local steakhouse, hurt, angry, and jealous. He let Steve lead him into the restaurant and to their table. His feet dragged as if he'd just finished a marathon.

At the table Steve was high with nervous energy. "If you have trouble penetrating the female mind, talk to that geek who wrote the computer program that apprises writers of what gender they are. He supposedly knows all about women—and men."

"That's different." Tom, still sulking, sank into a chair.

"How do you know? When I write, each of my *nom de plumes* has a different style of writing and a different persona. To me, they are a lot more interesting than ordinary people. When I write as Bullet or Cleo I don't even know the definition of half the words in Claude's vocabulary. Are they parts of me? Or spirits? Or am I merely a genius?"

"You think?" Tom yawned. "Angie says you are either schizophrenic or have dissociate identity disorder."

Steve ignored him. "How do you feel when you're writing?"

"In the zone. If the phone rings..." Tom's eyelids drooped.

"You ignore your phone or don't hear it," Steve finished for him.

"Like I'm someone or somewhere else for a while." Tom's face twitched. He snapped his eyes open. "I feel too tired to eat." His head nodded, then bounced back. One eyelid jerked with a tic and both eyes closed, then reopened. "I don't know what's wrong with me." He lifted his water glass to drink and let it slip from his grasp. A widening blot of soaked white tablecloth circled shards of glass and a lemon slice.

Steve raised his palms in surrender. "Old buddy, if I'm that wearisome, I'm taking you back to your room. You get some sleep. I'll go out and find a club. Even in this ethereal town, there must be such a mundane place."

\*\*\*\*

Rebecca sat on the edge of the hotel bed examining her pedicure. She jumped up to smooth the satin coverlet. She plumped the feather pillows. Opening the bedside table drawer, she removed a zippered travel case containing a tube of lubricant, a box of condoms, and her mini-vibrator. She took two foil-wrapped condoms from the box and placed them near the front of the drawer. Just in case. In case Max didn't bring any. Sometimes he seemed very single-minded. His old-fashioned, courtly words reminded her of lines in a historical romance novel, but she became impatient when Max seemed unaware of ordinary things invented in the last one hundred years.

She closed the cottage drapes, rearranged vases of roses, and lit one small lamp to spread a warm glow throughout the room. Piles of legal documents were stuffed in the closet, a closed laptop and printer the only reminder of the obsessive technology which ruled her life as an attorney. Even her cell phone was turned off.

Not until Rebecca firmly closed her mind had Little Rebecca given up nagging her to cancel the date. She would not let that childish voice ruin her exciting evening. Even Aries had gotten into the spirit and helped like a girlfriend. Her hairstyling turned out pretty good.

She'd spent the entire day preparing for this romantic evening. Besides the massage and manicure, George, the hotel's psychic concierge, had arranged for a yoga teacher to give her a private in-room class to relax her. Also on George's recommendation, she'd ordered the restaurant's world famous *Romantic In-Room Hide-Away Dinner for Two*.

In addition to the wines to accompany dinner, the chief wine steward had, at Max's request, delivered and set to chill two bottles of red wine and a quart of white rum. There was so much wine, buckets and ice everywhere, Rebecca decided to sample a little of each in order to select which was best. After two hours of sipping, she was still not sure, but no voices disturbed her thoughts.

Opening the rum bottle, her hand slipped and she snapped her right thumbnail. She intended to pour herself just a tiny taste, but the sweet smell reminded her of Max and she drank more.

At eight o'clock, she circled the room one final time to be certain everything was perfect. She removed a condom packet from the drawer. She lay down on the bed, rolled to the center, stretched out her arm and casually dropped the foil an arm's reach from the left side of the bed. Just in case.

She stroked her transparent white gown and adjusted the folds. Max's gift of this hand-stitched, vintage nightgown had excited her most of all. She decided long dresses must affect women's brains and turn them into emotional wrecks. During the last few days in

Sedona, wearing long skirts had definitely turned her into a woman she'd have previously labeled a hopeless ditz. So what? Tonight she felt like a princess waiting for her prince.

All week she anticipated Max inviting her out for a gourmet dinner at some romantic restaurant. She wanted a chance to show off her handsome beau. But this would be so much better. She giggled. She couldn't very well wear this dress in public.

A knock on the door startled her. Barefoot, she ran across the floor. Suddenly shy, she looked out the peephole. The porch light over the door was lit, but she could see no one in front of the door. She called, "Who is it?" her voice squeaky like a girl's.

"It is I, Max, my love," replied the deep, familiar voice.

Rebecca pulled open the door. The light was on. A tall, solidly masculine form to the right of the door stood in the shadows. There was just enough light to see Max again wore the silky black shirt and pants that reminded her of an expensive pirate costume. Thunder smacked. She gasped. The lights flickered and went out.

Max strode in. "Quite a storm brewing out there this evening, Rebecca, my love. Never fear. We will be safe and wonderfully happy here." With a kick of his boot, he closed the door behind him and swept her into his arms.

As she melted against his chest, she smelled the heady scent of spicy rum.

"I have waited so long for this moment." He breathed the words along her neck.

She felt his cool hands through the dress's fragile fabric. "Me too," she choked, her feet dangling above the floor. Max's powerful arms were clasped around her, yet she felt far from safe.

In the darkness, there was something wonderfully familiar about his body. The way she fit against him reminded her of...someone...someone warmer? She tried to remember.

Oh well, her hope to at last see her mystery man's face had been destroyed by a power outage on this dark and stormy night. Why hadn't she thought of candles?

Max began to kiss her neck and stroke her shoulders,

forcing visions of candlelight and romance novel scenes out of her mind. She felt the cool, thick folds of his silky shirt pressed against her breasts and she let out an involuntary swoon. So that's what a swoon felt like.

The entire day's preparations and her every thought had been intensely focused on being with this man. Progressively, she'd become more and more excited until now she was extremely aroused. She was also aware that she'd had too much wine and his embrace—or the rum warming in her belly—seemed to have made her knees quite weak. Her practical brain told her she needed fresh air and food.

She took a deep breath and felt Max pressed harder against her, crushing the air from her chest. As he cradled her head her hair felt deliciously free. He buried his hands in her hair and each curl came alive as his fingers touched and stroked. She needed to remember to thank Aries for creating this hairstyle. Her usual tight chignon would have been pulled out into a sticky mess by now.

Opening her lips with his, Max searched for her tongue. He lowered her to the ground until her bare toes touched the floor. Their teeth clicked together, her knees collapsed and she slumped in his arms. Her entire body hummed and a loud buzz spiraled inside her head.

Hungry to stay close to him, she stretched up along his length. Her hands slid up the flowing silk of his shirt and touched his face. Hesitantly, her fingers traced his jaw and cheekbones, trying to picture her romantic lover. She felt a scar on the left cheek and let out a breath.

Fighting to regain control, she said, "Max, I have wine and a lovely dinner for us. Do you like Chateaubriand? I could have ordered New York Strip." She giggled at her own joke.

"I am hungry only for you, my darling. I have waited too long."

Little Rebecca's voice almost screamed in her head. *No! Send him away.* Rebecca closed her foggy mind as best she could.

He picked her up. Her head nestled against his shoulder and her gown billowed around them as he carried her across the room. She was sure he must hear her heart thumping. Perhaps the couple in the next cottage could also hear every beat.

Setting her down beside the bed, Max whispered, "Rebecca, I adore you. No mere words can express my devotion or the ecstasy you create in my body." He placed his hands on her shoulders and let them slide along the delicate straps of her nightdress, fingering the material until they reached the swelling of her breasts. "We are destined, you and I, throughout eternity."

She gasped as his cool fingers moved along the thin fabric of the low neckline. "Oh Max," she whispered. "You...I...never..." She had never been good at foreplay talk. Preferring silent partners, she'd hated when Tristan insisted she speak. And that CPA who wanted her to talk dirty found himself out in her hallway. This was different. She wanted Max to know her body ached for him.

"My body aches for you," she finally gasped. Did that sound hokey?

He was undoing the tiny buttons that held the delicate fabric taunt across her breasts. At her words, he took hold of either side and pulled. Pearl buttons pop...pop...popped into the air.

"You ripped my...my bodice. My beautiful..." She drew back and held the pieces together to cover her bare breasts.

"My darling, do not worry. A gown can be repaired, whereas my zealous heart is forever rent in two with desire for you. My passion will make you, my own divine goddess, infinitely happy."

"I really wish I could see you," she pleaded, pushing one palm against his chest as she clutched her torn dress. Even as her body melted, her foggy mind still wanted to know what her mystery lover looked like.

His lips closed on hers and he continued to kiss her while his hands undid the sash at her waist. The last wisps of the soft fabric fell on either side of Rebecca's naked body.

"Our souls are our eyes, my love," he said and again silenced her words with his mouth and lifted her onto the feather bed.

His kisses were hypnotic. She fought to stay awake. She was so sleepy and...she wanted him so badly.

He pulled back and she heard his shirt swish onto

the floor and then another swoosh. The image of his slinky black pants sliding over his hips and pooling on the floor made her swoon again. She wondered if he were going to remove his boots. She waited. There was no thump.

Moonlight shone through a high window behind Max and she saw him silhouetted above her moonlit body. She blushed with embarrassment. Though thin from dieting and working out, her body wasn't perfect. Her hips were too hippy and her belly squishy. She promised herself she'd spend more time at the gym. And why hadn't she found time for the tanning bed? Skin cancer risk be damned, she wanted to look good.

"Perfectly beautiful, my love," Max sighed as he knelt over her. "You are mine at last. No one will ever come between us—again."

Every cell in her body whirled with heavenly sensation—especially her head. Things were progressing really fast and he hadn't noticed the condom. She gestured with her elbow to the nightstand and grunted, "Ugh. Ugh."

His lips covered her mouth. She couldn't talk or hold back much longer. Her last iota of common sense surfaced and she lifted the left side of her body, and inch by inch pulled her arm free. Pointing at the foil square, she smiled up at Max with a shy grimace. He didn't respond. Instead he nibbled at her earlobe, unfortunately the very spot she'd over-doused with perfume.

He pulled back with a sputter to grab the big bottle of rum from the other bed table. He lifted it to his lips and gulped a few swallows to wash down the taste of *Evening in Paris*. While he drank, Rebecca had space to rise up and twist to reach for the condom. Her fingers found it.

Max turned back to her. She held the condom out towards him. "Condom. Please," she said with what she hoped was a licentious smile.

He grabbed the thing from her hand. "Why ask for one of those expensive apartments at a time like this? Soon, I'll give you anything you want." He tossed the packet over his shoulder and reached for her.

Rebecca knew the condom was lost. She pushed his hand away and her right thumbnail, sharp as a knife, drew blood from the back of his left hand. Hearing Little Rebecca's vice and seeing the blood shocked her awake. She would not be treated like that by anyone and instinctively used Close Encounters with Attackers Technique #3—and brought her knee up—hard.

She heard a sharp cry that sounded like "Aargh! Zounds! Damn poppet!" and a loud angry groan.

Crying out, she came in wild, thrashing spasms and the sounds in the room were silenced by the quake that engulfed her body.

She collapsed and closed her eyes and rolled onto her side. As she groggily fell into an uneasy sleep she heard a door slam. Little Rebecca whispered, *Now rest. You are safe.*

## Chapter 13

Rebecca awoke. Her head ached. She took a breath and gagged at the smell of roses that filled the room. She slid her hand under the covers expecting to find a deliciously warm body next to hers. But she was alone. The cozy duvet was tucked under her chin, the sheets were soft, the featherbed luxurious, but she was alone. She opened her eyes. Had last night been a dream?

She inhaled the scent of rum and spicy cinnamon clinging to the pillow and stretched her sated body. Last night had been no dream. From the table the odor of roast beef and crème brûlée drifted toward her, smelling more like garbage than delicious dinner.

Shaking off a vague feeling of unease—last night had been perfect, hadn't it?—she watched a sunbeam shine through the high window onto her beautiful dress, draped over a chair. On the mahogany bedside table, her pearl buttons lay, encircled by a pearl necklace—a gift from Max!

She heard a knock on the door.

A voice called out, "Room service."

"Come in." She pulled the covers to her chin and watched Josch roll in a cart and remove uneaten dinners and empty bottles.

She wondered if he knew what happened here last night. Why should she be embarrassed? She was Rebecca Dumaurier, partner at Bankhead, Blanding and Gillimesh, not Rebecca of Sunnybrook Farm. But what had actually happened here last night? Did it matter?

She'd always said sex was like hair—you never got that quite right either.

Josch smiled. "Hope the storm didn't keep you up. Don't usually have monsoons this late in the season. Lucky we didn't lose power." He settled a tray of coffee and pastries near her bed and kicked the unused condom packet on the floor under the bed.

Rebecca thanked him and he left. Despite his age, he was good at his job, efficient and hopefully discreet. She noticed her computer and printer and wondered why they were in her bedroom. She poured coffee and ate a pastry, but she couldn't stay still.

Vague memories of the night before floated in her head. Or was that her imagination? She was unwilling to think of that and despite a mussy head, moved around the room, inhaling the scent of a rose, touching a petal, admiring the reflection of sunlight on pearls. Then she fell back on her bed and wriggled into the sensual softness of feathery comforter and expensive linens.

Not knowing what to do with her blissfully energized body, she jumped up and took a perfect scarlet rose from the vase. She searched for paper and finding only small sheets of embossed hotel stationery, tried to smooth the rose between two sheets of Aries' aunt's e-mail.

Her broken nail made pressing a rose not as easy as she had imagined. A thorn pricked her finger and blood dripped onto the paper and her white robe. Quickly she stacked heavy things on top of the lumpy paper: Godiva boxes, books she was currently reading, the thin Sedona phone book, a Gideon Bible, and on top of it all, the book of love poetry.

"Yes! Poetry!" she cried aloud. "I can do that, too." She took a small sheet of the hotel stationery and located her lucky fountain pen, the one kept for signing important contracts. She threw a bed pillow on the chaise lounge, or fainting couch, as her mother would have called it.

Pen. Paper. She would write a love poem. "I feel wonderful..." Not good enough. "Love...dove...moon...June?" No, this was September. Determined to be a poet, she tried again.

\*\*\*\*

*My heart flies to love,*

119

*When you are above*
*Me.*

\*\*\*\*

"That wasn't good. Max...Max...sax...backs...lacks...sex." She giggled. Unstacking books, she uncovered the new Godiva box. For inspiration, she popped a chocolate into her mouth.

\*\*\*\*

*You melt in my mouth*
*I twinkle like stars in the sky.*

\*\*\*\*

What was that poem Max had e-mailed to her? She opened her laptop and located his message:

\*\*\*\*

*The Moon will shine more brightly when you are mine.*
*When I possess you, both Sun and Moon will join.*
*My love and I will walk our dove white beach.*
*When I regain the love time can never breach.*

\*\*\*\*

"His poem rhymes! Why can't I write love poetry like that?" She paused. Was she truly in love? Max excited her. Was this just a...a...romantic fling. There, she'd said that hateful word, "romantic." Little Rebecca added helpfully that "lunatic" also rhymed.

Rebecca ignored her. She still wanted to send a love poem to Max. She opened the book of poetry and copied the first one she found. She'd e-mail it to him later.

The phone rang. She'd promised herself she would not talk to Heather this morning—not when she felt so deliciously...delicious. She answered.

"The usual," Heather chirped. "Xailana is upset that her latest cover is a cartoon, not a candy box. Yvette is complaining that her editor changed her spellings. Zora is complaining that her editor did not change her spellings. I suggest we send all our clients dictionaries for Christmas!"

"Cute, but a bad idea. Tell X, Y, and Z that those are not my problems. Refer them to their agents."

"I did. I was reading this article—"

"I don't pay you to read."

Heather ignored Rebecca. "As I was saying, this authoritative business psychology article said powerful control freak women need some part of their life to be in control. If you relinquish control in your bedroom—"

"In my bedroom?"

"Who's talking about you?"

"Do you mean whips? Chains? That sort of stuff?"

"No. Just letting someone else do it. Women with high-powered careers—you know, doctors, stockbrokers, judges, even lawyers—can't let down. Their personal fantasy could be submissive behavior."

"You are crazy!"

"It's just an article. I thought it might explain why some publishers go for the more erotic stuff. Why are you so testy? As the article said, submission in a safe, committed relationship isn't politically correct, but makes sense."

"Get back to work." Rebecca hung up the phone. What drivel. Erotica demeaned women. Strong women didn't get involved in demeaning relationships. The average bodice-ripper romance was different, but right now she couldn't think why that was true. Heather was such a troublemaker. She had more important things to think about than the personal fantasies of women. She looked at her broken thumbnail. "I need a manicure."

****

Tom stretched lazily across his bed. He heard a car door slam in the parking lot and his eyes flew open. He groped for his travel alarm. It was already nine o'clock. Angie must have left for the workshop hours ago.

He did a mental check of his body. Head...foggy. He felt a little hung-over but lately every morning was like that. Face...achy. Back...pain between the shoulder blades. Chest...sore. Stomach...empty. And...he got as far as his privates. They felt like he'd had sex or had been aroused all night. His entire body felt like the morning after passionate lovemaking. Even after a long time, he remembered that feeling.

He snapped awake and threw back the covers. The warm, delicious smell of woman clung to his body. He

stood and headed for the shower, trying to replay last
night. He'd planned to have dinner with Steve. He
remembered sitting in a restaurant and spilling his
water. He had been so tired. After Steve brought him back
here, he must have crashed.

Now that he thought about it, he'd fallen into a deep
sleep at an incredibly early hour every night for the last
few nights. Why did he need so much sleep? Why did he
feel hung over? Again. And why did the linens smell like
rum? Again.

But sex? Could Angie have come into his bed? He
wouldn't put it past her. His anger flared. He knew she'd
never be able to suppress gloating. But it was not Angie's
scent that clung to him. This one reminded him of apples
like...no. That would be impossible.

He stepped into the shower. He reached to turn on
the hot water and noticed dried blood, rinsed it, and saw
the dark line of a recent scratch on his left hand.
Wondering how that happened, he let the hot water
pummel his body. He began to soap himself in his usual
routine and felt the sting. He stepped back and covered
his manhood, turned his back to the spray, and let the
water massage his back. He soaped more gently. "What
the..?" The delicate skin felt raw and the muscles of his
thighs and groin were tender. "I feel like I had sex after a
long bout of celibacy or had been kicked in the balls."

He stepped from the shower, lightly toweled, and
gingerly dressed, choosing sweatpants instead of snug
jeans.

****

Rebecca opened the door. Elise stepped in carrying
her folding massage table.

"The hotel paged me. You look like you need a
massage again." She checked her hotel purchase order.
"Requested by Max Winter. Two full hours. And an
emergency manicure."

Rebecca held out her broken nail.

"Umm, this Mr. Winter must want you to be very
happy."

Rebecca nodded. "I guess."

"Oh, and the desk said to give you this." She handed
Rebecca a copy of *Many Lives, Many Loves*.

122

"Another romance novel?"

"Not exactly. A psychologist's case studies about reincarnation and the enduring nature of love through time."

Rebecca looked at the book with a glimmer of understanding, while Elsie put the Do Not Disturb sign on the outside doorknob and set up her massage table.

Max was always taking about love transcending time.

Two hours later Elise carried her table out, telling Aries, who waited on the porch, that Rebecca was resting.

Aries shrugged and kept reading until a Calamity Jane look-alike with boots and buckskin ruffles approached. That floppy brimmed hat and long ringlets hadn't been in fashion since the West was won. "Who are you?" Aries asked.

"Who are *you*?" the older woman in exotic western wear replied. "I am here to see Rebecca Jane Dumaurier!"

"She cannot be disturbed."

"She will see me. I am her mother!"

"You're a mother."

"Watch your mouth, little girl! I'm Charlotte Dumaurier and you are...?"

"I'm Aries Blessing Paxton. I am a harpist diva with my own CD. My parents are famous and I am Rebecca's best friend." Aries looked down at the petite older woman two steps below her. Charlotte's outfit did make her look more like a docent at The Rodeo Hall of Fame than anyone's mother.

Charlotte raised her chin. "I doubt my daughter has an eleven-year-old friend."

"I'm fifteen...fourteen...thirteen. And I *am* her best friend. She and I do things together every morning. My dad is a client of hers."

"Oh, she babysits?" The back of Charlotte's small hand flew to her mouth. "That is even more impossible. My Rebecca would never..."

"She does not babysit. She likes me."

"Well, never mind. Let me by." Charlotte stepped a booted foot onto the porch.

Aries blocked her way to the door. "I said Rebecca is resting. Her masseuse just left. She had an exhausting night, if you know what I mean."

Charlotte's lower lip fell open.

A young steward carried two dozen roses and a large box of Godiva chocolates up the cottage steps.

"Hi, Josch." Aries gave him a grownup smile. "Leave them here, Ms. Dumaurier is indisposed." Aries opened the box and offered the assortment to Charlotte.

After they had each eaten a few chocolates, Charlotte said, "May I invite you to the restaurant for a cup of tea?"

Aries smiled. "Of course, Mrs. Dumaurier."

At a table for two in the hotel restaurant Charlotte ordered *pan au chocolat* and mint tea for two, then discreetly began to pump Aries. "Who is her uh...boyfriend?"

"Rebecca is very mysterious. Yet, I do know he sends her lovely presents."

"Tell me more." Charlotte leaned forward.

"A book of poetry and romance novels. Of course, lots of chocolate and roses. You saw the latest delivery."

Charlotte nodded. "How does Rebecca respond?"

"She floats around kind of totally dreamy. Yesterday she got this totally great nightgown and I fixed her hair. Did I tell you I help her pick out clothes?"

"Aries, dear, you are quite precocious, but we cannot be talking about the same woman. My daughter is, sadly, a most unromantic woman. *Quelle disappointment.*"

"Miss Charlotte, I totally—"

"Aries, ladies do not say 'totally.'"

"I truly..." She watched for Charlotte's approving smile, then continued, "...wish Rebecca were less romantic. My dad really likes her and she treats him like a friend. He is a nice man, but not the classic romantic alpha male hero type, if you know what I mean."

"I know. I was married to an alpha." Her eyelashes fluttered. "Alphas are overwhelming, but so compelling."

"So, you want to talk about...?"

"No! Let us go back and wake my daughter."

Charlotte led the way back to the cottage and knocked. Rebecca opened the door. "Charlotte! What are you doing here?"

"That's no way to greet your mother." Charlotte swept in with Aries in her wake. Looking around, she observed the disarray. "Almost noon and Housekeeping hasn't been here? What have you been doing?"

"None of your business." Rebecca scooped the string of pearls into the pocket of her robe, swept the buttons into the bedside table drawer, and began to neaten the bed.

Charlotte watched in amazement as Rebecca went out to the deck, brought in the new roses, and set out the ones that were beginning to fade. "This place smells like a...rose garden. What is going on?" She squinted. "You've gained weight. And what have you done to your hair? Do you have a lover?"

"None of your business. I have lots of work to do. Could we meet for an early dinner? I'll make reservations." Rebecca herded her mother out the door.

Aries stood her ground.

"You too. Out!"

"I have another installment." She waved a few sheets of paper. "This one looks totally romantic."

Rebecca closed the door. "Fine. Read."

\*\*\*\*

*August 30, 1864*

*St. Albans Island, British West Indies*

*St. Albans Island is the most beautiful place on earth. I shall never forget my first sight of St. Albans and The Moon, for that is the name of our lovely plantation house. The Windswept came about and I saw the white sand beach of St. Albans harbor, the forested mountains, and two plantation homes set like jewels on twin bluffs.*

*As a newly married woman floating with the joy of being with my new husband, I was overcome with delight. Thomas put his arm about me and pointed to the house which would be our home. I took it all in—the terraced fields, the pineapples and cotton bales piled high near the dock waiting to be loaded onto the ship, and the staring black faces seeking a first look at their new mistress.*

*I became impatient to step off this ship, my home from the day after my marriage. But like a silly twit, I swooned in the heat without the sea breeze. My beloved Thomas carried me to dry land.*

\*\*\*\*

*September 1, 1864*
*St. Albans Island, British West Indies*
*This morning I insisted Thomas take me all over our island so I should know my home.*

*St. Albans is very long and quite wide. The beach has sand as white as snow, palm trees tall and heavy with coconuts, on both sides of a welcoming pier. On a map the island resembles a half-grown moon with a large black stone on each point. The protected harbor is as placid as a lagoon, while the ocean side has rocky outcroppings of white and black rock. The original Settlers' Cabin is on the ocean side. Thomas tells me his ancestor wanted to be reminded of the hard side of life. Not for me. I love the white sand and gentle waves. Thomas showed me a pool under a lush rainforest waterfall and has promised to teach me to swim.*

*We have horses, mules, and goats. There are slaves to work the fields, and each slave family has a nutmeg tree for shade. When the tree bears fruit, the family harvests and dries the nuts, makes sauce from the fruit, and sells the mace and dried nutmegs to trading ships.*

*Thomas had told me the houses were built by his father and uncle when they divided the half moon-shaped island into two equal shares, one white house on each promontory.*

\*\*\*\*

Another knock interrupted their reading. Aries answered and George, the hotel concierge, walked in.

"Sorry to bother you, Ms. Dumaurier. But I wanted to make sure all went well last night." Her efficient demeanor showed no emotion as she handed Rebecca her card. "Call me if you need anything else."

"Everything was fine. You seem to have a knack for knowing what guests want. Even before they ask." Rebecca thought George's burgundy pantsuit was more flattering to her solid figure than those paisley dresses, but decided not to get into a fashion discussion. The young woman with the mousy pageboy still reminded her of a librarian.

George smiled. "Being psychic helps. I knew you wouldn't eat dinner, so it didn't matter what you ordered, but the hotel pushes the *Romantic Dinner for Two* deal. I knew you needed a yoga session and I knew you were making a mistake by skipping lunch."

"You're good." Rebecca looked at the card with formal black print. "But I keep thinking some guy named George Rotfels is the real concierge."

"I'm George, the real concierge."

"Georgia? Georgeanne?" Rebecca surprised herself by asking a hotel staff person such a personal question. Usually she ignored those that she paid for services.

"George."

"Why don't you change your name?" Rebecca realized that had been a rude question. Why hadn't she changed her own name?

"The hotel had these cards printed. This is my other card." She handed Rebecca a card with metallic gold print over a red rock scene.

"Joy Sedona, Psychic?"

"That's the name I'm going to use for my Spiritual Concierge Service. People who come to Sedona on vacation need help choosing the right psychic and healing modalities. Who better to help than a psychic who knows all the sights and shopping tips?" She watched Rebecca for her reaction. "I suppose you think the name is dumb?"

"No. But I think Joy of Sedona has a better ring."

George nodded. "You're right."

"I help a lot of writers find the perfect *nom de plume*."

"So, Joy of Sedona will be my *nom de spirit*."

The young woman smiled and looked so much younger, so Rebecca chanced another question. "Why is your name George?"

"My father's name. So, why Rebecca?" George shot back.

"My mother's favorite book. At least she wasn't enamored with *Ulysses*."

"Why R.J.?"

"A better lawyer's name," Rebecca admitted. "Why Joy?"

"A better psychic's name. And better to become a new person in Sedona."

"I'm back to the name Rebecca and becoming a new person—in Sedona."

They both grinned.

"Sedona does that, doesn't it?" George said. "Change."

Chapter 14

Steve paced in front of Tom's cottage door. "Hey, come on. Let's go get coffee. You need a jolt of caffeine."

"I sure do, but this puzzle is making me crazy. I bought a copy of *Many Lives, Many Loves* to give to Rebecca. I believed that book would be an opening to talk about a connection stronger than this lifetime. Now, the book is gone. No one except me, Angie, and Aries has been in this room since dinner last night."

"Would Angie...?"

"No." Tom shook his head. "She would have no reason."

"Forget the damn book. Let's go."

Tom stopped shuffling papers and shifting books and followed Steve out to the van.

At the coffee shop, Steve pushed the latest issue of *Variety* across the table. "Hey, hey, Tom, take a look at this."

"That's your sister!" Tom pointed to the picture on the legal news page under the headline "Study Claims Cleo is a Man!"

"My fans think that sweet face, framed in blonde curls, is me. If only people knew how much makeup hides her scars from ten years on the pro wrestling circuit. And the wig cost a fortune."

Tom smiled. "She always seemed a little tough."

"Tough? She would have killed me if I hadn't hid her steroids the first time she pinned me."

Tom chuckled. "Your life would make a great novel."

129

"No publisher would touch it. Readers couldn't suspend belief long enough to get through chapter one."

"But readers believe that Amazon is capable of writing delicate female stories? While you are..." Tom stopped.

"Say it, buddy. I'm the sensitive type. I'm also smart enough to write books women adore. I know more about women—and men—than most women." He shook his head. "That's why I'm fed up waiting for my agents and lawyers to allow me reveal my real identity. Now I look good and want my mug shot on all my books. Damn it. I can write for women and men. Every reader in the country loves at least one of my genres. Intellectual snobs can't get enough of Claude Festerman's *opera*. One critic called me the interpretive genius of modern society. What a crock!"

"You are a genius. Always have been. Your essays in high school blew teachers away."

Steve shrugged. "I only gave them what they wanted. Not that my talent ever helped my social life. No girl would date me. Even the nerdy girls made eyes at you."

Tom waved away the words. "But what about this article that claims Cleo St. Cloud uses pronouns like a man?"

"When I write as Cleo, I feel like a woman and write like a woman."

"Not just different e-mail addresses and websites?"

"I have different desks, computers, and hats for each alias persona. Hey, it works for me."

"Think getting separate bedrooms for each entity that grabs my body might help me keep them straight?"

"I'm serious. In the morning, I write in my library at a Regency desk with a pink monitor, wearing a big floppy hat and sipping froufrou tea. After breakfast, I drink coffee in the library and write erudite trash with lots of Brobdingnagian words in impressive urbane phrases. After lunch and a stint with my personal trainer, I get down and dirty on my latest Bullet novel, and pump out wild explosion scenes. After dinner I edit the manuscript closest to deadline and, if I can't sleep, work on my new project for fun. Screw that computer program. My books are great."

"Amazing. What new stuff are you working on?"

Steve looked over his shoulder at the other diners. "My agents don't even know." He leaned close to Tom. "A cyber-punk trilogy."

"Neat. No horror?"

"Are you kidding? With a real name like Steve King, that's the last thing I'd try."

Steve walked Tom back to his cottage. With still a half hour to kill before he was due to pick up Aries, Tom started putting away the mess he'd made searching for the lost book. He might as well do it now. If tonight was the same as the last few nights, he'd be too exhausted later.

His fatigue was affecting his memory. He wanted so badly to know what he looked like during a trance, but when he started to watch the video he'd fallen asleep, twice.

Hanging clothes in the closet, he noticed the black silk outfit Angie had bought him for formal appearances. Identical to the white one, the black reminded him of a marauding pirate or a bad Shakespearean actor. He never wore black because it made him feel awful. Pulling out the hanger, he saw the pants looked as wrinkled as if someone had slept in them. He noticed a rip and smelled what reminded him of Captain Somebody's spicy rum.

Who wore his clothes? He turned on the closet light and examined the rest. All seemed to be in order, until he noticed a pair of black boots in the back. Other than hiking boots, he'd brought only sandals. He picked up one knee-high boot. Did a previous guest leave it? Though the leather was elegant, soft, and expensive, the style looked more like a Halloween accessory than practical footwear. He found the other boot stuffed with a half-empty bottle of *Jolly Roger White Rum*.

He heard a knock on the door and hoped Steve had come back. Steve was smart enough to make sense of this. But instead, that familiar waiter, his head bent in such a way the eyebrow ring hung loose, stood waiting. Tom wondered what he would do if Aries pierced anything.

"Sir..." the thin boy in the oversized jacket stammered without meeting Tom's eyes, "I came to tell you I'm working in the kitchen 'til eight tonight."

"So…"

"Don't get angry again. I really want the job." He tucked his chin even more as if he couldn't stand to look at Tom and just stared at the boot Tom held.

"What job?"

"You know, the e-mail tutorial. I promise I'll bring your scanned documents tonight. I put all the images on a CD and we can e-mail everything with no problem."

"I don't know what you're talking about." Tom was ready to shut the door or call Hotel Security. The kid had seemed nice enough, but now was acting confused, like he was on drugs.

The boy looked up and directly at Tom for the first time. "Oh, sorry, you're Aries' father. I thought you were the other guy. Please tell him I'll be back at eight."

Tom watched the back of Josch's green jacket. "Kids." He decided not to call the front desk and report the confused teenager. He had enough on his mind.

****

Rebecca decided to spend the afternoon taking a long hike around Courthouse Butte without her cell phone. She'd already hiked two and a half miles in the heat of the day and the sunshine and fresh air were restoring her. The smell of roses, perfume, and food in her cottage had been so nauseating she'd requested Housekeeping do a good cleaning while she was out.

Everything was mixed up. Maxed up? Max never called her during the day and she sure did not want to talk to Heather. She especially didn't want to run into Tom. Though Tom wasn't her boyfriend, or had any right to become jealous, she just didn't want him to know about her relationship with Max.

Away from her room she was able to admit that last night may not have been the perfect romantic evening she'd hoped for. First, she had drunk way too much wine. And the rum had been a very bad idea. She had learned that her idea of a romantic evening was very different from Max's. She'd envisioned a little wine, good food, and lots of quiet talk. But was that any reason for Little Rebecca to behave like a scared heroine?

Rebecca was certainly not adverse to the more physical part of romance. Actually, by the time he arrived,

132

she had been very, very hot. But he'd barged in and headed for the bed. He hadn't paid any attention to her. That's the part that bothered her. And his disregard for the condom showed a definite lack of respect.

He sent presents and spoke like an old-fashioned lover, but didn't take time to know who she was. Like the pearls. They were beautiful and very expensive, but she just wasn't a pearls kind of girl. Plain gold with a large, but dignified, diamond or two that she could wear to the office was her style.

She was embarrassed that she had no idea how the evening actually ended. What had Max thought? A girl who couldn't hold her liquor? Had they actually had sex? She didn't think so but she couldn't ask him. That would be more embarrassing.

Had she ever before not known? There was that party after she'd passed the Bar. She never had much time for parties. Until she started dating Tristan, if she needed sex, she'd call an old friend from law school. He was, like her, too busy for a social life, and they'd grab a quick take-out dinner and go to a hotel near their offices. The arrangement was convenient and, if it wasn't too late, they could be back at work by 9 p.m.

Rebecca finished her second bottle of water and kept walking. Nothing was any clearer.

****

Shortly before ten that evening, Max called Rebecca. His voice was, as usual, smooth and sexy, though a little slurred. "My darling, how are you after our wonderful evening?"

He spoke as if last night had been perfect. Perhaps she'd missed the good parts? "I'm fine. Thank you for the pearls. What a wonderful gift!" She hoped she sounded thrilled.

"They reminded me of your ivory skin and silver hair."

Rebecca knew her skin was olive and, though her hair had lightened since she stopped using her special gel, far from silver. So, how did she ask him how it was for him? "So, how was it for you?"

"Perfect! Now you are mine! My Rebecca! Again!"

"When will I see you? Why can't we be together

during the day?"

"For now, that is not possible. I am working very hard so we will be together forever on my island. You will love my island."

"Where is—"

"I need first to regain my fortune. Your winning my plagiarism lawsuit is most important for me to receive what is properly mine. Then I will reclaim my island from the interlopers."

Rebecca spoke slowly and clearly into the phone, "Max, do you understand what plagiarism is?"

"Of course, stealing the rights to my property."

"First, you have to prove the work is your property."

"I sent you copies of the documents," he said with a touch of impatience. "You said you were a competent attorney."

"What you sent looks like legal records written in Danish and French. I can't read them. "

"They are land deeds and business contracts. What matters the language?"

"What do these documents have to do with plagiarism?" In this conversation, she was determined to keep Max focused.

"They prove who I am and that I am the only person who could have written the book."

"You still have not told me what book. How can I represent you if you will not confide in me?" She thought he was acting like a typical petulant client.

"Rebecca, my darling, please understand I also do not want to harm our love affair. I just want you to prove that I wrote the book."

"To prove that, I'd need to use the Epping cryptomnesia test. Ghost writers use this computer program in court to prove who actually wrote a book."

"Ghost...writers?"

"People who write books for other people, like celebrity autobiographies. Often the celebrity will claim to have written their book alone. Then tests are needed."

"Oh, that kind of ghost. What if a celebrity wrote about himself and another celebrity took the words down on paper—"

"—Max, stop. This is getting too confusing. Give me

two writing samples. One from this mysterious book you claim was stolen from you and one of your writing. I can have your normal style, syntax, and vocabulary tested and compared to the book. Then I will determine if we have a case."

"Rebecca. You are my dearest love, but as my solicitor, I tell you I want to sue the man who has stolen my life story. That is all you need to know."

Max sounded angry. What had he to be angry about? Had he been drinking? She was familiar with what rum could do.

"Do you hear me?" he asked.

"Yes," she replied. She never allowed clients to talk to her like that.

"I will e-mail new attachments to you. Read them and prepare your case." He hung up.

She turned off her phone and her computer and picked up a book. "I give up," she told Aries' copy of *Jane Eyre*. "Why can't life be easy?"

Chapter 15

Rebecca groaned and covered her head with her pillow until the ringing phone became quiet. Only Heather would dare call so early. Turning off her cell phone never deterred Heather. Heather never gave up.

Rebecca had slept fitfully after her telephone conversation with Max. He was obsessively focused on his plagiarism case but refused to give her the basic information to lay the groundwork for a lawsuit.

Max's behavior had changed after the night in her room. His constant use of the words "mine" and "forever" were beginning to offend her. She felt he treated her like a prize.

As his lawyer, she was seeing another side to her mystery man. She knew she couldn't expect people to behave the same in a business relationship as with a lover. Tristan had been a clever lover—sometimes sneaky—at getting what he wanted. She believed she used her time efficiently. If they both got satisfied in twenty minutes, why take two hours when you could be doing something else, like reading briefs or prepping for a morning court appearance. She and Tristan had been the same, in or out of bed.

She'd never taken his teasing taunts about being unromantic seriously. She had no time for romance. Then suddenly there was no relationship. If Max, the most exciting man she'd ever met, made her feel and behave like a romantic, wasn't that proof there was nothing wrong with her?

In a way Max's changeable moods made him more human. No one could be perfectly romantic all the time. He was impatient about some things and a bit aggressive at times. And didn't all men have one-track minds? He'd had sex—sort of—with her, now he'd gone back to work. She could understand that.

Only Tom was the same nice guy all the time. He cared for his daughter and worried about this thing taking over his body, but he still was a nice guy. She could not imagine him being anyone else. She couldn't imagine him wanting to hurt Angie. He might be one of those rare people who only could hurt someone if someone he loved was in danger.

The phone rang again. This time Rebecca was ready. "Good morning, Heather dear," she answered in her syrupy client-pleasing voice.

The line was silent. At last Heather spoke. "Why, good morning, R.J. Aren't we in a good mood this morning? Of course, you were out of pocket for an entire day while I, your slave back here in the Big Apple, covered for you."

"You made your point. What's new?"

"What's new? What's new is Cora-what-have-you-done-for-me-lately has decided she wants bigger movie deals and in the next contract—are you sitting down?—she wants a starring role. Star as in movie star. Star as in box office suicide."

"I get it. Give Cora Ayne my number and I'll talk to her."

"Surprise. Cora Ayne's on her way to Sedona like everyone else, except me, who we know is not on vacation, but here in the City during an Indian summer heat wave, but that doesn't matter of course, since I never get out of the air-conditioned office—"

"—Stuff it, Heather. Cora's here in Sedona?"

"According to her P.A., she's in a meeting in Phoenix and will arrive at your hotel at six this evening."

"She'll find me." Rebecca set down the phone. It rang. She picked it up. "R.J. here. Hi, Cora."

"Are you psychic?" Cora asked.

"Sedona does that to everyone. I'll meet you in the hotel lobby at six. Looking forward and all that."

137

Rebecca printed out the current day's e-mails from Heather, including copies of Cora's contract and Tom's pre-nup. As she finished, Aries arrived.

"Give me a minute to look these over," she told Aries. She covered up Aries' parents' pre-nup. No reason for the kid to read that document.

"No problem. I'll read these new pages from Aunt Arianna all by myself."

Rebecca put down the contracts. "So, read to me."

"The plot thickens," Aries said gleefully and began to read.

**** 

*August 24, 1865*
*St. Albans Island, British West Indies*
*This glorious tropical morning, I realized it had been one entire delightful year since I first set foot on St. Albans, the home I know now and love so well.*

*My life is filled with flowers and beautiful birds. Parrots and macaws and occasionally orange-pink flamingos and scarlet ibis delight me.*

*My Thomas and I swim in the moonlight like natives. This morning I ate my breakfast of Cook's sweet bread spread with the jam of the nutmeg fruit and grated cinnamon accompanied by fine English tea while listening to a nightingale.*

*This world has become my paradise. I manage the household in the mornings, have lunch with my adoring husband and in the heat of the afternoon we work on account books and argue about new crops to plant. When business is not pressing, we retire to our rooms and enjoy each other's company or swim in the cool waterfall pool. After dinner we walk the moonlit beach and swim in the smooth, salty water of our secluded cove.*

*This morning as I tended my roses and watched hummingbirds fly to the brightest frangipani bloom, Thomas rode his horse right into my garden. "Arianna," he called, "I have received a letter from my sister. She has married and she with her husband will be on the next ship to St. Albans. I will have my dear Penelope close and you will have a gentlewoman for a sister and companion.*

*My heart leapt at the news. Dear Thomas has no other relative in the entire world. When he began his studies, he regrettably left his delicate young sister with a cousin. He had confided in me that he worries about her, for all the usual reasons, but also because as a child she would hear voices and he has had reports that the wily cousin exploits her talents.*

*Thomas told me that when they arrive Penelope's husband will become master of half our little island paradise and his sister will become the mistress of the other plantation house, the one that belonged to Thomas's uncle before he died. We immediately set about preparing that house, The Sun, as it was always called. Much needed to be done.*

*Thomas was too exuberant to even wonder what kind of man would arrive to share our island. Then Thomas's tender lips spoke the name of Penelope's husband. I was certain that man was The Major, the very man who wooed me in London. My paradise was sullied.*

\*\*\*\*

*November 2, 1865*

*St. Albans Island, British West Indies*

*Today The Windswept arrived with Penelope and the man called The Major. When our eyes first met, Penelope and I became true sisters. I loved her more since I immediately recognized her as the sad young woman at that disastrous séance. She was Thomas' double, though so feminine and dainty, I wondered if plantation life might prove too difficult for her temperament. As for The Major, I avoid his eyes and pretend we had never met previously.*

\*\*\*\*

*November 25, 1865*

139

*St. Albans Island, British West Indies*
*At first Penelope appeared intensely in love
with her new husband, but after only a few weeks
on the island she has been devising many
reasons to be at our home. I thought she loved the
company of another woman and, of course, she
and her only brother were closely bonded. Yet on
those evenings Penelope and her husband dine
with us, I see no sign of true affection no matter
how much she struggles to please him. We seldom
visit their home, for Penelope says it needs
renovation. Yet she seems uninterested in the
task, while her husband orders fine English
furniture, draperies, and all manner of
decoration.*

*I look forward to seeing the changes in The
Sun, though Thomas said he thought the harvest
would not pay the debts of such extravagance. I
prefer Moon's West Indian style with honey-
colored wooden floors, and windows that open
without heavy draperies.*

*\*\*\*\**

*January 12, 1866*
*St. Albans Island, British West Indies*
*Penelope seems happier when The Major is
away. Often he travels to other islands, trading
and doing who knows what kind of business,
while his overseer runs their plantation.*

*\*\*\*\**

Reading Arianna's e-mail did not settle Rebecca. She
could not work on the custody issues while Aries was in
the room. By default she agreed to take Aries to a yoga
class and since the instructor required the thirteen-year-
old to attend with an adult, Rebecca had no choice but to
stay for the class.

Sitting in the peaceful studio in a pair of stretchy
black yoga pants and a cute top printed with an elephant-
headed Hindu god, Rebecca was glad she'd come. Yoga
was getting easier for her. More and more she enjoyed the
way she felt after a class, though she still preferred a
place in the back of the room.

The red formaldehyde-free nail polish from her latest

pedicure made her toes look spectacular. Between sandals and yoga, her feet were always exposed in Arizona. She was beginning to feel freer wearing clothing that did not turn every body surface into armor-like barriers. Some of the clothing she brought to Sedona seemed tight and constricting compared to flowing dresses and stretchy yoga pants.

Karunananda, the blissful instructor, led the class in the first breathing exercise. Rebecca never imagined breathing could be anything but easy and boring, but this was neither. A few minutes into the exercises, while the instructor reminded them they did this 23,000 times a day, the side door opened and Tom slipped in carrying a worn mat and blanket. Aries waved to him and Rebecca tried to ignore him. As if the only man in the class—especially a tall, handsome one—could ever be ignored. He found a place, unrolled his mat with a whoosh, and folded into a cross-legged position Rebecca envied. She wanted to be that flexible.

Karunananda closed the drapes and, in the dim light, Rebecca concentrated on stretching, and almost forgot about Tom. Karunananda's reminders to breathe, watch alignment, and not compete were slowly sinking in. She was learning to relax and her body felt more open.

After the usual sequence of poses, Karunananda announced, "I'd like to try something different for the optional pose part of today's class. We will work on partner poses."

Rebecca hated team activities of any kind. Individual competition was great. She had always been competitive, but she dreaded the words "pick a partner." She turned to Aries, hoping to pair off with her. Instead their instructor did the matching, first choosing Aries for herself and pairing the other women. She pointed at Tom and Rebecca, and Tom scooted over to share Rebecca's mat.

Aware that any woman in the room would have killed to pair with Tom, she accepted her fate with a smile. The instructor asked them to center themselves and then synchronize their breaths by placing their left hand on their partner's heart. She hesitantly reached out to touch his chest. Before her fingers made contact, the heat from his body warmed her palm.

Tom and Rebecca sat facing each other. Rebecca closed her eyes and tried to ignore Tom's fingers against her chest. She found it easy to anticipate Tom's breath. After a few minutes, she began to feel as if they were one person—the point of the exercise. With this thought she panicked and couldn't get back into sync with him.

Tom said, "Relax," and placed his right hand on her shoulder. Immediately she had difficulty keeping her breath slow. She breathed faster and faster. Tom kept up with her until they both began to hyperventilate and then laugh.

The next exercise was called Double Chair. Its purpose, according to Karunananda, was to build trust and explore the need for commitment and cooperation. Tom and Rebecca sat on the mat, backs pushed against each other until they rose to standing. After a few false starts—the back to back, butt to butt pose felt very intimate—they mastered the tricks of weight distribution and worked together perfectly.

Next, Double Warrior, *Virabhadrasana*, required that they stand back to back, link hands, then turn sideways and bend their front knees and look out over their joined arms. Compared to the Chair pose, this one was a piece of cake. Standing strong with Tom, Rebecca felt powerful and safe, as if together they could defeat anything or anyone. For the first time she understood why this was called Warrior Pose.

The last partner pose, Double Boat, was supposed to bring up feelings of vulnerability. It did. Partners sat facing with knees bent, holding each other's wrists, then placed the soles of their feet together and raised their feet between their linked hands until their legs straightened. As soon as Rebecca got over looking around her legs at Tom's smiling face, they achieved a perfect pose.

The class ended with the familiar yoga nidra relaxation. This time partners lay next to each other. Rebecca felt wonderfully relaxed next to Tom. When her conscious mind let go, she imagined the two of them floating high in the cloudless sky over Sedona.

After relaxation, Rebecca felt so peaceful and exhilarated she could hardly stand. Tom helped her up, then rolled her mat. "You're doing so well."

"Maybe I was a yogi in a previous life," was her quick answer.

He laughed. "You're beginning to talk like a true Sedonan."

## Chapter 16

After the yoga class, Tom followed Rebecca and Aries back to the hotel. While Rebecca changed, he delivered Aries, despite her protests, to her mother. Then he drove to New Frontiers to select a picnic lunch and to Safeway for three Starbucks House Blend grandes with extra shots. Even when the coffee cooled, he'd have enough caffeine to keep him awake through the afternoon.

"Let's take my SUV," Rebecca suggested.

"My van's just as comfortable."

She wrinkled her nose.

He got it. "Oh, you don't like riding in the Beloved buggy."

"Your guru van is very recognizable. The word 'Beloved' is scrolled all over it. It reminds me of our meeting."

Tom laughed. "You'll never forget the accident."

"I don't like being reminded that I'm a New York driver."

He watched her transfer picnic supplies into her Cherokee. "You don't look much like a New Yorker anymore."

The sun beat warm on her thin t-shirt while she dabbed sunblock on her face and arms. Her cell phone was back in her room with the laptop and she hadn't even stopped to check her e-mail. She'd have to go back to old habits soon, but today her main concern had been getting into her jeans. They fit tight, but she knew she looked good.

She settled into the passenger seat and let Tom drive without an argument. The hotel laundry must have shrunk her new jeans. She could hardly bend enough to sit. "Do you really think I've changed?" She leaned back, sucking in her belly to stop the waistband from cutting her stomach in two.

He roared. "Changed? Oh, yes. You've changed."

The wind blew in her window and swirled her hair. She didn't lift a finger to smooth it. "Where are we going? Bell Rock?" she asked, not really caring, as he drove towards the Village of Oak Creek.

"A picnic," he replied, smugly.

The yoga class partner poses had definitely broken down the invisible wall between them, though Rebecca wasn't willing to give all the credit to those trust and vulnerability exercises. For some reason, today Tom didn't feel just like a client or a friend. This felt like a date.

She reached over and teasingly touched his arm. They'd both noticed the sparks. "Static electricity," she said and pulled back.

"Vortex lightning. Happens all the time to us extra-mystical types."

"Extra-terrestrial is more like it. I've never met anyone like you. Perhaps you aren't human?"

"Me? I am human and don't you ever forget it."

She smiled. Tom was acting more confident. He held his head high and looked absolutely delicious. How could she have refused to think of him as more than a friend?

They crossed the bridge over Oak Creek and turned left up Schnebly Hill Road. After a short bumpy drive, Tom pulled into a parking area and helped Rebecca out. Taking her hat from the back seat, he placed it on her head and pulled it down over her eyes.

"Stop it. I can't see." She pushed the hat brim back up.

"That's the idea. Close your eyes and let me lead you to the trail."

"No way. I could fall." Little Rebecca told her, *Trust him.*

His hands firm on her shoulders, he looked at the red rocks reflected in her brown eyes. "Do you trust me?"

"Well, sure." She had never trusted anyone

145

completely. Some may have deserved her trust, but her strong independence never allowed that door to open. But right now she did trust Tom. "No one's ever asked me that. At least not seriously." She brushed a tear from her cheek, explaining, "The wind."

"I am serious. I am telling you, you can trust me. Now, eyes closed."

She nodded. Not trusting herself to say more, she allowed him to lead.

Fifty yards along the path, she felt a breeze.

He stopped and faced her into the wind. "Now open."

She opened her eyes and gasped, "This is...this is..." Little Rebecca sighed, *Oh, so beautiful!*

"Yes, it is."

"Oh, Tom. I thought I'd seen every spectacular, gorgeous, amazing view in Sedona. I'd almost gotten used to seeing a more beautiful red rock panorama at every turn, but this is..."

"The best," he finished her thought. He draped his arm over her shoulders and snugged her close as they both looked out over the town of Sedona below. A Shangri-la village in a pine-rimmed red mountain canyon shimmered as the sun cut through the canyon.

"If I blink, will it disappear?" she asked.

"I felt that way the first time I came up here. But no, it changes but does not disappear. And we can come back any time we want to."

She liked the way his voice sounded when he said "we." She slid her arm around his waist. "Thank you for bringing me here." Her head felt so natural leaning against Tom's shoulder, and feeling his warm strength.

He turned and leaned to kiss her. Their lips brushed. She pulled back, suddenly shy. What was she doing? She had to deflect this serious moment. Telling herself to keep it light, she teased, "Thank you for not throwing me off the mountain." This made no sense. Yet, she wanted to kiss Tom more than anything.

Tom looked disappointed, but teased, "I'd never do that...at least not before lunch." He grabbed her hand. "Let's have our picnic."

Rebecca wandered around the overlook while Tom laid out their lunch on an isolated ledge down a short trail

146

from the parking area. Before leaving the SUV, she'd seen him gulp the second Starbucks grande. Now he looked exhilarated, but his eyes had the glassy reflection of the sleep-deprived.

He called out and she joined him in a feast of tortilla-wrapped salads and fruit. He set out bottles of cold water and poured a bubbly burgundy liquid into wine glasses, explaining, "Sparkling pomegranate juice. It's too early for alcohol."

She thought wine would have been nice, but she also wanted to keep her head clear. Thinking clearly was getting more and more difficult. Since she never had problems in the city, she decided to blame it on the altitude.

Lunch in the sunshine was delicious and between bites they talked and laughed a lot. After they shared the darkest organic chocolate she'd ever tasted, she watched Tom pack away the picnic things and unfold a woolen blanket.

Tom stretched out and she followed his example. The sun warmed and relaxed her. The crispness that was Arizona late summer tickled her nose. A breeze carried the scent of pine down from the upper canyon. Rebecca awkwardly straightened her legs and lay back, even more sorry she'd worn these painfully tight jeans.

Rebecca's gaze followed Tom as he watched an eagle and a small plane cross the sky. He seemed not to have a care in the world.

She watched the plane swoop with the eagle, neither acknowledging the other. "I'd love to fly like that..." she whispered and turned toward Tom. He'd fallen asleep. "...before I leave Sedona." Leaving Sedona? After walking these canyons, the City would never feel the same again. She shook off an unexpected sadness and lay down, shading her face with the hat, and felt her consciousness falling away.

The next thing she knew she was waking up. She'd fallen asleep. Right outside. In the wilderness. What about bears, bobcats, coyotes? And those wild pigs, the javelina, would they hurt her?

She stretched against Tom. His easy breathing told her he was still asleep, but he was now pressed against her, one arm over her arm and the other cradling her head. They were spoons. She placed her hand over his and felt the warmth of his skin. The sun was intense and she smelled the delicious scent of burnt cinnamon.

He moved and she readjusted her hips to fit his length. She was certain they would both be embarrassed when he woke, but she was too contentedly lazy to move. She drifted back to sleep.

His breath on her neck woke her and he whispered, "Rebecca, my love."

That's what Max always called her. Tom must be talking in his sleep. She shivered. Here, surrounded by open spaces and sunshine, Max and his dark secrets seemed very far away.

Through the back of her t-shirt, she could feel Tom's heart beat. Her mouth was dry, but she couldn't reach for her water bottle without disturbing him.

He nuzzled her neck again and kissed her. His hand slid down her side and he carefully rolled her onto her back and moved on top of her. His eyes were open. He was not asleep. Without thinking, she arched up, flashed a happy smile, and kissed him, holding his face in her hands as he looked down at her. His gaze was gentle and questioning.

This was crazy. He was her client. And what about Max? Little Rebecca said, *Stop thinking! This is where you need to be.*

Still she felt happy and warm and wondered if it was the sun that heated her blood. Then she stopped thinking and pushed against Tom and sighed his name. She wanted her body closer to his.

She leaned back and began to pull her shirt up and felt the sun on her skin, almost as warm as the heat in her core. Tom lifted back and she let him help. His lips brushed her belly and his fingers, without hesitation, cupped her breasts.

"Oh, my." She reached for the zipper on his jeans. No belt. Thank goodness. She fumbled, then found the slider. One hand worked it down while the other stroked him.

"If you keep that up, they will never come off," he told her.

"Can't you do magic?"

"Some kinds of magic." He took her hands and gently pinned them above her head.

She felt the playfulness in his passion and pure joy in his slow movements. This felt more like teasing play than real sex. He was holding back to please her. Where was the pushing and sweating? And the fighting to be first to achieve orgasm? This was fun.

She stopped thinking. Her heat had turned to fire. All she wanted was him closer—a lot closer.

She lifted her hips, pulled her arms from his grasp, and began using both hands to work her jeans down. Damn jeans were stuck. They would not go lower than her pubic bone and would never make it down over her butt. The zipper cut into her skin and tangled in her hair.

Tom smiled. "You are a natural blonde."

"This isn't funny. Please. Help me take them off," she pleaded, squirming against the roughness of the blanket.

Tom laughed. "Anytime."

"It's really not funny. They're stuck. Really, really stuck." She gave up. Her jeans were going to stay on and she couldn't blame the hotel laundry. The truth—she'd gained weight from eating all that Godiva Max had sent her and the great hotel food. Maybe she should switch to wearing silky drawstring pants like Tom wore for his guru sessions?

Tom looked down at her breasts and belly totally exposed to the sun. She recognized desire behind the twinkle in his eyes.

"Do you trust me?" he asked.

"Yes! Yes! Now, can you get them off?" She was willing to try anything.

"I don't think I can."

This man was insane. He just grinned. Then began to kiss her. He teased kisses around her belly button and she arched up, wanting more. The zipper cut deeper into her flesh.

"Relax. Don't hurt yourself. Let me."

"Let you do what? You are crazy," she told him with a giggle, but settled back to see what he'd do. She tried some of that relaxing yoga breathing while he continued to kiss and stroke and raise the temperature of her blood past boiling.

Her nipples were ready to explode and her pelvis throbbed. She had to close her eyes. Seeing him touch her was just too much. She wanted to touch him, but when she reached for him, he again constrained her arms. Laying still like this and breathing was the hardest thing she'd ever done. For the first time in any sexual relationship, she was concentrating on her own feelings and giving someone else control. Could Heather have been right to call her a control freak?

Tom's right leg held her thighs to the blanket. His right hand kept a gentle pressure on her chest, holding her down while he stroked. Lightly when she wanted harder. Harder when she was sure she could take no more.

"More," she gasped even though she was sure she could take no more. This heavenly feeling must go on forever. Tom wasn't listening. He kept the slow steady pace that drove her mad.

The waves came from deep in her center, flooding into every cell of her body. And kept coming. And kept coming. Never had she felt such intensity, or for so long. Minutes? Hours? She had no idea.

She reached for Tom and he held her tight as shudders rocked her. Her brain had shut down and it felt wonderful. Over and over, powerful waves rolled through her from toes to head. Even the best vibrator had never made her feel this good.

At last exhausted, she fell back. "Hold me." Tears slid down her laughing face.

"I am," he told her, his eyes sparkling with joy. "Was that good?"

She laughed. "You're the guru. Read my mind."

Chapter 17

An hour later, Rebecca and Tom stood in the hotel lobby waiting for Aries. Both were uncomfortably silent and self-conscious. Separate showers had cooled them down, but the picnic had changed everything.

Rebecca wore her loose, long red dress. The hated jeans lay in shreds on the floor of her bedroom. She'd never tell anyone George had been waiting for her at her cottage with slippery gel, long pointy scissors, and homeopathic cream for abrasions.

"Aries is such a big fan of Cora's," Rebecca told Tom, "I promised to introduce her. Then I need to meet another client for dinner. After that I'm as busy as if I were in New York." She was talking to be talking. She needed time to figure out how she felt. Tom had been so quiet on the ride back, she wondered if he'd had regrets.

Tom saw Aries approaching in a black mini and sequined strapless bustier. He exploded, "No way! Go change."

"I totally don't want Cora to think I'm a kid."

"You are a kid," Tom and Rebecca said together.

"I could get a part in one of her movies. Don't you think I'd be a perfect made-for-TV movie heroine?" Aries said, striking a pose.

Rebecca grinned. "Careful. Cora wants the starring roles for herself. She considers her films Hollywood blockbusters, not made-for-TV movies."

Tom turned Aries and sent her back in the direction of their cottage to change.

Fifteen minutes late, a white stretch limo pulled up to the hotel lobby. The driver rushed around and with a flourish opened the door. Cora burst out with her arms raised and diaphanous butterfly jacket flapping over a black mini and tank top. Rebecca wondered what gel kept Cora's flaming red hair flaring out wider than her hips.

"R.J. darling, my gloriously brilliant legal eagle." She air-kissed Rebecca's cheeks. "You will save my so, so expensive butt, again." Her eyes narrowed. "Did you do something to your hair?"

Rebecca pulled back, ignoring the hair question. Cora was always dramatically overwhelming, but here in Sedona, the Hollywood superstar getup looked silly. She looked to see Tom's reaction to Cora. His eyes were wide. Was he awestruck at her beauty or her absurdity? She could not tell.

Aries scooted around the corner, saw Cora, and slowed from scamper to sway. Her jeans were low and her top cropped to show lots of innocent adolescent midriff. Her platform thongs created a mature sway to her back and added four inches to her height.

"Let me introduce you to my friends." Rebecca drew Aries to her side. "Aries Paxton, my friend, a promising musician, and a big fan of yours."

Cora fussed over Aries, not quite sure why this kid was important, then fastened her eyes on Tom. "Are you another big fan?" she asked, stepping into his space. "I'm Cora Ayne, darling. Call me anytime."

Cora's laugh said the quip was a joke, but Rebecca knew it was no such thing. "Cora, this is Tom Paxton, author and spiritual teacher. He's a new client of mine. Did I mention he's a spiritual teacher?" She stepped close to Tom's shoulder. "Aries is his thirteen-year-old daughter."

Cora fluttered impossibly long eyelashes. Could they be implants, too?

"Mr. Paxton, I should have known you from your jacket covers. I've seen all your books."

Tom frowned, obviously puzzled by her statement.

Rebecca explained, "Cora means she hasn't actually read your books, but knows you from bestseller lists and bookstore displays."

Cora lunged for Tom's arm. "Don't you listen to that silly woman, darling. We celebs have so, so much in common. We must have a private *tête-à-tête*."

"That would be good," Tom said, "but I have to take Aries to rehearsal."

He backed up, but Cora was too quick. She leaned into him and, wrapping her butterfly sleeves around him in a rainbow cocoon, hugged him. Gazing up into his eyes, she sighed, "Spiritually, we must be so fated to be here—together." Then she kissed him.

Rebecca's eyes narrowed. She was certain that under that diaphanous jacket, Cora was thrusting her pelvis against Tom. Her first instinct was to rip them apart. But before she could do anything, Angie glided into the lobby in her white angelic robe, took in the tableau, and screamed, "Tom, why aren't you driving Aries to rehearsal...I mean the harmonic run-through. This is no way for a responsible father to behave. Another woman? Now a fake redhead. I'll be sure my lawyer adds this to the list of reasons I deserve total custody."

"But Angie. Mom..." Aries whined.

Angie spun on her heel and swept out to the parking lot in a cloud of white silk.

Tom pulled away from Cora, keeping his gentlemanly composure, despite his flushed face and the swatch of crimson lipstick on his upper lip. "Please excuse me. So good to meet you." Cora raised her eyebrows and tossed her mane. He turned to Aries. "Say goodbye. We are very late."

"*Enchanté.*" Aries followed Tom.

Cora dismissed Rebecca with a wave and led her entourage to the front desk.

Rebecca tapped her toe. She'd seen Cora's performances before, but that scene with Tom was excessive. Only a shameless, shallow woman would behave like that. He'd never fall for her. Or would he? He wasn't as innocent as she'd thought. Their picnic showed her a new side. A side she sure didn't want Cora to see.

A classically handsome man in a lounge chair stared in the direction Cora had gone, clearly dazed. Cora did have that effect on some men.

Rebecca continued to pace the lobby, then stepped up

to the desk and told the clerk, "Please ring Claude Festerman's room."

The seated man stood and said in a voice which didn't quite match the rest of him, "Hi, R.J. It's me, Claude. Don't you recognize me?"

Rebecca, surprised out of her professional nothing-can-surprise-me poise, did a double take. "Claude, is that you?"

"You don't know your biggest client?" He winked. One eyelid closed while his face stayed immobile, creating a cartoonish wink whose action and sound were out of sync.

"There is not one thing about you that looks like the Claude Festerman I know. You...you...you're taller!"

"Medical technology and money create miracles." Claude grinned.

"I'm in shock. Speechless."

He tossed back his head. "The peerless R.J. Dumaurier, the most loquacious intellectual property attorney in this bibliophagic business, at a loss for words. I'll take that as high praise."

If she closed her eyes, the cocky attitude, voice, and over-the-top vocabulary reminded her of the old Claude.

He crooked his arm and bowed. "May I escort you to dinner?"

She took his arm, trying to reconcile her memory of the mole man with this too-handsome hunk.

Seated at their table, he leaned forward. "It might be easier if you called me Steve."

"Steve? Who's Steve?" Her voice rose. "Another pseudonym? I represent Claude Festerman and Cleo St. Cloud. I hear Bullet has another lawyer and I am not pleased with that." Her voice rose another notch. "Who the hell is Steve?"

"R.J., or Rebecca as you seem to be called now, relax. You are way too excited."

She exploded. "I am not excited."

"Then lower your voice." He indicated the crowded dining room and she looked around. All faces watched them.

"Fine," she whispered and reminded herself to breathe, then slowly said, "Now, please tell me who Steve is."

"Steve is me. My name. My real, true name. Claude has been my legal name for the last ten years, but Steve is my, how do you say it, my 'birth name.'"

"Why the hell..." Rebecca took a breath and continued in a forced whisper, "Why didn't you use your real name as your legal name from the beginning?"

"What publisher would publish, or what agent would represent me, if..." He paused for dramatic effect and grinned. "...my name were Steve King?"

"Oh," Rebecca breathed in. "That name's sort of taken."

"Right, counselor."

They ate dinner and shared a bottle of wine as they talked about minor contract issues. Rebecca expected Steve to bring up demands for book tours to reveal sweet Cleo was a guy with liposuctioned love handles. So far he hadn't mentioned either. She hoped this meant he had come to his senses.

On the way back to her room, Rebecca looked up at the gorgeous man she now called Steve. His cheeky façade was not much different from hers. Par for this business. Why hadn't she noticed he was bright and interesting and a nice guy? Probably because she didn't date moles. Was she as shallow as women who judged men solely on looks and clothes?

They swayed toward the rosemary bush in front of her cottage. Steve put his arm around her shoulders to steady her and steady himself and they giggled. Just then, Tom and Cora walked under a light nearer the lobby and they heard Cora say to Tom, "I'm so, so glad we accidentally met."

Steve and Rebecca watched Tom and Cora turn towards Cora's cottage. Steve's low keening moan interrupted Rebecca's spontaneous jealous thoughts.

"What's the matter?" Rebecca asked.

"I love her and he is my best friend." He sat down on her cottage step, holding his head in his hands.

"She's my client and he's my...best friend." She sat next to him and they looked in the direction where Tom and Cora had disappeared.

After a few minutes of silent mutual commiseration,

Steve said, "I know Heather told you I want to come out as a man. I am serious. I'm tired of being a genre cross-dresser. I have to do it. Then Cora will love me."

Rebecca gulped and shook her head. "Claude or Steve or whoever, you need to understand that would be professional and financial suicide. No way, José!"

"My agent said I needed to clear the legal issues with you."

"And he begged me to talk sense into you. He'll have to take his kids out of private school and mortgage his house in Boca if you tell the world you're a man."

"I am a man. Don't you think my readers want honesty?"

"No!"

"Come on, R.J. I don't need your permission to have a press conference."

"No, but you'll need me when the lawsuits are filed."

"From?"

"Your agents and publishers will claim fraud, misrepresentation, anything they can think of to get a chunk of your money—while there's some left. You'll end up autographing remainders in Wal-Mart."

"Give it up, Rebecca. I'm through taking orders from hacks who only care about their percentage."

Rebecca sighed. "Remember how much you like the Mazerati and the villa. Bestselling authors with loyal fans—lots of loyal fans—enjoy those perks." She rubbed the center of her forehead with the heel of her hand. She felt a headache starting.

"I'm not saying that I'll trash my past in the tabloids. I want babes who see my new bod to know I'm famous."

Rebecca stifled a gag. This was the same mole-like man who, clutching a manuscript and a contract, crept into her office begging her to represent him because she was the best in romance genre publishing. Now, this muscular peacock was ready to thumb his nose at her in order to get laid.

****

Cora hung on Tom's arm, smothering him in masses of red hair. "Please darling, come in. I have books I'll sign for your sweet daughter, A-R-I-E-S?"

"Sure," he yawned. That heavy, tired feeling was

coming over him earlier every evening. Every morning he slept later, but was as exhausted as if he'd been up all night. The past few mornings he'd needed a minimum of three cups of strong coffee before he could function. Tomorrow he'd try an espresso instead of breakfast. After Angie left early for the workshop and Aries went off to Rebecca's cottage, he was supposed to be working on his new book, but his body was all screwed up and he had no clue how to straighten things out.

He should be walking on air after the wonderful picnic with Rebecca, but he wondered if he'd made everything worse. She'd been quiet on the drive back and all business later. Maybe he'd made a mistake. The signs she sent to him told him she really liked him as more than a friend. He wanted to show her how he felt and that he was not just a nice shy guy.

Cora pulled at his arm, urging him up the steps to her cottage. What was going on? He'd just seen Rebecca in front of her cottage with Steve, his best friend. They looked very cozy, not at all like client and lawyer. He wanted to interrupt them but he'd allowed himself to be led off by this pseudo-superstar.

Inside the door, he yawned again and Cora interpreted that as a sign of encouragement and began to massage his back.

"What about those books?" he asked.

"They're right over here, next to the bed," she cooed. "Bring your pen...and I'll inscribe you, I mean them."

Tom stopped, stiffened and jerked his arm away. "Get off me." His voice was suddenly harsh and his eyes shot daggers at Cora.

Cora stepped back against the foot of her four-poster and raised her hands theatrically in front of her face.

Tom shook his head and looked around. "Who said that?"

"You," she squeaked. "You did."

"Sorry, I'm really tired. I need some sleep." He backed to the door, opened it, but before he slipped through, he heard Cora say, "You are crazy." He fled towards his cottage.

Within five minutes Tom was asleep.

Max got up and began pacing. He called Rebecca's

room. No answer. He'd seen her earlier with that Steve person who was a friend of Tom's. There was something very wrong with Steve...and that Cora woman. She was beautiful in the way of wild harlots who'd attracted him in his younger days. But she and Steve reminded him of stage actors. Something about their bodies, voices, and manner was wrong. Regardless, if he had the time, he'd consider a fling with the redhead. But he had bigger issues to resolve and soon.

He had never expected his plan to be easy. There were many inconveniences, but Tom—he spat the name—was getting to be a great nuisance. He knew Tom was in love with Rebecca and he was not about to allow that whelp to spoil his plans or steal her away from him. During the day Tom was usually strong enough to block him completely, like this afternoon. Sunlight took all Max's power away and Tom had spent the afternoon in the sun with Rebecca. Max sensed something important had happened.

He pulled a box from under the bed and changed into the black smoking jacket which made him feel more like himself. He found the boots in the closet but his rum was missing. He called the desk and ordered another bottle to be delivered to the room.

That busboy with the hole in his eyebrow had taught him to shop on the computer with Tom's plastic money. He didn't know how, but packages arrived.

He found the bottle of *Evening in Paris* the steward had delivered earlier. Gifts these days were more expensive than he remembered, but every time he signed Tom's name, he knew securing Rebecca was worth any amount.

He wondered if *Chanel No. 5* would have been a better choice for a serious woman like Rebecca. But he didn't have much time and had to rely on the wounded busboy's research.

He was certain that Rebecca was in love with him. She accepted his gifts, welcomed him into her boudoir, and certainly did not behave like a lady. Other than that talk about a condo, she acted just like any low-bred strumpet. Now he needed to complete the seduction that would make her completely his. He took out one of the thick hotel notecards and wrote:

****

*My Dearest Love,*

*I detest every moment you are not in my arms. Our love has been destined. Can you doubt we were once lovers in another life dancing in the Paris moonlight? Never doubt my love for you, nor doubt that I will find a way for us to be together forever.*

*Your most devoted Max*

****

Now, where was that tutor?

Chapter 18

Aries opened the blue glass bottle and sniffed. "This perfume is so totally not me. Tell him to keep the Godiva coming and forget perfume that smells like my great-grandmother."

"Be quiet. I'm busy." Rebecca tapped nervously on her laptop. She must have been crazy to agree to go with Aries to visit a psychic and now wanted desperately to get out of it. Aries insisted a reading would straighten out Rebecca's love life, as though the girl had any idea how complicated her life and loves had become.

Aries went back to reading, then, looked up from her Jennifer Crusie novel. "Rebecca? At what age do mothers start treating daughters like grownups? I don't know if I can wait."

Rebecca didn't blink or interrupt the e-mail she was composing. "Never. One minute my mother treats me like I'm younger than you are, the next tells me I'm old and better hurry and get married and give her grandchildren." She rolled her eyes. "I'm the best lawyer in my business. She criticizes my wardrobe and my boyfriends. She adored Tristan because he was good-looking and well-dressed, but I think she liked his name best."

"That's a cruel thing to say. Why did you break off your engagement? Was he boring and unromantic? All work and no play?"

"Not exactly." Rebecca was convinced Aries was a forty-year-old in a teen body. But she certainly was not going to tell this child about her boring engagement and its exciting end.

"But why? Did you fall in love with someone else or go off looking for your soulmate, like in one of Cora's novels? Did you know, like a Nora Roberts heroine, that you were going to meet someone like my dad?"

"My life is not like a romance novel. Well, maybe one of Jennifer Crusie's."

"Are you sure the sex is *that* that hot or just that funny?"

"Between me and Tris?"

"Between romance novels and real life."

Rebecca shut down her computer. "Enough questions. Let's read the latest in Arianna's diary."

\*\*\*\*

*June 10, 1866*
*St. Albans Island, British West Indies*
*This morning I ran down to my waterfall for a swim wearing a calico dress as simple as that of a house slave. One month ago, the pineapple fields smelled delightful, but after harvest the rotted fruit is too unpleasant, so I took the path near Penelope's house. I heard her husband roar at the servants and I ran the rest of the way.*

*Gentle Penelope avoids being alone with her husband, for his moods frighten her. One day I heard him accuse her of being a witch. He is mad to have an heir and her delicate constitution vexes him greatly. Penelope is now with child and asks if I would accompany her back to England, but The Major will not hear of it. He says she may visit after their son is born.*

*I am happy for her and hope that soon I too will be with child.*

*I spy Penelope at the waterfall and am about to call her name. But I see she sits so still I think she is asleep. Her eyes are open and she stares into the tumbling water. I push through the bushes and lean against a large palm tree.*

*Penelope's face twitches like she is being tickled by an ostrich plume. She throws her shoulders back and lifts her face to the sky. Then the strangest thing happens. A large woman's voice comes out of her mouth, accented like a Greek servant I once had. Her light hair appears to grow darker. Her bosom strains at the bodice of her dress. Her eyes look deep and kohl-rimmed.*

*"O woman," the not-Penelope voice cries. "Follow the course of freedom. The world is for your children."*

*I crawl across the rocks and ask Penelope if she is well and the voice responds. "Penelope is not here, Arianna." You can imagine my surprise. Was Penelope playing a trick? I am sure not.*

*"Beware of the dark man. Find the red rocks to reunite with your true love," it said. How silly. Rocks are not red and I have my Thomas. I am perfectly happy.*

*"The dark man plots to possess you," the voice continued. "Be careful. Warn Thomas."*

*Just then The Major crashed through the trees. He used a coconut shell to scoop water from the waterfall and splashed his wife's face. He screamed at her to get up. Seeing me, his manner softened. I dare say, even in his temper, he looked too long at my light shift. He picked her up, saying to me, "Arianna, my wife is not herself," and carried Penelope back to their home.*

*Later when I sought her out, she did not know what she said. I remember the séance in London and wonder if she is truly possessed.*

\*\*\*\*

Rebecca shook her head. "This is not a romance." Little Rebecca whispered, *For Arianna this is the story of the great love of her life. For Penelope the story is her great tragedy.*

"But it's so totally gothic. I love it."

"Look. The heroine found her perfect man. Romance over. She and her lover are in the happily ever after part. The story could be a mystery. Or if poor abused Penelope is the heroine, it could be a woman in peril story. Unless her husband gets lost in a storm or she is kidnapped, there isn't much chance of romance for her."

162

"But remember it's not a story. Aunt Arianna said it's my family history. She's transcribing this diary she found in her father's—that's my grandfather's—trash years ago. He threw it out for some reason. She says the entries start in London, then go on in The British West Indies and end in Paris. Because some pages are in bad condition and the handwriting is very old-fashioned, she put off working on it until she could get a sabbatical. She thinks she can get it published."

"I hope she won't settle for one of those stodgy presses that make wonderful books look boring and refuse to advertise in the bigger market. This is good stuff. She could get a really big advance if it were handled the right way. Tell her not to sign anything until she talks to me."

"First, she wants to go to the British Virgin Islands and find St. Albans. The island is not on maps, but she thinks she's found it. She wants Dad and me to go with her at Christmas."

"That would be great." Rebecca wondered if, since this Sedona trip had turned out so well, she would take regular vacations, too. She could go to the Caribbean for the holidays, or any place. Not that she was thinking about going with Aries and Tom. "Wait. Are you saying she found a real island called St. Albans that your family owned?"

"Of course. It's part of family history. My family did not live on an imaginary island."

Still thinking about Arianna's story and imagining the publicity opportunities for a book tour for the famous trance guru's sister, Rebecca drove Aries to the crystal shop for their readings.

"How did you find this psychic?" Rebecca asked. "Is she a friend of your dad's? Or your mom's?" If the psychic was Angie's friend, Rebecca was ready to cancel.

"I Googled 'Sedona Psychics,'" Aries said with a shrug.

"How do you know this one's any good?"

"Didn't I tell you I'm psychic? If she's the not the real thing, we leave."

Aries approached the jewelry counter. A woman directed them to draped cubicles in the back. A plump white-haired gypsy in a purple robe and Aladdin slippers sat at a small table with a crystal ball.

Rebecca began, "I'm not sure—"

The back door burst open and a young woman in a paisley business dress entered. "Sorry. My other job...traffic..." she gasped. "I'm Joy."

"You're...George...the hotel concierge," Rebecca said.

"And Joy of Sedona, remember." George beamed at Rebecca and Aries. "Welcome. I'm so glad you both came." She indicated the tiny table barely big enough for two people in the second cubicle. "This is very cramped. Let's go out to the back garden."

Settled between a pyramid and a rose bush, George offered them bottles of water. "I'm moving into my own office. Between the hotel job, appointments here, and getting my own place ready I'm swamped, and on top of everything else my meditation group's having this big Mabon celebration and potluck on the night of the Equinox." George fumbled in her bag, pulled out a tape recorder, Jeep tour brochures, and a bundle of sage. With a dismissive wave she told them, "Enough about me." She took a deep breath, lit the sage, and waved the bundle around, letting the calming smoke curl over them and breathing in a lot herself.

Rebecca and Aries sat listening to the fountain until George was satisfied that they were properly smudged and asked, "So, Rebecca, what are you looking for?"

"You sound like you did when I arrived and you asked what kind of activities I was looking for, hiking, shopping, Jeep tours, or a timeshare purchase."

George's laugh was relaxed and mellow. "Sorry. Let's begin with a standard reading and see what happens."

Rebecca knew George was a great concierge, but wondered if this young, disorganized woman was a competent psychic. Was there a Sedona Licensing Board of Psychics?

George closed her eyes.

Aries explained, "She's getting into her psychic space, calling in her guides, that sort of thing."

Rebecca whispered to Aries, "She can see the future, can't she? I want her to tell me if this man I'm seeing is the right one." She sounded like a letter to Dear Abby.

George opened her eyes and took Rebecca's hand.

"Ah, the man you are seeing? Or the man you are not seeing? A wonderful man has come into your life. You and he are destined to be together. Why don't you just enjoy him? You may need to lighten up a little."

Rebecca leaned forward. "But he's so mysterious!" Why had she come with Aries? This was too adult for a kid. "He only comes to me at night."

"Do you enjoy the romance with your lover?"

Aries giggled.

Rebecca shot her a keep-quiet look. "No. Yes. I guess. I do find him very exciting."

George closed her eyes again. "Your lover's name is Thomas."

Aries covered her mouth to stifle a laugh.

"No!" Coming with Aries was definitely not a good idea.

"Yes." George sounded sure. "You have a lover named Tom."

"No. I have a friend named Tom, this girl's father." Rebecca was firm. "You know that from the hotel gossip."

Aries shushed her. "Right now she's not exactly the same person as when she's working at the hotel. She doesn't know the same things."

"Child, is your father mysterious?" George took Aries' hand with her free hand.

"No. He's your ordinary everyday psychic trance channeler. Actually, he's kind of shy."

"Ah...Tom Paxton, of course. I've read his books." She turned to Rebecca. "There is only one man in your life. He loves you and will be kind and loving to you always. Do not fear him. However, the dark spirit means you harm. HE must be vanquished." Turning back to Aries, she asked, "Now, what question do you have?"

"Will I ever have a real family?" Aries looked hopeful.

"Do not be sad. Soon you will have a happy home."

Rebecca paid George and took Aries directly to the parking lot without going back through the crystal shop.

"She's a total quack," Rebecca told Aries.

"I don't think so. I think she was confused. I can tell that in psychics. When they see things that don't make sense to them, they are afraid to say too much and scare the client. They do the best they can and then kind of end the reading real quick. I think we should go back again."

"And waste more money." Rebecca slipped into the parent voice.

"I have a credit card. I'm not a kid. Let's hurry back to the hotel. It was supposed to be a secret, but my dad's taking you for an airplane ride this afternoon. Grownups have all the fun."

****

Max heard an angry female voice outside Rebecca's cottage. He'd been waiting impatiently for that infuriating Rebecca woman to return. She was too damned independent for her own good. He opened the door and looked down, not at Rebecca, but at the diminutive Charlotte Dumaurier garbed in the popular Sedona goddess style.

He bowed. "You must be dear Rebecca's sister," he said with the automatic lie of a gentleman.

Charlotte instinctively raised her right hand and Max took her fingers and kissed them.

"Maximilian Winter, at your service, madam. Dear Rebecca is not here. I seldom have a free morning to visit with her and today I am bereft to have missed her. Please come in."

"*Monsieur* Winter, I am charmed. What a handsome name." Charlotte visibly quivered with pleasure as she floated through the door. "If I had had a second son, I would have named him Maximilian."

"But surely, you are too young to have children." This woman was ridiculous. He knew her kind, the aging coquette, living through her grown children. Stupid, but easy to manipulate.

"You are kind. I am, I must say, Rebecca's mother. She is my eldest."

He shot her his practiced disbelieving stare. He knew he played the gentleman's flirting and flattering game extremely well.

"Though I was but a child when she was born. Swept off my feet...as you gentlemen are so apt to do."

"Then you are the renowned Mrs. Dumaurier. Charming madam, may I offer you a cup of tea and perhaps a chocolate, this brand named after a bold equestrienne." Perhaps he could learn something useful

166

from this silly woman.

"You are too kind."

Max poured tea and removed the lid from the Godiva box. He knew she was noticing his black smoking jacket and knee-high boots. He thought this former beauty would appreciate that he dressed like a 19th century rake, moved like a gentleman, and fawned as naturally as other men shook hands.

"You dress well," she said. "May I ask why you are in my daughter's room, sir?"

"As soon as I can complete the formalities—I have not enquired where I can find my dear Rebecca's father—I expect to be her fiancé, and quite soon after her husband." He assumed that would make his presence appear proper.

"Rebecca has agreed to marry you!" Charlotte's hand flew to cover her open mouth.

"She would already be my bride, if my wish could make it so." He leaned toward Charlotte and whispered, "I do believe the darling girl does love me to distraction." This should keep her meddling mother from ruining everything.

"Are you sure we are talking about my daughter? Rebecca?"

"Oh, yes. If you would be so kind as to ask your husband, Rebecca's esteemed father, the head of the family to meet with me, the technicalities will be settled post haste. The dowry, the naming of our first son..."

"Rebecca's esteemed father is, um...not my husband...any longer. I consider myself the head of the family."

"But her father...I would prefer the traditional way."

"If you must..." Charlotte walked to Rebecca's desk and flipped open the address book. "Here." She pointed to the name John Dumaurier and a phone number. "Heaven knows where he is. He always traveled a lot..."

"What business is he in?" Max wondered if Rebecca's family had money and might settle a large dowry on their only daughter.

"Last I heard...real estate."

Though Charlotte's chin lifted to show her disinterest, Max detected the lady had feelings for this John Dumaurier.

Chapter 19

When Tom and Rebecca arrived at the Sedona Airport, he told her, "Aries wanted to come. But, this is for you. You need to get away from all those clients you're always meeting with or hiding from." He had been purposely mysterious about his plans for the afternoon, hoping he would be rested. He finished the travel mug of coffee and hoped his long morning nap would keep him alert for the flight.

She followed him into the terminal. "This doesn't look at all like a big jet airport."

"Sedona's airport is just for private planes and tours."

"Are we going to take a tour? That would be fun." Rebecca looked at the maps and aerial photo of Sedona's red rocks.

"I've rented a plane. We can go anywhere you want." Tom enjoyed Rebecca's expression of surprise and delight. He left her looking at the photos and walked to a desk to confer with a man in a blue baseball hat. They studied maps and Tom showed him his logbook. Rebecca came over to see what they were talking about as the counterman asked Tom how experienced a pilot he was and Tom replied that he had been flying for ten years and had a small Cessna 150 back in New Hampshire.

"No problem then," the man with the "Mr. Bill" nametag told him. "I'll put you in a plane just like yours. Come on, we'll do a quick checkride to be sure you can handle the 150 and then you're off. I'll brief you on the scenic route. Your wife will love seeing Sedona from the air."

Rebecca blushed. "I'm not..." she began, but Tom and Bill already were out the door to where the planes were tied down.

In twenty minutes, the men were back. Bill gave Tom a thumbs-up and Tom escorted Rebecca out to the two-seat Cessna. He showed her how to climb up and in, and then ran around to his own seat and buckled her into a harness-style seat belt.

She was still surprised at how different this experience was from big airlines. "No long lines or security checks?"

"And no frequent flyer miles." Tom was confident and exuberant. He wanted her to enjoy this. He smoothed back the bronze wisps of her hair and showed her how to adjust the headset and talk to him. He wrinkled his nose in the closed cabin. Perfume?

Before he turned his attention to starting the plane he held her hand and said, "I love you," knowing she was looking out the window and that until he turned on the radio, her headset blocked his words.

During the flight Tom enjoyed pointing out landmarks. He was familiar with how different roads and buildings looked from the air and had flown over Sedona many times. Her "ooohs" and "ahhhhs" made this the best flight since his first solo.

Looking down, he realized he did not want to leave Sedona. When he arrived, he'd been anxious to finish this workshop and take Aries home to New Hampshire and the beautiful fall colors. Autumn festivals made this his favorite time of year there. He knew they'd miss that great equinox festival that marked the end of every summer tourist season in their town.

Angie was determined to keep Aries in California, while he wanted her to stay with him in the house he'd built on Lake Winnipesaukee close to his friends at the nearby holistic camp. Rebecca hoped to negotiate a compromise or delay the move until Aries finished high school, but she had not sounded positive. Rebecca. He wanted to stay in Sedona and spend more time with Rebecca. Aries liked her and had become a nicer kid since she and Rebecca began spending time together. But

Rebecca would be returning to New York City any day.

He banked the plane towards Schnebly Hill, hoping she'd remember their picnic. How could she keep pretending it had not happened? They'd almost had sex! Well, she had—sort of. He'd had the most erotic experience of his life—and he hadn't taken his clothes off. Steve would probably say that proved he loved this woman.

An hour later, Tom helped her out of the plane. The flight had been smooth and perfect. He had wanted to show her something beautiful and exciting and hopefully romantic. He lifted her down and held her close. He tried to sense from her presence and smell if she were the woman he'd been with when he was not in his body. He felt kind of silly, but he had to know. The day of the picnic, he was too much in the moment to sort it all out.

She pulled away from his arms, but not before he smelled that old-fashioned perfume that reminded him of his grandmother. The scent was distracting, but underneath the perfume was a personal essence, like tart apples and maple syrup, that was distinctly Rebecca.

The quizzical look on her face made him wonder if she, too, was trying to remember. Or was she thinking about the picnic and expecting him to say something? Sometimes women needed to hear certain words at certain times. He wasn't good at saying the right thing at the right time because he preferred to think things through before he spoke. Didn't she know how he felt about her? After all those years with Angie, he had lost touch with women with subtler needs.

She smiled and took his hand. On the way back to the hotel he sensed that they both were avoiding saying anything personal.

****

Rebecca closed the cottage door and twirled around. The flight with Tom had been great. The scenery was amazing and she enjoyed flying in the small plane with him. She'd never met anyone who had their own plane. What lawyer had the time for lessons? Tom was bright and funny and tried to please her. He was honest and showed her he liked her without being pushy or using any woo-woo stuff. He hadn't mentioned the picnic and that bothered her. Perhaps they had gotten carried away and now he wanted to pretend it hadn't happened. She sure couldn't forget.

After the flight when Tom held her, she felt the queerest sensation. She felt the way she felt when she was close to Max. Not the wild scary part, but the good part—like the having been together before thing Max always talked about. Could she have known them both before?

Max insisted she had been with him in a previous life. Tom went into trances and talked to spirits all the time, but he never talked like that. What if she asked Tom to check his spirit connections and find out if Max was right?

She wasn't ready to talk to Tom about Max. Max hadn't exactly said not to tell Tom, but he treated their relationship as if it were clandestine and she had started out enjoying the intrigue. Now, she was afraid if Tom knew about Max and their meetings, he would misunderstand and she would lose him from her life. She did not want that. She couldn't make sense of her thoughts or feelings. She would sleep on it. Exhausted, she lay down to rest and immediately fell asleep.

When she awoke, the room was dark. She looked at the clock. It was almost 11:30. She'd promised to meet Max at the river at eleven o'clock. Changing into the Sedona goddess dress he liked best, she slipped out into the night.

Little Rebecca showed up again. *Listen to me! Stay away from that man. Do not go to the river.* Rebecca was tired of the little voice's arguments and snapped, "I don't have time to argue with you. Be quiet." Why did Little Rebecca hate Max without any reason?

Once again the light fixture closest to the river was out of order. She'd report it to the manager in the morning.

She saw the silhouette of a tall man at the river and ran towards him. Max turned. His face was tight and impatience hardened his eyes. He wore that black shirt and pants that reminded her of a pirate. He held a bottle in his hand.

"Is something wrong?" she asked.

171

"You're late." His voice was rough. He held the bottle to his lips and drained it. He continued in a gentler tone, "I've missed you so," and took a step closer.

"I missed you, too." She could not see his eyes but the shadows of his face would be what Heather called a Mr. Darcy look.

"Did you have a nice ride in that air ship?"

She didn't like the accusation in his voice. "Why, yes, I did. Is that a problem for you?"

"I want you all the time. We need to make plans. Your mother and I..." He came closer and tossed the bottle down the bank to the creek.

She heard the glass shatter on the river stones. "You were talking to my mother?"

"You were right. She is charming, but insignificant."

Rebecca snapped, "Only I can call my mother insignificant."

Max went on, "I had hoped to talk to your father. Before—"

"What would you want with my father? I haven't talked to him in years myself. He's a selfish, arrogant bast—man. All he ever cared about was success and pleasing himself. Look at my poor mother—turned into a caricature."

"So I do not need to ask your father for your hand?"

"My what?"

"I am so impatient." He swept her into his arms and kissed her hard. "Let us go to your boudoir. I will have you now. That will convince you."

"Max. Slow down." The smell of rum on his breath was overpowering. "I want to talk. We hardly know each other." What was he rushing her into? She'd made no commitment.

He held her tight to his chest. She struggled to free her chin and looked up at him. Backlit in the shadows, the bones of his face appeared sharp and his eyes dark and shadowed by prominent brows.

Rebecca felt she was with a stranger and she did not feel safe. She pushed him away. He pulled her back and pressed his face to hers until his beard scraped her cheek and she cried out. The more she squirmed, the closer he pressed. Using all her strength and a subtle move she'd learned in that "Street Safe Women of New York" class, she pulled away. Picking up that damned ruffled skirt, she ran to her cottage, let herself in, and bolted the door behind her.

Max thundered after her. "Rebecca my love, you misunderstand. Perhaps, I was impatient."

She heard his boots on the porch and turned on the light. "Go away," she called, "I'm tired." After a few minutes she looked through the peephole and saw his back striding away.

She was tired. The phone rang. She unplugged it and made sure her cell phone was off. Just for tonight, she told herself. She needed time to figure out what was going on without anyone's help or voices in her head.

She settled down to read and analyze Max's e-mail attachments. The first was a .jpg file of an illegible handwritten letter. The background was grey, but she recognized Max's old-fashioned script. The date looked like June 22, 1966, but it was blurred and too dark to be sure.

\*\*\*\*

*I dream of being master of my own island. But I not only dream I will be master, truly master. I write these words to show my plan. When all is in place, let no man claim I came upon my fortune through fortuitous means.*

*After payments to a few selected government officials, my island will be the domain of no country. It will be found on no map or chart. I will be my own country. No king nor queen will have power over me. To no petty governor nor absent lord do I swear fidelity.*

*I will acquire more armaments in case marauding pirates wash up upon my shore. And more slaves. Because as countries outlaw what they call the barbarous trade, I will possess sufficient breeding stock to supply wealthy plantation owners.*

*My present wife's weak brother worries about what crops to plant and the quality of the cotton. I will convert all fields to sugar cane and import more for the refinery I will build. Rum will be my fortune as my ships swiftly transport my "gold" to any harbour where the price be highest.*

*The shipping company in London that my second wife will bring as her dowry will be my legitimate business. My sons will need this to claim their place in society anywhere in the world they choose.*

*My weak wife carries my son and when that man-child first sees light of day, half the island becomes mine. It is likely that this frail woman will not long survive the birthing. She is not strong and many know that demons speak through her. These devils may call her to throw herself from the bluffs into the ocean. And if they don't, I will.*

*I expect my dear brother-in-law will not survive a slave uprising. He is too kind to his slaves and one day I fear they will take his life most brutally. Then I will be here upon this island with the fair widow of this simpering brother to my departed wife and I will hold power over her. She will see that becoming my wife and uniting the island is her desire. I am her destiny and this island will be truly my paradise found. I shall truly be Lord of Moon Island.*

*MW Esq.*
*Moon Island*

\*\*\*\*

She was tired, very tired. Was the next file supposed to be part of the book Max claimed he wrote? The format looked like a script. Parts sounded like the document she'd just read.

\*\*\*\*

*Revised Shooting Draft*
*Paradise Island: Somewhere in the Caribbean, ocean, palm trees, mountains, flowers*
*Superimpose Maxwell in profile in black pirate dress looking out past ships in harbor.*
*Script:*
*Voice of Maxwell: "I am master of the island.*

*I am my own country. No king nor queen has power over me."*

*Fade to scenes from last week's show: Sword fight, slave beatings, rape, cleavage and blood close-ups, voodoo ritual.*

*Voice of Maxwell: "I have cut marauding pirates in pieces and thrown them back into the sea. I use my slaves for breeding stock and for my own pleasures. Do my wife's demons call her to throw herself from the bluffs into the ocean? Or will I be her devil? Will the slave uprising kill my brother-in-law? Or will I end his life with my own hand to gain his fair widow?"*

*Fade to ad for Lord of the Island Rum™.*

*Voice of Maxwell begins commercial: "My fields produce the special sugar cane to fuel my rum refinery. My rum is shipped all over the world. Taste the flavor of my plantation and the heat of the Caribbean."*

*Fade to jungle waterfall*

*Break to superimpose Ari-Anne happy, then fearful.*

*Voice of Ari-Anne: "This island was my paradise, now I fear for my husband's safety...and mine."*

*Back to Maxwell profile:*

*Voice of Maxwell: "I will break her to my will and she will become my wife and unite this island. I shall be Lord of the Island, all powerful."*

****

Too tired to think, Rebecca forwarded both files to Heather with a note to send them to that Epping program expert for testing. Reading these documents left her with an uncomfortable feeling in the pit of her stomach. She liked romances better.

Chapter 20

Rebecca welcomed Aries the next morning, knowing her clever mind would offer her a distraction from last night's edgy scene with Max. "What do you think about plagiarism?" she asked the girl.

"Like cheating?"

Rebecca nodded and waited.

Aries wrinkled her nose. "Well, everyone knows cheating is bad, but everybody needs help. Like using the Internet to write papers for school? I'm smart enough to write them when I'm in regular school, but traveling with Mom is so boring, I'd rather read what I like than do research for dumb papers."

"Isn't cheating dishonest?"

"Well, it's not like real crime."

Rebecca stopped. "Plagiarism is stealing other people's words, their talent."

"But you're a lawyer and make money when people steal." She looked at Rebecca and saw her you-have-gone-over-the-line look, then relented. "You're right. I guess I never thought about it."

Rebecca and Aries had come a long way. Now the teenager had actually told her she was right.

"One time, someone broke into our hotel room. My clothes got dumped on the floor and my diary tossed in a corner. It turned out some spiritual stalker just wanted to touch Dad's things."

"What about your diary?"

"I don't think anybody read it. Even Mom wouldn't do

176

that."

"How did you feel?"

"Terrible. I throw my stuff on the floor all the time, but to think someone else did made me angry. This morning Dad asked me if I'd seen anyone go into his closet. He was angry. His clothes are all mixed up or something. My dad never gets angry, except at Mom."

"Some people say theft feels like rape."

"Yuck. I totally don't want to think about that." Aries shivered. "I have more pages from Aunt Arianna. *Tres interesant.*"

****

*March 14, 1867*
*St. Albans Island, British West Indies*
*This morning I walked along the beach at low tide looking for pretty shells. Thomas had taken men and a small boat to Tortola. Suddenly The Major darkened my path. He wore that ingratiating smile I detest. I have managed never to be alone with this man. Not easy on our small island. I confessed to Thomas that The Major had been an unwelcome suitor and I did not think well of him. Thomas now worries that Penelope will be hurt.*

*"Beautiful sister," The Major called out to me. "Favor me with a smile. Walk with me this pleasant morning."*

*"Sir..." I tried not to be rude as my heart beat against my bodice, but his eyes on me made me shiver. "Perhaps your wife, dear Penelope, would like to walk with us."*

*He sneered. "Penelope is a shadow of a woman compared to your bright light."*

*At that moment, I saw one of the housemaids carrying a basket from the pier up to the house and I told him I must inspect the fish for tonight's dinner to celebrate Thomas's return.*

*This evening I told Thomas The Major's words. Thomas says gossip in Tortola claims Penelope's husband bribed officials to take our island off sea charts in order to be free of both British and Danish rule and taxes.*

177

*Thomas's grandfather, who settled St. Albans, was a law-abiding man. He brought men and mules and laid fields and built houses. Charles Paxton treated his slaves well, educated his sons, and brought them back to St. Albans. This island is Thomas's heritage and he spent happy days here as a boy before beginning his education in Oxford.*

*He now completely distrusts The Major and fears the man will harm Penelope. As Penelope's husband, half the island belongs to him, but he cannot sell the plantation without Thomas's assent. Once Penelope produces a male heir, the land is his to do with as he chooses. It is clear he wants Penelope to bring forth this heir post haste. Last spring when she lost her babe, he was more angry than concerned about his poor wife.*

*Now that she is with child again, she begged to go to Tortola where there is a physician. He refused and bought a midwife from Martinique for £50. He gave this slave named Josephine the Settlers' Cabin on the rocky side of the island and there is gossip that he spends many nights there.*

****

Charlotte intercepted Tom on the hotel grounds as he walked to pick up Aries. "Sir," she said, holding her chin in the air with the confidence of a woman who knows her most photogenic angle. "You're Tom Paxton, the father of young Aries..."

Tom flashed his proud father smile, then grimaced in pain. This morning, he had all the symptoms of a killer hangover. He knew that was impossible since he hadn't even tasted wine since he'd begun experiencing those trances. Keeping control was more important than an occasional drink.

"...the young woman who says she is thirteen. And behaves as if she were were forty-five."

"That is my little girl." Tom looked at the older woman's perfect platinum blonde coiffeur, her large eyes, and beautiful mouth. "You must be Charlotte Dumaurier. You also have a lovely daughter." He saw her resemblance

178

to Rebecca. The strength. The sureness. The stubbornness. Though her hands moved in helpless female gestures, this was not a damsel needing rescue.

"Mr. Paxton, may we sit and chat? The café perhaps?"

"Of course, Mrs. Dumaurier, there is nothing I would enjoy more. I have arrived quite early to retrieve my daughter and, in fact, had hoped to have more coffee. She and Rebecca value their time. If I show up too soon, they treat me like an interloper." He offered his arm, happy to get out of the bright sunshine.

She slipped her arm under his and laid her hand on his. "My, what a nasty cut," she said, noticing the not yet healed scratch on his left hand.

"I don't even remember where I got it." He led her to the restaurant entrance and the waiter escorted them to a window table.

As soon as they ordered, Charlotte asked, "You and my daughter are friends?"

Tom was taken by surprise. "Well, yes. And I am her client."

"I know that. However, your daughter, the charming and precocious Aries, confided to me that you wish more."

"Ah. I don't know what to say. Your daughter has very definite ideas."

"As does yours, Mr. Paxton. Tom?" She smiled at him through thick, perfect lashes. "My Rebecca is very much like me. All her life she has claimed to be exactly like her father though she saw little of him during her youth. She has inherited his height and patrician bones—"

"—And your beauty."

"Hmm. If you spoke that way to her, perhaps you would become more than her friend."

"If I spoke like that to her, she would laugh at me."

"Perhaps. But Rebecca does crave romance." Charlotte raised her hand to silence him. "I am aware that everyone calls her the least romantic woman in the world. But then, why has she established herself as the lawyer to romance authors? Perhaps she protests too much?"

"I don't—"

"—Because she is like me. Why do you think she

179

hides her blonde hair?"

"Rebecca is a blonde?"

"Yes. Like me." She fluffed her hair. "She darkens it and rejects her feminine name by insisting everyone call her R.J. Everyone called her father J.R. instead of John Robert." Charlotte smiled a dreamy smile. "She has her father's dark eyes."

"I love her eyes." Tom's words just slipped out.

"So, your daughter is right."

"She thinks I am in love with Rebecca." Tom blushed. "I think I have—how do you say—I've had...made...love..."

"You just say you had sex or made love or whatever you wish. But young man, if you truly don't know, you may not be the man for my Rebecca."

"It's complicated. I'm a trance channeler. I may have been sort of unconscious."

"I am so sorry."

He took a breath, "Yes," and laughed. "I love the most unromantic woman in the world. Now that I have said the words aloud, what do I do?" His face turned serious, recognizing how complicated his love had become.

Charlotte smiled. "That is for you to figure out."

\*\*\*\*

Cora swept into the hotel lobby on long Barbie legs, artfully messy red hair billowing around her head. She spotted Rebecca talking to a man and accelerated the swaying walk that would have attracted attention even without the leopard catsuit. "Tom, darling," she interrupted Rebecca's conversation. The man turned. He was not Tom.

Rebecca said, "Cora, this is Claude...uh, Steve, he's a big fan..." Rebecca stopped. Steve and Cora stood, perfect as money and cosmetic surgery could create, posed dumbstruck like the children's game of statues. Her two most self-centered, babbling clients were speechless.

"Cora!" she called, "Steve!" She waved as if they were asleep or on another planet.

Steve, never breaking eye contact with Cora, asked, "Rebecca, please introduce me to the most ravishing woman in the universe."

Cora tittered. The sophisticated Hollywood star tittered.

"Steve, this is Cora Ayne, the famous bestselling author. Cora, this is Steve, also known as Claude Festerman, Cleo St. Cloud, and Bullet Shotman. He is the most prolific bestselling author in the world."

"Bullet?" Cora giggled.

"I met this divine apparition of unexcelled femininity on the plane," Steve gushed.

"Do you two want food?" Rebecca asked.

They turned to her and together said, "No," then returned to posturing and making faces at each other.

"I definitely feel redundant." Rebecca asked, "Any objections if I leave?"

Steve touched Cora's shoulder and she stroked his cheek with the back of her hand. They turned and left Rebecca without a word or glance.

Rebecca had just watched the two gorgeous, artificially created people fall in love. "Don't thank me for the introduction," she called after them.

Since her plans for this evening had been cancelled, what should she do? She didn't want to go back to her room and deal with messages and phone calls from Max. His tirades about plagiarism and his demands that she meet him late at night had gotten tiresome.

Tom had asked her to come to tonight's second-to-last trance session. She did want to see Tom in trance again and she needed to observe Angie and Aries one more time in their working relationship to prepare for the custody trial. At last she had a plan. She was working to transfer the custody hearing to New Hampshire where Tom and Angie lived during their marriage. Those courts would certainly side with Tom against the wild California woman. And if there were delays, Aries could stay with Tom. She hoped she could make it work just like that.

She drove to the workshop site and slipped into the large domed room as Aries finished a harp solo. Tonight Kevin ignored her and she found a cushion and sat directly across from Tom. She wanted a clear view of whatever was going to happen. He looked so good sitting beaming at Aries. He noticed Rebecca and smiled. He seemed very pleased that she was there.

Angie glared at Rebecca, then returned her expression to her interpretation of a blissful spiritual smile. "And now gods and goddesses, what you have been waiting for. Our Tom will be entering a trance state and..." Her voice crescendoed. "...Don Thomas will speak to you. Those of you who have requested messages already have departed loved ones waiting in our spiritual green room." She waited for the group to get her lame joke. She smiled at the obligatory laughs and continued. "You all will receive your messages this evening." She sent Tom a look that left no doubt that this had better happen. "And remember, if you have questions anytime after this workshop, send an e-mail to questions@Beloved.com." She nodded to Kevin and the lights dimmed.

Tom said, "Thank you, Angela." He smiled at his daughter. "Aries, thank you for the gift of your heavenly music." He closed his eyes. "I never know what spirits will come in, so let's see what happens tonight."

Rebecca watched Tom's face. At first nothing happened. His breathing was slow and steady. His face relaxed. Then that old Spanish accented voice began, "I am Don Thomas, here to bring you Beloveds answers from the spirit realm beyond." She listened carefully, certain now that voice came from a small speaker under Tom's cushion.

The Don Thomas voice continued and Rebecca kept her eyes on Tom. His head jerked back and when he straightened his face began to change. Soon she saw the visage of that familiar Asian instead of Tom's face.

"...Mrs. Wetterman," the Hispanic voice under Tom announced, "I have a spirit here, a white-haired man with a goatee by the name of Norris—"

"—Morris," cried the margarita woman. "My Morris..."

"Quiet," Tom spoke firmly in the Asian-accented voice Rebecca remembered from the sound studio.

Rebecca heard an electronic click. The Don Thomas voice broke off. She guessed Kevin had turned off the sound.

"I am Ku," a gentle voice, definitely coming from Tom's lips, told them. "Tom has asked me to help you find comfort and knowledge of the world beyond by speaking to spirits who will talk to me. Kindly ask your questions."

182

A woman stood. "Ku, sir, ask my departed husband, Manfred, if I should invest in gold or krugerrands?"

A woman on the left called out, "Ask my mother where she hid her diamond ring?"

Someone else shouted, "What diet will take off twenty pounds?"

Another asked, "Should I marry Albert or Sam?"

Group members rudely called out questions, until Tom's hand rose and the Ku voice said, "Enough. I have come through the body of this kind man to bring spiritual teachings to you. I know little of your time and your culture, yet I think all peoples have similar needs. I wanted to help you understand what life could be and to bring peace and clarity to your minds."

Rebecca noticed that Tom's shirt hung loose from his shoulders and he rocked back and forth as his lips moved with Ku's words.

"What I have learned from your questions is that you people are not sincere seekers. You are not here for true spiritual purpose. Your questions dub you as spiritual babble-dabblers, looking for a Miss Manners or a Dr. Ruth. I am no dating service nor investment brokerage. Go to the Internet for that." A shy smile played across his lips. "These terms come from Tom's vocabulary." His demeanor became serious. "I also sense the energy of this seminar is for financial gain and not true knowledge—"

"—Just one minute, buster," Angie got to her feet turning toward Tom. "You have gone too far."

Ku's voice became stronger. "You have gone too far, madam. Your heart is cold and closed. You are not a fit teacher."

Angie now stood in front of Tom. She slapped his face loud enough for the sound to echo through the room. He fell back, rolling off his cushion. The lights came on.

"Ladies and gentlemen," Angie announced. "Our dear Tom has been working much too hard on his new book. An aberrant spirit has stolen power from our wonderful Don Thomas. Tomorrow is the final workshop day. Optional Sunrise Past Life Vortex Experience participants meet at 5 a.m. in the hotel lobby. The wrap-up morning sessions will offer you alien visualization handouts to take home. Those of you who did not get to speak to your departed spirits tonight will be given personalized messages on a CD recorded earlier by Don Thomas. Tomorrow evening's trance session—I promise you—will be the most exciting Tom has ever given. So don't miss one minute. Kevin will be in the lobby to take orders for CDs you will be able to pick up at the end of the final session. Or order a personalized DVD to be mailed to you. Sleep well, Beloved gods and goddesses. Blessings." Her voice sounded pseudo-friendly, but her face was stiff without expression.

Kevin opened the door and workshop attendees began to file out.

Before Angie's speech ended, Rebecca was kneeling beside Tom. "Are you OK?" She took his left hand and noticed the half-healed scratch.

Tom shook his head and rubbed his eyes. "What happened?"

"Ku took on Angie. I have a feeling that part will not be included on the tapes and DVDs for sale." She helped Tom to his feet. "Let's get out of here."

Angie blocked their way. "Not so fast, R.J. I know your game. Leave him alone. This is none of your business." She turned to Tom. "You be here tomorrow evening and you had better play it straight. You follow my agenda or I am taking Aries and the entire damned Beloved operation out of the country. You'll never see her or another dime in royalties."

\*\*\*\*

Rebecca drove Tom back to the hotel in silence and made sure he was asleep before she returned to her own cottage.

Inside she found more roses and a note that read:

\*\*\*\*

*My Dearest Darling Rebecca,*

*Please forgive me. My passion overcame my manners and good sense. Only my deep love for you makes my life worth living. How can I make you love me again?*

*Your repentant Max*

\*\*\*\*

Rebecca frowned. She'd occasionally had boyfriends get out of hand. Was Max a psycho? He was so different from any man she'd ever met. His language, manners, and exuberant passion still excited her. He was definitely the most romantic lover she could imagine, but his recent rudeness and possessive language made her uncomfortable and his roughness the last time she was with him spooked her. He was so intense, maybe they just hadn't had time to understand each other.

She walked to her computer and wrote an e-mail to him:

\*\*\*\*

*From: rjd@bankheadfirm.com*
*To: maxwinter@yahoo.net*
*Subject: Cool*
*Dear Max,*
*I think we need to cool things down. How about lunch or a walk in the red rocks?*
*Call me,*
*Rebecca*

\*\*\*\*

Was this what she wanted? Little Rebecca's voice broke through the barrier and told her, *No. Do not send it. Erase. Please erase.* Rebecca closed her eyes and stubbornly hit "Send" anyway. That voice knew nothing. She wanted to risk a little more to find out if she and Max had the future he spoke of? She wanted more than flowers, romantic notes, and mysterious nocturnal phone calls. They needed to share ordinary things. She wanted quiet talks and pleasant afternoons...like those she spent with Tom.

She still had so many unanswered questions. Did Max still live in the Caribbean? How did he feel about her work? Would he move to New York? He kept talking of regaining his fortune. What did he do for a living? Or was he just rich? Did he have abusive tendencies or was he just high-strung? Would he consider counseling?

She fell asleep imaging Max piloting an open cockpit plane over Sedona with a white silk scarf billowing in the wind.

An hour later she awoke. She'd been dreaming of making love to Max on a cloud of roses. When the thorns pierced her she screamed. The cloud parted and she fell, spinning into space. Tom swooped out of the sky like Superman, caught her, and together they floated down to a tropical island. She reached up for him and watched his face change from Tom to Ku to Max and back to Tom.

Chapter 21

Rebecca's morning e-mail included a forwarded attachment from Aries containing another installment of the diary. Ignoring all her other work, she began to read.
\*\*\*\*

*September 13, 1867*
*St. Albans Island, British West Indies*
*This morning I pinned up my petticoats and went out to walk along the beach below The Sun plantation house. I knew Penelope was not well and The Major not yet back from St. Thomas. Tom had gone to Grenada to purchase a new boat. I was bored and set out to find a cave one of the slaves told me about.*

*When The Major was gone, I felt the island was all mine. I decided to take my adventurous self along the bluffs to reach the water level on the far beach. As I stepped down the slope from the cane fields a loose donkey followed me until I shooed him back. I crawled over the rough rocks near the Settlers' Cabin hoping to avoid Josephine.*

*I reached the narrow beach. My feet sunk into the sand and I removed my shoes and tucked them behind a boulder. The sun had begun to warm the sand and foam from the waves tickled my toes. A few tiny shells poked from the sugary sand and I bent to pick one.*

*When I stood I saw a cave hidden with*

*vines. Upon closer examination I saw vines had been woven into fishing nets which could cunningly be pulled out of the way. I knew someone must be very serious about keeping this cave secret.*

*I pulled the net away and saw wooden crates and casks stacked to the ceiling of an underground room as large as the ballroom in a fine London home.*

*I wanted to open a box at once but the flat stone beneath my bare feet was slick and sticky, and I slipped. The light was poor but I saw one metal trunk fine as any lady's chest.*

*Was this a pirate lair? I would tell Tom as soon as he returned. I heard a noise and backed out of the cave. I turned and saw a massive black man pulling a rope towing a boat in the shallows. He lifted the boat onto the sand. He saw me and spoke in a deep echoey bass that sounded like the depths of the earth. "Ah, oh, a lady!"*

\*\*\*\*

Rebecca's cell phone rang. She considered not answering, but knew it was the persistent Heather.

Heather immediately told Rebecca, "Two items on today's agenda."

"Make it quick." Rebecca tried to sound busy and efficient, rather than anxious to get back to reading an old diary.

"Number one: when are you coming back to the office? For almost two weeks I've been telling people you are on vacation. Since you haven't taken a vacation in five years, no one believes me. They think you've quit or have been in some awful accident. An associate asked me if you were despondent after your breakup with Tristan. The paralegals wanted to take bets that you were having cosmetic surgery, but no one thought you'd take the time."

"Do you think I should have cosmetic surgery?"

"What?"

"Never mind. Tell everyone I am *not* on vacation. I'm working out of the office. In fact, my clients are all here in Sedona, so this is where my work is."

"Don says your billable hours look like you're on vacation. Only forty-five hours last week. Don billed more when he was in the hospital for his triple bypass."

"What is problem number two?"

"I'm e-mailing a scanned copy of a letter that arrived today."

"Give me the story," Rebecca demanded, too impatient to wait.

"An anonymous person is threatening to expose one of your clients unless you pay blackmail."

Rebecca opened the attachment, set down the cell phone and read, then asked, "Who is Bertha Humpfelter?"

Heather's distant voice came from the cell phone, "Pick up the phone and listen to me."

When Rebecca was back, Heather continued, "My research shows this Bertha person wrote novels—if porn lit can be called novels—and scripts—that's a laugh—for movies."

"Who's accused?"

"This guy claims it's one of your biggest clients."

"Cora, Cleo, and Babs are my biggest properties. So far no one knows Tom's a client of mine. It couldn't be Tom, could it?"

"No, R.J. Not Mr. Clean."

"So that leaves the Unholy Three. Cleo/Claude/Bullet/Steve? Not Babs. I vote for Cora."

"Do you really believe dirty movies could hurt Cora's career?"

"A lot of Cora's mainstream romance readers get excited reading her sex scenes, then feel sanctimonious because the stories always end with marriage to the bad boy who turns out to be good."

"So, what are you going to do?"

"Claude is here, Cora is here. Babs is not. Set up a conference call with Babs and I'll pull Cora and Claude in. I'll question all three at once and if no one knows what this guy is talking about, we'll tell him no deal and no money."

She shut the phone and, instead of calling Cora and Steve, went back to reading Arianna's adventure.

\*\*\*\*

*I stopped and drew myself up and tried to*

189

*look like the mistress of the manor house and not a maid playing in the water. I said, "I am Mistress of The Moon."*

*"To be sure," he said most rudely. His shirt was covered with dried blood. I looked beyond him into the boat. Oh my, how can I describe my horror? The entire boat, except for where the brute had sat, was heaped high with white egrets with sad dead beady eyes, their bodies smeared with blood.*

*I screamed at the destruction of these delicate majestic creatures and scrambled up the slope without stopping to find my shoes. I heard the man's loud booming laugh behind me.*

*Back at The Moon, I called the housemaids to heat water and I slipped into a scalding tub without waiting for the temperature to moderate. My feet especially were caked with mud from the fields and blood from the floor of the cave. I scrubbed myself with a rough sea sponge until my skin was red.*

*This evening Thomas returned and I immediately told him of my misadventure. He stormed over to The Sun. The Major had returned and denied all knowledge of the sad birds and bloody feathers. Later, Thomas told me of men who purchased bird feathers and even whole birds from islanders and shipped them back to France and England to adorn ladies' bonnets and dresses in the newest fashions. I am glad I am no longer near that society. I would never wear parts of the gay birds that I have seen fly free on our island.*

*The next morning Thomas went to the cave and returned to tell me all the casks were gone, though he found the cave floor bloody with bits of feathers as I had described. He suspects The Major and worries about his poor sister Penelope married to this terrible man. He called him a devil scallywag. I have never known Thomas to speak so of any man.*

*I think of the voice within Penelope and*

*wonder if I should warn Thomas of the dark spirit she spoke of. But he already has many worries.*

\*\*\*\*

Steve watched Tom gulp his morning coffee. "You look like hell."

"I swear this hotel coffee is getting weaker every day. I'll have to switch to espresso to feel a kick." Tom poured the last from the carafe into his empty cup.

"Tom, it's not the coffee."

"I could be sick. I'm exhausted all the time. I want to spend more time with Rebecca, but I get so tired, I can't talk coherently or even think of going out in the evening. Maybe the trances are ruining my life?"

"Going to see a doctor?"

"It's not physical. This fatigue is like the feeling I get when Ku starts to come through. I nod off, but instead of feeling a gentle vibration in all my cells, there's this ripping in every muscle and painful twisting in my gut. Not a prelude to peaceful sleep."

Steve nodded. "That would sure keep me wide awake."

"But, I'm out like a light."

"What can you do?"

Tom lifted his cup and drained the last drop of coffee. "I'm going to a medium."

"You *are* a medium."

"That doesn't do me any good." Tom patted Steve's shoulder. "Thanks for listening, old buddy."

Tom headed for his van and Steve went back to his room to write a few chapters before lunch with Cora.

Halfway to the parking lot, Charlotte Dumaurier waylaid Tom and invited him to accompany her to the hotel restaurant for more coffee. She chatted about Sedona and the lovely Arizona weather until Tom said, "I would love to talk with you longer, but I need to find a medium." He grinned, waiting for her to reply with the same words as Steve.

"Mr. Paxton, I was informed that you are one of the best. If what you need is advice, perhaps I can help."

He noticed that when her eyes sparkled, she almost seemed younger than Rebecca. "Your lovely daughter is driving me crazy. When she arrived here, she wore black, had tight dark hair and seemed out of place this far from New York. Now she wears long dresses, New Age jewelry and half the time floats around completely distracted. We go for walks and she praises the beauty of nature. We had this fabulous picnic..." He decided not to share that memory with Charlotte.

"The change is truly amazing. Perhaps you are a good influence?"

He shook his head. "She seems to enjoy my company."

"Yes. But there is more going on in her life."

"Sometimes the change is unbelievable. The day she let Ariel fix her hair she was painting her nails and couldn't keep her mind on business. She doesn't seem as interested in her clients."

"Unheard of, to be sure." Charlotte raised her perfect eyebrows.

"You know more than you will share with me. Aries knows more, too. But female bonding prevents her from telling me what is going on with Rebecca. I wanted Aries and Rebecca to become friends, but now their loyalty is making me desperate."

"Rebecca has an admirer here in the hotel. A quite mysterious gentleman."

Tom shook his head. "Impossible. I've never seen her with another man. Only my friend Steve and he is gaga over Cora." His mind reviewed Rebecca's strange behavior. Had she been seeing some guy in the evenings?

"As I said, this man is quite mysterious. I met him once. He appears to be an old fashioned romantic gentleman."

"The roses?"

"Of course, the roses. You are a very smart man. Anyone can order flowers."

Tom nodded. "You met him. Did he look like me?"

Charlotte tilted her head and squinted, but not enough to create frown lines. "Perhaps a smidge taller, a little heavier build, darker longer hair, and more tan. But a *petit* basic resemblance."

"Do you think Rebecca has fallen for him?"

"I said he appears to be a gentleman. He is not.

Beneath his politeness, he is both unkind and dangerous. I would warn Rebecca but I know her too well. She would only hold on more tightly if I criticized this man."

"What can I do?"

"I am most observant of handsome gentlemen. I am also an expert on romantic heroes. They are fun to play with, but for the long haul, undependable. They are always looking for another conquest or another deal. Not the home and hearth kind of man."

"You married a romantic?"

"John Dumaurier was a storybook prince. And I, a willing Cinderella. But when our little princess and then another prince and princess arrived, he had other things to do."

"I am so sorry..."

"Charlotte waved her hand dismissively. It was a long time ago. I may look like—what do they say these days—an airhead, Mr. Paxton. But I have done quite well in my career."

"Rebecca never mentioned your career."

"She conveniently forgets. It serves her to see only the ruffles. I was an editor for a major romance publisher. They called me 'The Love Doctor,' I recognized a good story and I knew how to make a good story a great story. I made extra money reading from the slush pile. Rebecca learned to read from romance manuscripts."

"Why didn't you write your own?"

"Perhaps I did? But, back to Rebecca. At the age of twelve she suddenly began to hate anything to do with romance. She never understood how hard I worked to hide the tough side of life from her. I made her life easy and watched her go off to law school and become like her father and make fun of me and my lifestyle."

"What would you advise me to do?"

"Romance her." She looked deep into Tom's eyes. "You have more true romance in you than you know."

"I'm not a romantic hero."

"Oh, I think you are."

Tom thanked Charlotte and drove along Sedona's main street, Highway 89A. Every block had signs for psychic readings. He'd trusted his intuition to select a Sedona psychic. That did not work, so he found a small strip mall coffee shop. He entered Sedona Coffee Roasters and inhaled the aroma that verified its name. The deli counter and tables looked more comfortable than Starbucks, pretty much like places all over the country.

He ordered and got an empty white cup. A guy with a Nehru shirt and ponytail pointed to black plastic coffee dispensers near the window. Pouring from the one whose varietal name sounded strongest, Tom skipped both the half-and-half and sugar and settled at a table in the corner. He took a breath and relaxed.

Customers here looked fairly ordinary. More long, gauzy skirts than in cites, but most customers looked California business casual rather than East Coast. Glad he'd worn jeans and a dress shirt, he noticed a man in the identical white silk outfit Angie insisted he wear for workshops and no one seemed to notice.

He borrowed a copy of the local paper from the next table and scanned the news. Sedonans seemed to love tourists and their money but didn't want them in the way. He was reading an article about feng shui condos when he looked up and a solid thirty-something woman wearing a paisley business dress smiled down on him.

"May I join you?" she asked. "I'm Joy."

Tom looked around to see if all the tables were taken. Far from it. He nodded, unsure why he was making room for her.

The woman called Joy, who looked more like the town librarian than an autograph seeker, settled herself.

"Hello, Mr. Paxton." She smiled again and handed him a card.

Her face seemed familiar, but the card read "Joy of Sedona, Psychic." Then he recognized her—the concierge.

"I work at your hotel concierge desk. But I also am a psychic." She nodded as if Tom knew all of this. "As you left the hotel, my psychic beeper went off and I followed you here to see if I could be of help."

"Psychic Beeper?"

"That was going to be the name of my new business, but I changed it to Psychic Concierge Services. More classy, don't you think?"

Tom nodded. This woman made no sense. And she thought she could help him.

"You're tired." George put her hand over his, covering the scar.

"You don't have to be a psychic to see that."

"I see there are still residuals around you. Switching entities so often must be exhausting."

"I don't know what you're talking about." The woman's voice now sounded much older and more sure of herself.

She closed her eyes and her face glowed and softened. Now she looked a lot more like a medium. "Ku was one of my spirit guides. He's strong and wise with a sense of humor. He is a good entity to help you."

"You're talking about my Ku?"

"Isn't he the one who helped you write?"

"How do you know?"

"He talked through me back East. No one would believe me when I told them the things he said, but he started me on my spiritual path. Ku was the one who told me to leave my library job and come to Sedona. I'd always done readings on the side, but my new business will match tourists and real seekers with the right spiritual or healing practitioner. You know, the souls who need me."

Tom smiled. "Am I one of those souls?"

She looked concerned. "Oh, yes. I came to tell you that Ku is worried about you. He says you're in danger." George stood. "But now I've got to get back to work. I'm on my break." And she left.

Her card lay on the table. "Tomorrow" was written on the back and Tom knew this was his appointment with someone who might help him. She had found him. The card read "Joy of Sedona, President, Psychic Concierge Services, Information for Your Soul."

Chapter 22

Tom left Coffee Roasters and returned to the hotel. He passed George at her concierge desk on his way back to his cottage where he found Aries reading and Angie on the warpath.

As soon as he walked in, Angie waved a sheaf of papers in front of her. "Tom Paxton, don't think you can get away with this." He knew by her red blotchy face she was angry. "You will pay. I put up with a lot, but this..."

"Calm down. I don't know what you're talking about." Angie always had been hot tempered, but since the divorce, she'd get apoplectic at the smallest things. This time, she was spitting mad. Tom turned to Aries. "Honey, why don't you go to Rebecca's cottage?"

Angie yelled, "No!"

"Can I go see Charlotte?" Aries asked.

Tom nodded. "But if she's not in her room, come right back." He waited for Aries to leave, then turned to his ex-wife. "Let me see those papers."

"Don't play innocent with me. These hotel bills prove that you're an unfit father. You even have your New York bimbo taking care of my daughter."

"Watch your mouth. Rebecca is a better role model for a teenage girl than you could ever be."

"So that's why you're giving Mary Poppins all these expensive presents?"

Tom grabbed the papers from Angie's hand and tried to focus while she circled like an angry cat. He noticed a lot of items in addition to room charges. At least ten charges for flowers in one week. Angie ordered flowers for the workshop all the time. Then he looked closer. Chocolates, books, jewelry, and wine. A massage therapist sent to Room 201. That was Rebecca's room. No way Angie would give a Rebecca a two hour massage.

"Look. Look," Angie screamed, now holding his credit card statement. She pointed with a shaking finger. "*Evening in Paris* perfume! My God, Tom, have you no taste?" She seized the papers from his hands. "I'm taking these to Tristan. He will protect me and make sure you will never see Aries again."

"No one can protect you from yourself."

"Damn you." She stomped out and slammed the door.

Tom was stunned. His mind hurriedly reviewed the possibilities but could think of no explanation. Then, it struck him. There was one possible implausible explanation. He could have authorized these charges, sort of. The spirit who was forcing him to fall asleep, the one who made him feel hard and cold right before he lost control, could be taking his body and his credit card.

Tom told himself that spirits don't use credit cards, but there must be an explanation. With Rebecca's help, he now had a video. He inserted the tape into the VCR and watched his body transform into Ku, and then into that other savvier spirit who fiercely took possession of his body. Ku was gentle and respectful. The dark spirit was abusive and dangerous.

Tom stripped and stepped into the shower. He was angry. Angry at himself for being so stupid. He was the weak channel who let homeless entities take over his body whenever they pleased. But no more. He had met a lot of very spiritual people on the workshop circuit and studied with great teachers. He'd learned a variety of techniques to explore the mind, body, and spirit.

Letting the cold water pummel his chest, he searched for an answer. He recalled a workshop with a guru who practiced out-of-body meditation and another given by that military guy who taught remote viewing. That could be the answer. Before he could begin to fight, he had to prove to himself what was happening. And now he knew how. He stepped out of the shower and dressed.

He drew the drapes, locked the door, unplugged the

phone, lit a candle, and turned off the lights. Punching one of the throw pillows into a zafu, he folded onto the floor in a cross-legged position.

Instantly focused on what he must do, he had more trouble than usual getting into a meditative state. He began to breathe deeply. He forced his breaths to become longer and slower. His mind calmed. After a few minutes he allowed his conscious mind to fade and his corporal body to separate from his ethereal body. He could no longer feel where his body ended and the air around him began. He moved slightly so that the two bodies no longer lined up precisely. So far, so good.

He floated free, leaving the physical Tom sitting cross-legged on the pillow. Without judging, he watched himself from a few feet away, then rose to the ceiling. The Tom on the floor looked pale and empty. The floating Tom observed a slight quiver like he'd seen on the film as a precursor sign that Ku was coming in. But the quivers immediately became jerkier. The head shot back and the eyes looked up at him. He was looking at himself.

The head fell forward and when it came back up, the face had darkened, the hair was longer, and the nose thicker. The eyes sunk into shadow. Tom, near the ceiling, watched the man below, who was him and was not him.

As Tom's conscious mind became aware something was wrong, deep inside the primitive survival need stirred. He desperately wanted his body back. He knew, if given the chance, this dark entity would keep his body. At that frightening thought, Tom's eyes flew open. He was on the floor, his body tingling with pins and needles. He was fully back. He'd succeeded in proving his suspicions and now was more frightened than ever.

****

Rebecca was tired of dealing with Max as a client. His phone messages and repetitious e-mails were useless. Soon the test results would be back. She wanted to offer an opinion and put an end to his quest for a lawsuit or turn him over to another attorney. If he were no longer her client, it would be easier to sort out her feelings for him.

Determined to lose her Godiva weight, Rebecca lunched on boring salad without dressing and herb tea while scanning the copyright briefs. Most of the documents covered the basic stuff she knew from law school. Most of her clients were sued for using someone's name accidentally or by lost relatives and friends of authors who claimed they'd been slandered—or not slandered—in some romance novel.

Max continued to be so vague, she wasn't sure what legal precedents applied. Using her personal password, she logged into her firm's network of legal databases and began to search.

She limited her search to civil law. Criminal sanctions could only be aimed at serious counterfeiting activity. In most of the world, the default length of copyright for the majority of works was the life of the author plus 50 or 70 years. And in the U.S., registering a copyright after an infringement only enabled the plaintiff to receive actual damages and lost profits. Had Max lost money? So far nothing he said proved that.

Max was adamant that an editor had changed his words. A work must meet minimal standards of originality in order to qualify for copyright, and even then the copyright expired after a set period of time. Different countries imposed different tests, although generally requirements were low. She thought Max's accent was British. The U.K. required that there had to be some "skill, originality and work involved." However, even a trivial amount of "work" was often sufficient to determine if a work was original and whether a particular act of copying constituted infringement of an author's original expression.

Max never told her when the work was produced or when the changes were made. This was getting nowhere. Without information she could go no further. She sent an e-mail to Max.

****

*From: rjd@bankheadfirm.com*
*To: maxwinter@yahoo.net*
*Subject: Your case.*

*In order to advise you I need more information.*

*Please provide me with the following data as soon as possible.*

*Your date and place of birth:*
*Current country of citizenship:*
*Date the "book" in question was written by*
*you and where:*
*Date the "book" in question was published*
*by them and where:*
****

Rebecca red-flagged the message as highest priority and hit Send. She had done all she could. Let him respond.

Curious, she went back into the database and entered "CHANNELED." She had a channel as a client and it was about time she familiarize herself with that aspect of copyright law, just in case Tom's books were ever questioned.

The hit list of results included a lot more interesting references than most legal research topics.

First she found cases regarding the book *A Course in Miracles,* said to have been dictated by the spirit of Jesus. That book sold a lot of copies and generated a lot of controversy as well as motions, counter-motions, and fair use issues. Finally in 2004, the U.S. District Court ruled that the book had originally been placed in the public domain in 1975 and therefore could not be copyrighted later, so who wrote it became a moot point.

*Oh look at that!* Little Rebecca's voice interrupted Rebecca's research. "What do you want?"

*I like this quotation from William Shakespeare's Hamlet. "Why may not that be the skull of a lawyer? Where may be his quiddites now, his quillets, his cases, his tentures, and his tricks?*

"That is not so funny. They just put quotes on the website to make fun of the lawyers' copyright arguments."

*Well, it is pretty funny that spiritual people violate their principles with messy litigation.* Rebecca noticed that Little Rebecca did always talk like a child. This comment showed she was reading the website information and thinking about what was written.

The case citation, *White v. Kimmell et al. United States Court of Appeals Ninth Circuit [2] No 12762 [3] 183 F.2 744 [4] January 7, 1965,* involved a defendant who wrote down in a manuscript the communications between his wife and a "spirit of an individual who had departed this world and become an invisible non-material entity." A court in California heard it. Imagine a judge listening to that testimony. Here again the material had gotten into the public domain through mimeographed stencils and therefore couldn't be copyrighted later.

It appeared that once a work was in the public domain it was impossible to restrict copyright. The cat was out of the bag. It also seems that at first spiritual people couldn't wait to pass around what they had to anyone who had interest, then later when channeled material was more mainstream they wanted to profit and control the authenticity of the text.

Next she read about a long-running case tried in Oklahoma City against the non-profit foundation publisher of *The Urantia Book*. Supposedly no human author was associated with the content of the book, but rather numerous celestial beings. It was claimed that a "sleeping subject" received the material from these intelligences. Rebecca found that in 2001 The Urantia Foundation lost the U.S. copyright and the book went into the public domain. In 2006 the English copyright expired and now the complete edition of 2,097 pages is available on the Internet along with free audio versions.

Many of her more paranoid clients feared that their works would be stolen and turned into pirated e-books. She doubted they had much to fear, but carefully checked contracts for electronic rights.

One website article estimated that about 100 channeled works were published each year. Channeled works were defined as either anonymously published or with the name of an unembodied being, clearly using a spiritual name, but even that could not keep the work free from dispute. If the channeler took credit or kept the source a secret, problems always developed later for both publishers and authors who claimed the knowledge was from another realm and needed to be kept available. What were the copyright laws in other levels of consciousness? Or what would happen if two channelers channeled the same entity and published the same material?

Tom had been wise to hide his channeled work. When

Angie found a publisher, she carefully stated the channeled authorship and took the good advice from both lawyers and publishers.

She stopped and finished her unsatisfying salad. Checking her e-mail, she found a reply from Max already in her inbox.

\*\*\*\*

*From: maxwinter@yahoo.net*
*To: rjd@bankheadfirm.com*
*Subject: Re: Your case*

*MS. REBECCA. IT'S ME JOSCH. I WAS WORKING ON FIXING MR. MAX'S E-MAIL AND I SAW YOUR MESSAGE. MR. MAX IS NEVER AROUND DURING THE DAY SO I TOOK THE LIBERTY OF READING YOUR MESSAGE. SINCE IT'S SO IMPORTANT I TRIED TO HELP CAUSE YOU WERE SO NICE ABOUT THE FRUIT STAND, EVEN THOUGH I LOST MY JOB. AND ARIES LIKES YOU.*

*I TAUGHT MR. MAX TO USE THE INTERNET AND ONE WEBSITE ASKED FOR HIS BIRTH DATE. HE SAID IT WAS 06/13/39.*

*I GOOGLED HIM AND THIS IS REALLY WEIRD. THE ONLY MAX OR MAXIMILIAN WINTER I FOUND WITH THE JUNE 13TH BIRTHDAY WAS BORN IN LONDON ENGLAND IN 1839. AND HE DIED SEPT. 13, 1867!! IT MUST BE LIKE HIS GREAT GREAT OR SOMETHING.*

*ABOUT THE BOOK. I CAN'T HELP. I'VE NEVER SEEN HIM READ BOOKS, BUT HE SURE LIKES THE DVD OF THE VOODOO ISLAND TV SHOW. WHEN I WAS A KID MY MOM NEVER LET ME WATCH IT SHE SAID IT WAS TOO GRUESOME AND HAD NAKED PEOPLE SO I LIKE WATCHING WITH HIM NOW.*

*YOUR FRIEND JOSCH*
\*\*\*\*

Rebecca pushed back from her laptop. Josch's e-mail

made no sense. Yet, pieces were beginning to fit together. Take Max's old-fashioned way of talking, the way he dressed like a romance novel cover boy, and his behavior towards her and add that to the things he did not know that made him a misfit in the modern world. Something was seriously wrong and she needed help.

She walked to the closet and pulled out clothes, boxes, and shoes until she uncovered the box of Godiva she'd hidden for an emergency.

Chapter 23

Cora and Steve sat on Rebecca's loveseat holding
hands and gazing hypnotically into each other's eyes.
Steve leaned forward, buried his head in Cora's hair and
nuzzled her neck. Cora's perfectly constructed nose
touched Steve's perfectly augmented cheekbones. They
were disgusting. Rebecca sneered at the living Barbie and
Ken couple, glad she'd sent Aries outside to read.

The phone rang and Heather informed her that Babs
was on the line for the conference call. She instructed
Heather to listen and take notes. "Let's get down to
business," Rebecca interrupted Cora and Steve's
marathon kiss, "before I get nauseated," then switched on
the phone's speaker. "Hello, Babs. This is R.J. I'm here
with Claude Festerman and Cora Ayne. Some blackmailer
is threatening to leak dirt on one of you. I need to ask you
all one question and I need the complete, absolute truth—
if you want me to save your butts. Understand?"

Cora and Steve broke their lip-lock long enough to
grunt and nod.

Babs squeaked, "Of course, R.J."

"Let's get this over. Which one of you wrote
pornography under the name Bertha Humpfelter?"

Cora and Steve's collagen-enlarged lips popped apart.
The speakerphone was silent.

Rebecca turned to the lovebirds. Cora's eyes glazed
like a deer facing headlights. Steve looked ready to bolt
for the door.

"What is wrong with you people?" Rebecca asked.

204

"Just answer my question."

The speakerphone clicked.

Rebecca grabbed the phone. "Heather, get Babs back. Tell her not to hang up on me. Ever." Rebecca didn't usually lose her patience with clients, but all three were acting odd—odder.

In a few minutes the phone rang and Heather and Babs checked in.

Rebecca began again. "Steve first. If your real name is Steve King, who is Bertha Humpfelter?"

Steve rubbed his forehead. "My sister is Bertha. When I was a teenager, I used her name 'cause I was underage."

"You wrote porn?" Rebecca glared at him. "And you never told me?"

He nodded.

"I'm your lawyer. How can I protect you if you lie to me?"

Cora sputtered. "But...but...but..."

"What?"

"I...I...I wrote as Bertha Humpfelter."

"I'm Bertha," came a weepy voice from the phone. "Please, R.J., no one must know. Never. Especially the children—and Oprah."

"All three of you are Bertha Humpfelter?" Rebecca asked. The two in the room nodded and the phone sniffed.

Cora and Claude went back to nuzzling.

Three of Rebecca's clients had used the same name to write porn, probably for the same publisher. If this wasn't such a mess, it would be funny. "What can we do?" she asked, not expecting help from anyone.

Cora said, "Let him leak the story. I'll take the blame."

"No. I'll take the credit," said Steve.

Cora sighed. "Our first fight."

The phone sobbed.

Steve held up his hand. "I have many identities, no one will notice one more. I was only sixteen when I pitched my idea to write a series of pulps and X-rated movies based on romance novels. The publisher liked my concept so much he also paid others to write under Bertha's name. I did all the movie scripts, parodies of romances like *Withering Bites* and *Jane Errs*. The DVD series became quite popular with erotica collectors."

Rebecca shook her head and made a quick decision. "Fine. I'll write the press release." Then she realized Steve's maneuver. "So, I have to agree to tell the world you're a guy to get all three of you out of trouble."

He grinned his new stiff, handsome smile, took Cora's arm, and pulled her to her feet. "*Hasta la vista.*"

Cora waved. "*Ciao!*"

Cora and Steve walked out Rebecca's door and collided with a tall cowboy.

"You are...a big one," Cora cooed, admiring the chest of the handsome older man. In fitted jeans, leather sport coat, and matching cowboy boots, he looked the Hollywood image of a prosperous rancher.

Steve flinched. "Cora, baby."

She turned back to him. "Sorry, darling, I forgot myself."

Steve steered her around the man and down the steps.

Rebecca stared at the man in her doorway. "What are you doing here?"

"'Becca, is that any way to greet your old dad?" He took off the white Stetson and ran his fingers through his hair.

She noticed silver mixed into his raven hair, creating a perfect contrast to his magnificent tan and piercing charcoal eyes. Her father had always looked more like a movie star than any movie star she'd met. "You sure don't look old." She affected a disinterested toss of her head.

"You look tired, 'Becca honey." He walked to her. "But your hair is nice. And a few extra pounds look good on you."

Ignoring the hair and weight comment, she tolerated his hug. She'd forgotten how safe he made her feel. She inhaled and backed away.

"My little girl. Still trying so hard to be tough?" He settled into one of the Adirondack chairs, stretched out his legs, raised one boot, then the other to the railing. "Sit and tell your old dad what's going on."

Rebecca sat on the steps looking up at her father. Responding to his *Father Knows Best* voice, despite her best intentions, she felt like a little girl. "I'm the youngest partner in the firm. Most of my work is contract—"

"—I know that stuff. I follow your career. How are *you*?"

"You're a lawyer. I thought you would be interested in my career."

"You were always wrong about that. I've never been a real lawyer. I sell real estate as an excuse to have fun. Just flew back from where I'm building an island resort. I love the Caribbean, but it feels good to be back in Sedona."

"You have business in Sedona?"

"A few years back I turned a ranch near Page Springs into an upscale development. Liked it so much, I built myself a place. You might like it. Though it's real quiet. Not like New York."

"I would love to see it." She never remembered her father looking so content. She always imagined him rushing to airports and meetings. Was he slowing down? Sick? He sat next to her as if he had all the time in the world. "Why are you here?" she asked.

"Right down to business. That's my girl." He smiled. "I received a phone message from a man who said he wanted your hand?"

"My...my what?"

"The cell connection on the island is not good. At first I thought he said he wanted your land. He told me you were in Sedona at this resort. Last time I talked with Charlotte she told me you were engaged. I expected you'd found some successful accountant or stockbroker, though I'd choose someone more exciting for you."

"You'd choose..."

"'Becca, when your mother and I divorced, you began to pretend to be like the me you thought I was. You got this bee in your bonnet that your mother's ideas were hooey."

"I am not like Charlotte." Rebecca raised her chin. "And...I am *not* like you."

"You are like both of us." He reached out and put his hand on top of her head. "You just got it all mixed up."

She shook off his hand. "So, why are you here?"

"I'm here because I want to be sure this Max fellow is

good enough for my baby."

"Max?"

****

Tom walked toward Rebecca's cottage and froze when he saw a tall man sitting on the deck with Rebecca. Could this be her mysterious lover? Then he heard her call the man Dad, and saw the resemblance as they turned and watched him approach. They both had the same strong manner of facing the world, though Rebecca raised her chin to show her mother's determination.

When Tom reached the porch, the tall man offered his hand. "John Dumaurier, Rebecca's father. You must be Max?"

"Ah...no. I'm Tom Paxton, sir."

Rebecca blushed. "Tom is my client and my friend."

After a short, strange, but polite conversation, Tom excused himself to leave for his appointment with George. Meeting Rebecca's father and having John Dumaurier call him Max unnerved him. He needed to fit more pieces together and talking with George might help.

Tom arrived at the address on George's psychic business card clutching an extra large Coffee Roasters takeout. She ushered him into her new "office," a cubby-sized room with a small table and two chairs. A laptop case shared a table with a small Ganesha statue, a boom box and a stack of CDs, and lots of books.

"I'm so glad you've come," she said. "Please sit down." She indicated the more comfortable chair. You are my first client in my new office." When they were knee to knee, she said, "Let's begin."

"Do you want me to do anything? Close my eyes? Breathe in some special way?" Tom was used to complicated rituals psychics devised to add to their client's experience.

George smiled, "No. Unless you want to?" She slipped a CD into the boom box, and waited for the sounds of ocean waves to fill the small office. "That'll cover our voices in case anyone in the hall is listening." She leaned forward and took his hand.

Tom felt uncomfortable and for a moment regretted he'd come. He knew a lot of psychics and mediums from the workshop circuit and none made him as nervous as

208

this strange woman, probably because she didn't look strange at all. When he and Angie socialized with gurus and TV psychics, they talked New Age business and he'd long ago lost any illusions that it wasn't a business. Each spiritual personality had a basic cultural style, like Indian, Native American, or Peruvian, and wore unique combinations of ethnic garments. To that they added special gewgaws, crystal accoutrements, or music to their routine.

This woman was different. He felt she knew what he was thinking without gimmicks.

"Do you have questions?" George asked.

"I'm attracted to a woman and I can't think straight," he blurted out, sounding like a letter to Dear Abby. "She says she likes me as a friend. I don't know what to do."

George closed her eyes. "Rebecca is confused right now. I sense her body essence close to you. You two have been intimate. Yes?"

"No. I mean, I..." Tom wanted answers, not questions. "I think we may have had a connection in a past life."

"Bingo." George nodded.

"She may have been my daughter or my mother or even my husband. Please tell me if, in this lifetime, we were only meant to be friends."

"Oh no, not only friends. Your instincts are right. You were lovers. You are lovers..." She looked up and watched him shake his head. "...or will be. If you don't mess up."

"Thanks." Tom let sarcasm creep into his voice, then asked politely, "Anything else?" though he was ready to leave. He felt he'd already messed up. He was testing George. He didn't trust her enough to tell her about his theory and he didn't want the tabloids to pick up some story about the big trance guy needing an exorcism.

"You and Rebecca are in danger."

This got his attention. "Does it have anything to do with how I feel...physically?" he asked.

George turned her head to the right, mumbled, then listened. "Ku is here. He says you are not listening to him. He is tired of your stage shows. He says he is neither a dog nor a pony."

Tom asked, "You are talking to him right now?" George nodded. He believed her. He felt Ku's presence.

Not the same as when Ku was inside him, but the same essence in the room. "Tell him I am truly sorry. That workshop fiasco was not my fault."

"He says not to mind that. He is trying to help you and Rebecca. He tells me he is fighting with another spirit for your body. Does that make sense?"

"Yes! Yes. I know my body is a battleground. But what do I do?"

George turned, mumbled, and listened. "There is more. Ku says you must fight for Rebecca. But he cannot tell you how. You understand spirits can't interfere."

"Not interfere? A spirit is messing with me and with Rebecca, too. I need to know how to fight and win."

George looked over her shoulder, then back at Tom. "Ku's gone. I wish there were more that I could do." She had a tear on her cheek but her voice was strong. "Ku can't help you. There are rules."

Tom felt as if he'd been chastised for failing to return his library books. "The spirit world just threw in the towel? You're telling me it's the old excuse, I'd like to help, but I'm only a spirit? How come spirits are all-powerful only when they want to be?"

"Sometimes, a warning is all you are allowed to receive." She lowered her voice conspiratorially. "*Consider the Autumnal Equinox.*"

"Is that one of those foreboding paradoxical prophecies?" His voice didn't hide his sarcasm.

"Listen. There's more. *Light and dark are balanced in preparation for winter. Dark is poised to take over.*" She looked at him as if the sheer force of her will could make him understand.

Tom thanked George and paid her. He knew she had helped as much as she could, but her words had made as much sense as sorting through bloody sheep entrails.

****

John's cowboy boots kicked rugs as he paced circles around Rebecca's cottage. She had never seen her father like this, though she had to admit, she'd never seen much of her dad at all.

"What is wrong?" she asked.

"Charlotte won't return my phone calls. She is such a...drama queen. Isn't that the new term for what she's always been?"

"Mom's always been a little dramatic. That is who she is." Rebecca defended Charlotte. No one else could call her mother a drama queen. "And romantic."

"Of course," John almost shouted, "she's romantic. The most romantic woman in the world. I loved that about her."

"You did? She always said you wanted her to be sensible and practical."

"Whatever for? Next to Charlotte, I appeared sensible and practical, but I was more of a romantic than she ever was. I've spent my life finding excuses to travel all over the world looking for adventure. I've been lucky enough to make money doing what I love."

"But..." Rebecca did not want to hear his honest opinions. She was more comfortable having an absent, uncaring father.

"We had so much fun until there were three babies. She wanted me to stay in one place. Don't tell her I told you, but Charlotte would have made a damn fine attorney, better than I could ever be. Anyway, she didn't give me time to adjust. I went off to Thailand to do a hotel deal and when I came back she'd filed for divorce."

He paced faster, circling the room. Suddenly, he stopped and pointed to the stack of papers next to her laptop. "Where the hell did you get that?"

Rebecca cocked her head. "What are you talking about?"

He picked a dark sheet off the top. "No one knows about this. Where did you get it?"

"I'm doing work for a client. What is it?" She examined the print which looked like a photocopy of a nautical chart.

"It's a map of the island where I'm building my hotel. A clerical error took it off the nautical charts a hundred years ago."

"Moon Island?"

"Some called it that. Before it got erased, it was officially St. Albans. Getting official status back has been a bitch."

"Is it, by chance, moon-shaped?" Rebecca's mind began snapping puzzle pieces into place.

"Why else would it be called Moon Island?"

"You said it was your island? You bought it?"

"Didn't have to. I inherited half and an abandoned plantation from my grandfather and bought the other half from some distant relation on the East Coast. No one had set foot on the island for seventy-five years."

"Tell me more," Rebecca began, then was interrupted by a knock followed by the door bursting open.

Charlotte walked in and glared at the two of them. "Aries told me she saw a handsome man here with Rebecca. She described the ever absent John Dumaurier." Behind her Aries peeked in the door.

John laughed. "Still the same old Char. Can't resist a good-looking guy." He crossed the room and lifted her until her small feet flutter-kicked the air.

"Put me down or I'll..." she said, but her protest sounded more tease than threat.

Instead of putting her down, John held her closer until she stopped fighting and melted into his arms. He began to kiss her and she kissed him back.

Aries stood in the open door. "Wow. That's romantic. Totally romantic alpha male and beautiful heroine behavior. Way to go, Charlotte."

The two did not respond.

Rebecca put a finger to her lips and guided Aries outside. Hanging up the Do Not Disturb sign, she said, "Let's go to a yoga class. I've got some thinking to do."

Aries asked, "Do they always act like that?"

"I'm not sure."

Settled in the SUV, Aries said, "On the way I'll read you the latest Arianna entry."

****

*September 21, 1867*

*St. Albans Island, British West Indies*

*The night the baby was ready to be born, Penelope cried out while Josephine, the midwife, and I stayed by her bed. The painful labour went on and on until The Major burst in and asked what was keeping his son. Josephine told him Penelope was weak and the birthing slow, and Penelope needed to conserve her strength or the baby would die. The Major told her to save his son at all costs.*

*Josephine had hoped the baby would come early or late but not on this particular night. Her voodoo beliefs warned of male children born on the Fall Equinox. When The Major told her that was the exact day of his own birth, she looked more fearful.*

*Thomas heard his sister's husband's heartless words and challenged the man. They took pistols and went out onto the stormy beach.*

*I wish with all my heart I would have warned him of the words the oracle spoke through Penelope.*

\*\*\*\*

Aries finished. "Oh my God, a duel. How exciting!"

Chapter 24

After the yoga class, Rebecca and Aries returned to the cottage, now thankfully empty of both of Rebecca's parents. Rebecca's brain was spinning. During the class she realized that a few weeks ago her life was fine. She lived in New York and was engaged to a successful, attractive attorney. She was a partner in a great firm. Her career was secure. She knew who she was. Now she was having an affair with a mysterious man who she knew almost nothing about. She thought lewd thoughts about a client who happened to be a trance channeler possessed by a couple of other guys. Her best friend wasn't old enough to drink or vote. Everything she thought she knew about her parents—dimwit mother and selfish father—had just been revised. She didn't know who anyone was.

Starving, she called Room Service and ordered tea and plain crudités. She didn't care where the greens came from, she was determined to lose a few pounds before going back to New York or else she would have to replace her entire business wardrobe. She would reclaim her life.

When Josch delivered their tea, Aries, usually so bold, smiled an I'm-shy-but-I-really-like-you grin. He now wore a better fitting green jacket and matching pants.

Rebecca looked at Josch and demanded, "Why are you here this morning?"

"The hotel gave me more hours because I lost my morning job. The fruit stand closed." He pumped his fist in the air and Aries hugged Rebecca.

"So, the veggie vendor vamoosed?" Rebecca preened. "Not my biggest case, but another success."

As soon as Josch left, Rebecca began pacing. After that e-mail, she'd wanted to question Josch, but not while Aries was around. She did not want Aries to know she suspected her secret lover had been dead for one hundred and forty years. And she couldn't tell Tom and ask him for help. She wasn't ready to get Tom involved. Just because there was no trace of Max on the Internet did not mean there was any reason to panic. She supposed he could be one of those rich techno-paranoid freaks. She could deal with Max by herself.

Aries looked up from *Jane Eyre*. "I'm beginning to think that the alpha male romance novel hero is out of fashion."

Rebecca cocked her head and recalled recent novels she'd read. Could this child have observed a new publishing trend? "My clients all have alpha male heroes. Cleo, Cora, and Babs each have their own version. Since Cleo writes historical fiction, hers...ah...his are the most classic. The noble savage or tribal lord conquers the sassy heroine. No matter how feisty she is, she needs the hero's muscles and power to survive. Cora's heroines require the alpha male hero for sex. Even if he's a heart surgeon, lawyer, or computer geek, he must be gorgeous and a little apelike."

"Babs' heroes aren't very alpha."

Rebecca nodded. "Babs' heroes only have to discover the secret baby. Then they convince the heroine, who is never particularly bright or successful, that they are necessary to lead the pack—I mean family."

"But some romance writers don't use the alpha male hero at all. Sometimes the heroine is the hero and the hero is a smart, gentle nice guy. Sometimes the heroine has to chase the nice guy until he sees that he can conquer her." Aries stared at Rebecca, then whispered, "Like my dad."

Rebecca ignored her subtle suggestion. "Wait a minute. Let's go back to the traditional alpha male model and take it one step farther. The alpha male woos the heroine, overcomes the competition, and carries her off to possess her, have sex, and marry her. She becomes his property. She acquiesces because she really wants him to be all-powerful."

"Because she can't have babies and fight the bad guys at the same time." Aries grinned.

"Right. But the new American heroine is too old for babies anyway. The hero admires her abilities and strength. Why would he want to turn her into a wimp who can only pour tea or make baby food?"

"Exactly." Aries looked smug. "Heroines are changing."

Rebecca realized Aries was helping her see inscrutable industry trends that publishers used consultants with powerful number-crunching programs to decipher. "And I don't think young heroines are particularly interesting." She watched Aries reluctantly nod. "You told me your friends want to read about girls...women at least a few years older than they are. Readers age. Chick lit turns into hen lit. Older women don't want to read about some teenager's problems."

That settled, Aries went back to reading and Rebecca rechecked her e-mail and found the latest message from Max. She was determined to logically understand her feelings for him and the highly emotional state she'd been in since the night she met him.
****

> From: maxwinter@yahoo.net
> To: rjd@bankheadfirm.com
> Subject: My Love
> Dearest Rebecca,
> As usual you are right. We need to find more common ground. I propose we begin by taking a walk and perhaps a late dinner. Meet me at 6 p.m. at the Bell Rock Trailhead parking lot.
> Your new Max

****

A walk with Max? Was he at last ready to drop his mystery man disguise? Or was this another mood swing. She remembered her dream. Why did she feel she needed to choose between Tom and Max? Tom was her good friend and Max was the romantic lover all women—most women—desired. No need at all to choose.

She had no desire to turn wild, unpredictable Max

into a gentle Tom. But a walk with Max would be a way of getting him out of the shadows and into the sunshine. She wanted to get to know him in a safe place, and when she found out who he really was, everything would become clear.

Josch returned with another delivery, this time for Aries. Her Aunt Arianna had FedExed a book called *Diary of a Slave Woman of the Islands*. Aries handed Rebecca the book while she read her aunt's letter.

The book looked like a boring university press publication. Inside, most pages had more footnotes than text. She read the introduction and learned that the author was a black woman who became the toast of Paris for her spiritual gifts and curative potions and mentioned the addenda contained letters by the slave's former mistress who had brought her to Paris.

Aries squealed. "This is part of the Arianna story! Aunt Arianna writes, 'Imagine my luck at finding this book. I am sure the letters in the back are from our ancestor Penelope Paxton before she went into that French convent.'"

Rebecca flipped to the Appendix and read the last entry aloud.

****

*September 13, 1867*
*Moon Island*
*Last night the spirits came to me again. I could not sleep and I wandered the portico listening to the ocean. My husband was at the Settlers' Cabin and the slaves in their quarters. I was peaceful in my solitude. The spirits of my mother and father came to me and warned me of danger and told me to find a protector.*

*I know there is danger. I fear my husband wants me only for the child I bear, a male child that will give him half of this island my family loved. He is polite to me whenever Thomas and Arianna are present, dismissive of me in front of the servants, and cruel when we are alone.*

*The servants, I hate to think of them as slaves though that is what they are, do not obey my orders, for they know that I am not truly the*

217

*mistress of this house. They know Josephine, the slave midwife who lives in the Settlers' Cabin, has more power than I and they fear her voodoo.*

*They have seen me talking to spirits and know my spirits are no match for her spells and her power over my husband.*

*My husband will not allow me to go where a doctor can attend to me. I must hope Josephine's herbs and teas will bring me through this childbearing time. I know she does not hate me.*

*Today I told Josephine of my spirits. She sat with me and asked me to let the spirits come through me to talk to her. I did so and Josephine told me that I spoke to her in several voices. One voice was my sweet mother warning me that my brother Thomas was in danger.*

*Another was an old, old man spirit. Josephine said his name was Que and he instructed her to watch over me. A third spirit spoke in French and told Josephine to care for me, for I would make her free. Since my French is only that of a schoolgirl, Josephine was sure that this spirit spoke especially for her. This spirit assured her that my brother's children would find love and peace in the red mountains.*

*I am now less afraid. Josephine is my friend and I trust her despite her powers over my husband. My heart is lighter.*

*Penelope*

\*\*\*\*

Rebecca paged back to the main portion of the book and read the final entry in the slave woman's dairy.

\*\*\*\*

*September 21, 1888*
*Paris*
*As my life comes to an end, I bless the woman I called Mistress, then Penelope, and finally Friend. She forgave me and saved me by bringing me from cursed Moon Island to Paris, the most wonderful city in the world where I found a new life.*

*I write this on the day called Alban Elfred,*

218

*once honored by the French as the beginning of a New Year. It's the Druids' time for finding balance and settling old debts. A harvest festival for all. As day and night are equal, it marks the beginning of the move toward the darkest, coldest time of year.*

*My own days of sunshine are over. I leave my writings, not for my children and their children, but for those that come to learn about Penelope and her story and most of all for the descendants of dear Penelope who are still in danger.*

Chapter 25

Tom phoned Bill at the Sedona Airport FBO and made arrangements to rent a plane. He had to get away and an hour in the air could calm his mind and sort out his thoughts better than anything.

A half hour later he climbed into the same Cessna 150 he'd rented to show Rebecca the red rocks and taxied out. The Sedona Airport mesa always reminded him of what it must feel like to take off from an aircraft carrier—what a rush.

Flying was one thing that had kept him sane during his marriage to Angie. Taking lessons and flying his own plane gave him an escape. He and Angie had bought the Cessna for Beloved Ltd. and often used the white plane with "Beloved" painted in gold script on the side to fly to workshops, interviews, and book signings. Angie considered the plane a status symbol and made sure it qualified as a business expense, but for him, every minute in the cockpit was pure pleasure. Often with Angie in the right seat he turned off the feed to her headset and ignored her silent screams to purchase better radio equipment.

Looking down on Bell Rock, Cathedral Rock, and Courthouse Butte lifted his spirits and caused a frisson of excitement to pass through his body. With a pleasant shiver—he always thought of this as the vortex effect—he banked and headed northeast away from Sedona, Flagstaff, and the Grand Canyon out over the Mogollon Rim.

Out here, he felt like he was on autopilot. One part of him was alert, listening for radio calls, watching for planes, adjusting, trimming, ever conscious of controlling the airplane. This part was totally aware of the unnaturalness of flying and respectful of the inherent danger of his frail human body eight thousand feet above the ground.

The other part of him accepted flight as perfectly natural. This aspect allowed his creative brain to soar. He often touched back down to earth with answers to problems as if waking from a dream, the path ahead clear.

That's exactly what he craved now. Just for a few minutes he needed to let go of trying so hard to figure out what was happening to his body and what was going on with Rebecca. Then he could figure out how to fight that dark spirit.

He pulled the brim of his Beloved baseball hat lower to keep the sun out of his eyes. Through the windscreen he watched patterns of clouds in the sky and soft colors of the Painted Desert below.

He was hopelessly in love with Rebecca. But the closer he got to her, the more she pushed him away or something moved between them. He wanted to shake her to convince her how perfect they were together, but she had to see herself.

He centered himself. This desire to overpower her scared him. He was not the kind of man who would take a woman by force or trick her into loving him. But for a moment those thoughts rose up and he considered them. Doing that would be unethical, as bad as, or worse than, using his talent as a medium to gain power over others.

The plane bounced in an unexpected pocket of turbulence. His head brushed the roof. "Fly the plane," he told himself out loud. "Fly the plane."

After the flight, Tom finished his paperwork, found George's business card, and called the psychic's cell phone. After seven rings, he was sure he was going to get her voice mail. On the eighth, she answered.

"This is Joy," she whispered.

"Tom Paxton. I need to talk to you."

"My next office hours are tomorrow morning."

221

"I must see you as soon as possible. That problem I told you about." He knew he sounded desperate.

"I understand, Mr. Paxton. Come to the concierge desk. But if my boss sees you, pretend to be booking one of the new Vortex Photo Jeep Tours."

By the time Tom got back to the hotel, he was less sure about George. The hotel lobby seemed too public for psychic work. Tom waited while George talked with Steve and Cora, their interest in each other too obsessive to even notice Tom. George finished telling them about the nearby casino, then waved and called Tom over.

"Mr. Paxton. Sit down and tell me what I can do for you?" George asked. "You sounded very upset."

"Tom, please. I finally know who that spirit is."

"Good. You needed to find out for yourself. You know the drill. A psychic can't give information before the client is ready to receive it."

"You are a strange psychic," he told her, after she handed cowboy dinner show tickets to a family of five and discount massage coupons to a newlywed couple.

"I'm tight with the afterlife clique. Ku sends me tons of data and I have a couple of other guides who hang around. I'm a very good librarian, so I know how to use research for background and fact checking. And I have a lot of common sense." She lowered her voice. "My new Spirit Concierge Service will be great when I get it off the ground."

The smarmy hotel manager came into the lobby. She smiled at him and he nodded in greeting, then recognized Tom.

Tom raised his voice. "Miss, it's imperative that you make these reservations for me and my entire party immediately. Or I could never recommend this hotel."

"Yes, sir," George picked up the telephone and pretended to make a call until the manager detoured to his office. "Now, tell me what you know."

"The spirit called Max used my body to make love to Rebecca and I am mad with jealousy. Does she love him or love me?"

George grinned. "Wow! He did that! Amazing!" She noticed Tom's grimace, closed her eyes and mumbled to her guides, then told Tom, "You are correct. But the spirit has no body. My sources say he was in your body at the time."

"That's exactly what I said. But I wasn't in there. So who did she sleep with and who did she think she was sleeping with and who thought...God, this is confusing and crazy. See why I need help?"

"When spirit guides are not clear I like to try common sense to reason it out. Max used your body to seduce Rebecca. Without your body and without your soul essence, which hung around that body, she would have been repelled by him. He's what one of my guides called a bad spirit dude. If Rebecca had seen the real Max, she could never have been fooled into thinking she'd fallen in love with him."

Tom nodded. "That could be true. But..."

George looked into his eyes. "Tell me what in your heart you truly believe."

"I believe Rebecca loves me. But has been hypnotized by romance."

George nodded. "She told me you took her on an airplane ride over Sedona. That was so cool. When she's with you, she forgets the other guy. He's just a fantasy."

"I want to be her fantasy."

"Of course you do, but you are real. And that's what Rebecca wants too. But she's never been in love, so she's not quite sure what love should feel like."

"You know that? Her mother said Rebecca read romance novels when she was a kid."

"Yes. My guides say she was raised by a single mother with a father figure right out of a storybook, who popped in from time to time and treated her like a princess, then disappeared. She strives to succeed and doesn't trust anyone enough to let her guard down enough to truly fall in love."

"Are you sure she's never been in love?"

"Rebecca thought she was in love with Tristan, but even he was more real than she was. He wanted a real woman. As despicable as he treated her, he knew Rebecca's heart was never in it. When the relationship ended, she didn't really care."

"Why is she so different here in Sedona?"

"My guess? The Sedona vortexes. The first vacation

she's ever taken. Letting her hair down. Wearing a long dress. Going to a psychic. Having a thirteen-year-old as her first real best friend. Finding a man who truly cares for her and loves her for who she really is."

"I understand, I guess." Tom held his head in his hands and talked to the desk. "Her world's been turned upside down here."

"Understanding is a good beginning. So, what's your problem?"

"I'm still jealous? Of me? Of what she wants that isn't me."

"What is that?"

"The wildly romantic lover, of course."

"That's not you? You seem pretty wildly romantic to me. You're a philosopher trance medium who wears silk pajamas in public, files a plane, is smarter, funnier, and lots more fun than some dead guy. Max doesn't own a plane, or a car, or even his own body. Not much of a catch. He has no job. He's just a deadbeat trying to get cash by suing you at the same time he's trying to kill you. He dreams about a lost fortune on an island that he never owned. I can't imagine Rebecca would stay interested for very long."

"But she betrayed me. She acted as if she was interested, then fell into bed with...with...me!"

"Whose body touched her skin? Whose lips kissed her? Whose arms held her? Max is cold. You know that about spirits. Your heart won her. Your rival is not taller nor better looking. You keep the body in shape and breathe the life into it, while he's been dead for over one hundred and forty years. Besides, he's not really in love with her."

"He's not? Are you sure?"

"He's in love with a woman who never loved him. That other Rebecca, Arianna Rebecca, married your ancestor and had his child. Haven't you been reading that diary? Max loved your great-great-grandmother and was a loser then, too."

"Max is such a total failure. I'm beginning to feel sorry for him."

"Tom. No." George stared into Tom's eyes. "Listen to me. No sympathy. Stop being such a nice guy. He is dangerous. He is a very, very dark spirit who has been prowling the ether for a long time, seeking revenge, building strength, and waiting for an opportunity. He is very smart, but does not understand today's world."

"Like using my credit card on the Internet."

"He stole your identity in cyberspace too! Cool! Seriously, imagine a vicious spirit looking for a body, then deciding to kill the owner, which will kill the only chance he has to live."

"So what do I do to win?"

George pursed her lips. "Sorry, that's all for now."

Tom stood and laid an immense tip on the concierge's desk. "You have saved my life."

****

Tom arrived in high spirits to pick up Aries. Rebecca watched him literally dance in the cottage door and greet Aries with a hug as if they'd been separated for months.

"Everything is going to be wonderful," he announced. He looked at their intense faces. "So, what serious topics have you two beautiful women been discussing?"

Aries gathered her books. "Clothes, what else?"

He turned to Rebecca and without hesitation, took her in his arms and kissed her. He waited until she softened and responded. He felt the excitement between them and he held her until she heard Aries say, "Totally."

Pretending to ignore the kiss as friendly fooling around, Rebecca laughed and watched them leave.

****

Back in their cottage, Tom described his plan to his daughter. Aries whined, "Don't make me. I'm just a kid. You could get hurt."

"I need your help. There is no one else I can trust." Tom used his parental voice. "You've been telling me that you are grown up. You said your mother treats you like an adult and I must also."

"I was wrong. I want to be a kid. Go to school, the mall, have friends, my own ordinary life. And have a father who is the same person all the time." She scrunched her face. "I love you, Dad. Please don't do anything dangerous. Please talk to Rebecca. She is really smart and won't let anything bad happen to you. You said so yourself. She's a super lawyer."

225

"Aries, baby, this isn't a problem for lawyers. Rebecca can't help. I'm doing this for her because she's in danger."

"From that guy?"

"If by 'that guy,' you mean the man called Max, yes, I believe she is in mortal danger and I am the only one who can save her. To help me do that, you must lock me in this cottage and not open the door for anything. I need to have it out with this Max."

"But Dad, if I lock you in by yourself, how can you fight someone who isn't there?"

"I think Max is..." He refused to explain this to his daughter. "I think I have some power over him. I'm going to try to go into a trance." Tom dangled his room key. "Please..."

Aries reluctantly held out her hand to accept the key. "I love you—and Rebecca." She looked very young and scared as she hugged Tom and scurried out the door.

Tom heard her turn the key in the lock and waited for sounds of her steps leaving the porch. He sat on the bed and stared at the locked door. Now that he was convinced Rebecca loved him, he was sure this was the right thing to do. He hated involving Aries, but there was no one else he trusted.

****

Aries obeyed her father and walked to the river and found a seat farthest from their cottage. She took out the latest e-mail from her Aunt Arianna, hoping it would distract her from running back and unlocking the door.

****

*From: ARIREBPaxton@STXEN.edu*
*To: pinkbabe@Beloved.com*
*Subject: News*
*Dear Aries,*

*My life as an historian has been very exciting (for a change). A colleague in France discovered another diary which was written by that same Arianna Rebecca later in her life in Paris. Attached is the English translation of an excerpt.*

*Hope you received the book I sent. It's a diary written by the former slave Josephine who later became a friend of Rebecca and Penelope.*

226

*Your father must take these letters seriously because I believe his talents as a medium have been inherited from Penelope.*

*Tell your father I have secured rooms in one of the plantation houses restored by the new resort owner. Won't we all have a great time in the Islands? Please hope your mother doesn't find a way to stop the trip.*

*Tell me more about your friend Rebecca? What an interesting name. Like the woman who wrote the diary. Would she like to travel with us? You said your father likes her. Likes as in "approves of one of your friends" or "likes her"?*

*Your Loving Aunt*

\*\*\*\*

*A "Diary of Arianna Rebecca Paxton Dumaurier" (English translation) Entry dated April, 30, 1876. Paris, France*

*Life is strange. I now live in Paris. My husband, Jean, is a lawyer, and we have a home in the country and a townhouse in London. I am mistress of three lovely houses, yet often, I remember my days as a bride on my beautiful St. Albans with its waterfalls, flowers, birds, and warm breezes.*

*Jean is, like Thomas, very smart and good at business. He, too, is a gentleman who is not too old-fashioned to appreciate a clever wife. He has taught me the law and I help him in his practice. He is a good father to my son, Charles Thomas, who is now eight. Our Jean Paul is three. The boys are not at all alike. Charles is blue-eyed and talks of the sea. Jean Paul, with his big dark eyes, looks like me and already has the bearing of a barrister.*

*Every September I visit Penelope. She lives in a convent in the south of France and grows stronger. On the day of the Autumn Equinox we take a carriage to the sea and walk on the beach and cry for Thomas, the man we both loved. In France, those who remember the Republic still celebrate this day as the beginning of the new*

227

*year. We both feel great sadness and regret that we did not warn him of mortal danger.*

*Penelope is happy with the sisters who are gentle with her when they come upon her speaking in voices. They call her touched by God.*

*We never talk of the night our Thomas and her husband Maximilian Winter, who we called The Major, and her infant son perished. As soon as she was able to travel, I took her back to London. On the journey to my great discomfort and greater joy, I discovered I was with child. Josephine accompanied us to care for Penelope and became my nursemaid as well.*

*When my baby Charles was a year old, Penelope went into the convent and I met my Jean. I knew I would never have a love like sweet Thomas, but my happiness in marriage with Jean is great. We work together and travel, but never to the Indies. Our sons give us great pleasure. I am almost thirty, a settled married woman with a good life and a sad history.*

*My Charles has inherited the family curse— or blessing—of talking to spirits and letting them talk through him. May God protect him.*

****

*October 12, 1876*
*Paris, France*
*Last month when I visited Penelope, she gave me the deed to her half of St. Albans. I told her I could never return to the island. She said her share would be a gift to my second son, Jean Paul. And in that way, my heirs would own both halves, The Sun and The Moon united. Jean Paul would be part of the heritage from her brother Thomas.*

*She now speaks freely of her red rock visions. She tells me that my descendants will meet one day in red mountains and when they do, they will need protection. When I asked how I can protect them, she tells me to write down these words from her visions and pass them on to my children. "Love is greater than time. True love protects. Learn from your first duel. Light not darkness. Call on the power of the moon."*

\*\*\*\*

"Oh!" Aries cried. "Rebecca *is* totally a part of all this. Her Max is...I have to help my dad."

Chapter 26

With the door locked and Aries safely away, Tom walked to the mirror and saw the same familiar face he shaved every morning. He stared into the mirror, hoping he could look deep enough into his own eyes to discover the secrets he sought.

His left eyelid twitched. He blinked. This was not getting him anywhere. He knew falling asleep would make it too easy for him—whoever or whatever "him" was to gain control.

Slipping off his shoes, Tom prepared for meditation. He drew his legs up and easily crossed them. He loosened his shirt collar and rubbed at the tightness in his neck muscles. He'd craved a massage for days, but feared if he relaxed he'd change right there on the massage table and frighten some innocent massage therapist.

These new trances had altered his life. Every time Ku came into his body, his mind became calm and his life easier, but when that dark force took him, he was filled with fear.

Shaking off those thoughts, he stretched his torso and let his shoulders slide back and down. He purposely slowed his breathing. He must begin.

His head began to feel lighter and lighter, until he imagined his entire body floating. Lighter, lighter, lighter. Holding that sensation, he let his eyelids open a crack. He looked out through his eyelashes at the wall mirror opposite the bed.

He wasn't close enough to the mirror to be sure but

he did look different. Shorter, smaller and his eyes were different. The Ku feeling began to fill his body from the base of his spine up his back, through his neck, and into his head. He relaxed, surrendering to the familiar change he knew was coming.

A stab of pain flashed through his temples. His face contorted. This was not Ku. His entire body jerked in pain as that dark entity pressed into every cell.

He fought the pain and tightened control. His left hand reached for the pad of paper he kept on the bedside table for recording ideas for his new book. He observed the hand as if it were not his own and noticed the skin appeared tanner and hairier than he remembered.

The hand. Somewhere in his mind Tom registered that he was right-handed. But now his left hand took the pencil and wrote, "Thomas Paxton, give up. I am more powerful than you could ever be." He heard a sneer from his own lips in a voice that was not his. "I am becoming stronger every day."

Tom fell back on the bed, afraid to close his eyes and lose what control he still held over his own body. He focused, forcing back rage, and brought back his clarity of mind to rise above the present power struggle. He let the principles of life taught by Ku flood his mind.

He rose from the bed and stared at the pad in his right hand and the pencil in the left. The words on the pad read, "You are my enemy." He had written those words. His first instinct was to cut off his own hand. He tried to consciously open his fingers. Nothing happened. He tried again with great intent until the left hand opened and the pencil fell.

"There." Tom exhaled. He did have enough power.

He took hold of the shaking left hand with his right and held the hand still. He had won. As soon as that thought passed through his mind, the left hand broke free, grabbed the right and pinned it to the table. His mouth said, "Mortal fool. You are a temporary impediment, beneath my concern."

With tremendous effort Tom fought the power that swept through his body. With each breath, his body cried out. Every cell felt blasted apart, but he kept control. He was real. He was the man who had lived in this body for thirty-five years and he owned it.

With his right hand he wrote, "I am more powerful. If you want to communicate with me I will give you permission to use my hand." He wasn't practiced in dominance. He hoped this would work. "Tell me who you are," he demanded.

His left hand wrote, "I am Maximilian Winter. The one who will soon take your body and leave what is left of you to be flotsam in the cosmos, soulless before it is your time to leave your body. You ripped life from me and threw my body in the ocean just when I would achieve my dreams. You will now know bodiless."

His right hand wrote, "I never hurt you, you devil spirit opportunist."

The left grabbed the pencil and wrote, "Devil? No. Unconquerable? Yes. Your love of Rebecca makes you faint-hearted."

The right hand immediately responded, "I am capable of great love and want no harm to those I love."

The left ripped the paper as it wrote, "You are truly a fool. I will use your body to get what I want, regardless of who will be harmed."

"No. I will protect—"

"You sniffling eunuch. You want this woman, but you have no idea how to possess her. I have come through time to have her and take her back with me."

"I do not want to possess her. I love her and want her to freely love me." The hand-shifting was making him dizzy.

"Fool. I have had her body and given her great pleasure. She will never settle for a pitiful mortal."

Tom hesitated. He had to ask the one question that held him back. "Am I your descendant?" Needing to know, but fearful that the answer would be yes, he waited.

"I have no descendants, thanks to Thomas Paxton! He killed me. You are the great-great-great grandson and reincarnation of that Thomas Paxton and Rebecca Arianna. The woman you think of as Rebecca is the descendant and reincarnation of Arianna Rebecca through her marriage to the Frenchman, Jean Dumaurier."

Tom shook his head. His own voice roared, echoing through the room. He fell back. He had the answer he desired. He was back in control. He scanned his body and felt the other was gone. He had won.

He heard Aries at the door. "Daddy, are you all right?" She sounded very afraid. "I have to talk to you! I can't find Rebecca. It's important."

Unwilling to open the door and risk Aries' safety, he called, "I'm fine, honey. Everything is fine. I'm going to nap for a while. Go stay with Rebecca."

He turned on Aries' harp solo CD and smudged the cabin with sage. He needed to clear the space and regain his strength. Exhausted, he lay back on the bed and let his eyelids close just for a moment. He needed just a second of rest. One breath. Maybe two.

Three breaths later, the body stirred and Max opened his eyes, shook his head, and smiled. He stood and walked to the closet. Stripping off Tom's clothes, he changed into black silk and high boots, muttering, "Fool. You thought you could win that easily?"

He found the box containing the black Stetson Josch had delivered last night and stared into the mirror at his reflection. "Thomas—if you are in there?—see me and know I own this body. You do not set rules for me. Who are you to tell me I may only write with your—your—your left hand." He laughed. "This body is mine and you will never have use of any of it again. Nor ever see your love, other than through my eyes. Ha! You fight by rules. I fight to win."

He unbolted the door and stepped out into the pre-sunset coolness. He shuddered at the light, then straightened. For extra protection he put on a pair of very dark sunglasses. His head bent and he pulled the black hat lower and walked toward Tom's white van.

Max allowed the body to go into auto pilot. It opened the van door, got in, and started the engine. Why couldn't this be as easy as riding a horse or sailing a boat? Those skills he knew from his world were so much easier to master. His difficult task was to let the body do what it knew how to do without giving it the power to connect to the consciousness that had taught it to do those things.

He drove out of the parking lot and headed to the Bell Rock rendezvous. Soon he would have his Rebecca all to himself.

Chapter 27

Rebecca, dressing for her sunset walk with Max, first put on the red New Age-y dress, then changed into a hiking outfit whose pants were so tight she couldn't sit to drive. At last she chose a white ankle-length dress which she accessorized with rose quartz earrings and a matching necklace. George had told her rose quartz possessed wonderful healing properties. She hoped the stones worked. She'd fussed with her makeup and added a dab of *Evening in Paris* between her breasts, knowing the desert breeze would soften the intense scent. Instead of sandals, she pulled on her red cowboy boots for protection against cactuses and snakes.

New pages of the diary excerpts lay on the floor. Aries must have come by while she was in the shower, thought she'd gone out, and stuffed them under the door. She read while her hair dried. On the last page Aries had scrawled, "Rebecca, this means you!" next to the final words:

\*\*\*\*

*Love is greater than time. True love protects.*
*Learn from your first duel. Light not darkness.*
*Call on the power of the moon.*

\*\*\*\*

This made no sense. Teenagers could be so dramatic and high-strung.

She heard Little Rebecca's voice cry, *Yes. Yes! Remember those words, and*—Rebecca told her to be quiet. Another childish voice. She hated those intrusive outbursts when Little Rebecca's advice jumped into her mind so loud and demanding. The voice was no longer playing the role of entertaining imaginary companion. Besides, how could words from an ancient diary be that important to her life now?

She looked in the mirror. If her New York friends saw her now, they would never recognize her. Shoulder length hair fell in soft waves around her face. The last of the temporary black dye had washed out and a natural honey-blonde color accentuated her large dark eyes. The low-cut bodice of the white dress was far from her black-suited city persona.

She had fantasized, imagining herself strolling in the sunshine with Max and now felt tricked. The sun would have set by the time she completed the drive to Bell Rock. This was supposed to be a date. Why couldn't he have picked her up?

As she pulled onto 89A, she forced her mind out of stress mode, took a breath, and looked up at the rock formations glowing in the late afternoon light. Sedona had taught her to slow down and smell the...mountains. Now each bend of 179 revealed an enchanting new vista.

The day after tomorrow she would be back home. City lights and high-rises would replace this full moon and monumental rocks. After only two weeks, New York felt a million miles away and Sedona felt like home.

She knew she had changed and not just in her wardrobe. She didn't feel like the same woman who'd gotten off that airplane in Phoenix. Since then everything had become so complicated. She wished Max would say the words that would make everything all right. What if he told her that he loved her and would give up everything to be with her? He could move to New York and they'd have time to get to know each other. Then she could find out if she loved him. She pushed away the thought that, sometimes, she didn't even like him. She supposed love was like that. Her parents always had emotional scenes and arguments, but she suspected they had once loved each other.

She and Max could vacation on his island, perhaps every weekend, or travel to Sedona for special occasions and stay in that same rose-filled cabin with the four-poster bed. They could walk along the river...wait. It was Tom who took her for walks and airplane rides...

Tom? She would be with Max. Of course, Tom would still be her friend and Aries was part of her life now and she'd see them often. She could visit New Hampshire. They'd come to New York. Tom was her client. She sensed Max wouldn't understand. He would be jealous. He'd make her choose.

What about her work? She'd been thinking about work less and less. Heather's last calls were unanswered and she didn't feel all that guilty, but her clients depended on her. She couldn't just abandon them. Paperwork for Tom's full custody hearing lay in the back seat with the results of the Epping test for Max's manuscripts. She still had business to take care of.

She turned left into the upper Bell Rock trailhead parking area, parked, and looked for Max. She didn't even know what kind of vehicle he drove.

Surprised to see Tom's Beloved van, she got out and straightened the folds of her dress and fluffed the ruffle around her plunging neckline. The rose quartz pendant sparkled up at her.

She noticed a group of people climbing up another trail. The leader reminded her of George, the psychic concierge. Perhaps this was her group's equinox potluck?

A voice behind her called, "Rebecca, my love."

She spun around and saw Max in a black cowboy hat and sunglasses standing next to Tom's van. Could he have borrowed the van? She started towards him and noticed something very wrong. Max's head bent down awkwardly. He shook with effort as he lifted one boot, heavy as if it were mired in quicksand. She called to him, but heard only a croak in response.

His back hunched. Then, with great effort, he threw back his shoulders. His entire body lurched, then settled. He stood straight and came towards her. By the time he reached her, he looked fine.

He took her in his arms and lifted her off her feet until her red boots kicked the air. "Rebecca. At last," he breathed. "Now you are mine."

"Max. Put me down. I want to look at you." She smiled up at him, delighted to see his face in the light, or at least in more light than ever before. In the sunset shadows, his face was strong and ruggedly handsome, and surprisingly familiar. The scar running diagonally across his left cheek was a light gash on his tanned skin. "Now we can talk. Let's take our walk."

"Yes, my love." He slid his arm protectively around her and led her to the trailhead entrance.

They followed a level path, then took the left fork up to the next level. She felt she was being led up a huge red wedding cake. On the next tier, she looked down on cars halted along the highway. Tourists peering into cameras clamoring for the perfect shot missed the true magnificence of the formation at dusk.

Below on a path at the base of the rock, she saw a couple holding hands. In the fading light, she thought she recognized her mother—and her father. This was a very strange night.

Max, intense but now silent, took her hand and helped her over another outcropping to the next higher cake layer.

"Why are we going so high?" Rebecca asked as he pulled her up onto a shelf fifteen feet long and only ten feet deep. She looked out over the steepest cliff in the Bell Rock formation. Cars and people below appeared like miniatures in a child's train village.

Red dust streaked Rebecca's white dress and covered her boots. She wanted to sit, look at the moon, and talk with Max.

"This place is perfect," Max told her. His voice sounded rough and forced, no longer heavy with that elegant European accent she loved.

The full moon lit the panorama. Breathtaking, Rebecca thought, although she'd become accustomed to the high altitude. She now felt more lightheaded than lighthearted. She was no longer the New Yorker who kept her emotions under control.

Max stood before her and gathered her into his arms. "My own. At last you are mine."

Romantic words were great, but she wished he'd stop saying that she was his. She'd come a long way towards accepting the language of romantic talk, but she did not belong to anyone.

237

But instead of objecting, she said, "Max, this is so wonderful. I love being with you." And she meant it, mostly, though she realized she was forcing herself to use more romantic words to fit the occasion and encourage him to again become the courtly romantic lover.

"You shall be with me forever on my island and never concern yourself with the world again."

"Does your island have Internet service or satellite phones? Can I telecommute?" She laughed as if it were a silly question but really did want to know.

"There is no need for things like that. I am all you need."

"But...I thought—"

"No need for you to think, my love." He gripped her to his chest. "When you win my lawsuit, I will have my fortune. Everything we need."

"I forgot to tell you. I got the test results and I can't take the case to court. There's not enough evidence and no legal precedents."

His face instantly reddened. "You must! You cannot fail me!"

"Max, the law can not support your claim."

He began to pace and gesture at the moon. Max was out of control. She looked over the ledge and knew this was no place for a hot-tempered business meeting.

With no warning, he stopped and reached out to hold her again, but she stepped out of his reach.

He sneered. "Then never mind. I was wrong to ask you to be my lawyer. You are merely a woman—"

"—A woman and a damn good attorney. Better than any man in the business. You had no case. You were not honest with me." Her anger flared and her whole body tensed. Many times in court she'd had cause to become angry, but always kept her cool. Now, she could feel her heart beat faster and her face flush. No longer merely indignant, she was furious.

"Rebecca my love, don't trouble your pretty little head about this." He took her in his arms again. "I also have my secret treasure, buried in a safe cave on my island. When that treasure is sold I will have a fortune and then I will find an attorney competent to handle these affairs—"

"—We have to talk—" She struggled.

"—No need—" He held her tighter.

"—But I want to talk." He was holding her so tight she couldn't breathe. Rebecca raised her right foot and brought the heel of her red cowboy boot down hard on Max's instep. Close Encounters with Attackers Technique #2.

She pushed him and, caught off guard, he stumbled back, giving her a moment to think. Where was Little Rebecca, that voice of good advice? She relaxed her control and asked Little Rebecca, "Why did you let me come here? You didn't warn me!"

Little Rebecca whispered, *I couldn't save you from this danger. Anyway, you wouldn't have listened. Your destiny is here. Tonight!*

Rebecca watched Max's face tighten. She hadn't wanted to make him more angry. She just wanted to get his attention so he would listen to her. She wanted to tell him his behavior was way beyond her comfort level.

His face twisted and his body heaved. When his mouth opened, she was sure she heard Tom's voice say, "Rebecca, be careful. He plans to harm you."

"Tom?" But that was impossible. She stepped back, but Max's left hand grabbed her and pulled her nearer to the edge.

"I can control him. He has always been weak," Max's deep voice told her. "If you are truly committed to me, he will have no power over either of us."

"Who are you talking about?"

"Thomas Paxton stole you from me and now he tries to poison your thoughts against me—again. I will not stand for it."

"Tom? You know Tom?"

"He enchanted you and married you and I took Penelope, his weak, sniveling sister. She was crazy, just as this Tom is crazy."

"No." Rebecca's analytic legal mind at last took over. His words proved the diary held the answer. What did that last diary entry say about saving Thomas? She tried to remember. She knew she must remember the phrases exactly. Where was Little Rebecca when she needed her?

"I have taken advantage of the weakness that allows

spirits to use his mind and body. I own that body now and will not give it back," Max yelled, spreading his arms and looking up to the moon.

Rebecca screamed, "You can't just take someone else's body." What was she saying? Now she was certain that the diary held the answers.

She watched as a human body became a ghastly battleground. That body looked both tortured and possessed, much worse than anything she'd seen during Tom's trances. Even the trances with the most intense shifts were gentle transitions compared to these gut-wrenching jolts and anguished grimaces. Tom's entire body shuddered in agony as spasms shook every cell. She saw Max hold firm while Tom tried to regain control. Then she watched the power shift back and forth between Tom and Max. No horror movie effects could be this frightening. It was the most bizarre thing she had ever seen and she could do nothing to help.

Max turned. She was sure it was Max for his eyes were crazed.

He grabbed her arm and pulled her to the edge. "If we cannot have happiness in this time, we will not stay. If I cannot possess the weakling's body, neither will he. Come. We will go on to the next world. From there we can return to my island."

"His island!" Rebecca looked down. Tourists were pointing and taking photos of them.

Now she was certain Max intended to jump and take her with him. She would die. Tom would die. Max didn't care. But Tom could not die. She loved Tom and would not let him go. Aries needed him. She needed him.

Max grabbed her. "We go together."

With more strength than she thought she possessed, she pushed away from Max and moved back to the shadow of the rock and pressed her body against the cooling stone's face.

She pulled herself up tall. The evening breeze ballooned her skirt off to one side like a romance novel cover girl. "I will not come with you. I love Tom Paxton. And so did your Rebecca. I know because I read Arianna Rebecca Paxton's diary. You are only a petulant ghost. Tom killed you once. You cannot make me love you. Only

Tom can win my heart and soul."

What a speech! The classic heroine struggling to save her hero. Now, all she had to do was remember the words that would save them both.

Chapter 28

As he struggled, Tom heard Rebecca's words and his strength rallied. She loved him. She really loved him. Immediately he felt Max's power over him weaken.

Max roared as a cloud covered the moon. The night had been clear, the moon large and soft, and the breeze gentle. Now the sky was dark and masses of clouds shadowed the sky. Without warning the wind came up and daggers of monsoon rain pelted the ledge.

Max stood in front of Rebecca. His hand pressed into her shoulders as her soaked white dress slapped against her legs. "You will obey me!" he demanded, but for the first time, his voice lacked complete certainty.

Tom heard Rebecca call out to Little Rebecca, "Please, remember the words that will help me." And then she shouted, "*Love is greater than time,*" as lightning streaked across the sky.

He saw her try to pull away from Max to get off the ledge and out of danger, but her red boots slipped on the rain-slicked rock. Max reached for her and grasped the ruffle of her dress. It ripped as sheets of rain washed the ledge and ran down on them in rivers from the rocks above. He grabbed her shoulders and pulled her to her feet and towards the edge.

Rebecca cried out, "*Learn from your first duel!*"

Tom heard her words and from deep within his cells, he pulled a memory of how Max had lured his ancestor to the shore and tricked him.

The desert storm's rain blew like ocean waves in a

hurricane wind. Did they stand on a mountain or on a beach? The danger was the same. To die by drowning or to fall from the cliff, the result was death.

"We will go to our destiny," Max cried out. "I will take you to my island. In death we will be together."

"You're crazy! I want to live, not die." Rebecca paused. "I remember." Then she screamed above the storm with all her strength, "True love protects!"

Tom watched Rebecca through Max's eyes as he pushed her back against the rocks, expecting Max to drag her forward. Tom focused on his right hand and forced it to open and free her. She bounced forward, then back.

Little Rebecca said, *Say "Light. Not darkness!" It's like a spell. It will free Tom.* And Rebecca yelled up to the cloud-covered moon, "Light. Not darkness! Damn it." Max thrust her back and her head hit rock. She crumpled unconscious. Strong arms caught her.

Tom looked up to the moon. Lightning flashed across the blackness. He knew it would take more to banish that devil. He felt the presence of Ku within him. Ku who was not, by the rules of the universe, supposed to aid him, was giving his body and will strength and sending him the words he needed. Tom cried, "Descend Dread Lord of Shadows into the Darkness!"

Max's demented roar came from Tom's lips and the possessed body writhed and went limp, releasing Rebecca and allowing her body to fall to the ground. She rolled away, pulled herself to her knees and carefully crawled forward, still fearful that Max would jump up, grab her, and carry her over the edge to crash onto the rocks below.

As suddenly as the rain began, it stopped. Clouds uncovered the moon and moonlight shone on them.

A siren shrieked down the canyon towards them. Rebecca knelt and looked at the face of the man lying on the ground in front of her. It was Tom's face. Tears ran down her cheeks. "Please, do not die. I love you." In an instant, she knew she truly loved him. Love flowed through every cell in her body. She knew the false feelings generated by Max were only a shadow of what she felt now. In some sick way the two men had been one, but now it was clear only one could live. And that had to be Tom. Tom was good. Tom was love.

He stirred. His eyes opened. He took a deep breath. "Good," he gasped. "For I love you."

She hugged him. "I thought I was going to lose you," she cried between kisses.

"That will never happen." He tried to sit up, but fell back.

She smiled. "You must be tired." He nodded. Somehow she'd have to get him down the trail and back to the car.

Rebecca looked up. Three men and a woman in uniform stood watching from the other side of the ledge. Her father, looking more than ever like John Wayne, stood next to Steve King and Josch, as Officer O'Hara moved towards them.

Officer O'Hara reached for the radio at her belt. "Mr. Paxton! Are you hurt? Can you stand or shall I call for a stretcher?"

"No." Tom raised his hand. "I'm just tired. And it looks like we've lots of help here."

The officer gave Tom a bottle of water. She recognized Rebecca, and said to the others, "Who are you people?"

Rebecca's father stepped forward. "I'll take this man down. Looks like he's going to be in my family."

Steve said, "I'll help. He's my oldest friend."

"He's my girlfriend's father," said Josch.

Rebecca and Tom stared at Josch.

## Chapter 29

Back at the trailhead, the EMTs checked Tom over, while friends, family and curious tourists milled around. When he was released, Rebecca drove his van back to the hotel. The caravan behind consisted of her father and mother, Aries and Josch, Steve and Cora who also had been enjoying a sunset walk, and Angie and Tristan who'd showed up with the crowd.

Rebecca insisted Tom stay in her cottage. She put him to bed in the four-poster and he immediately fell asleep. She sat close to him and watched him through the rest of the night, and panicked each time she noticed subtle changes or twitches.

George stopped by on her way to work and told Rebecca, "Let him sleep. Tom's processing the last vestiges of that dark entity. Think of this rest as body detoxification. Max has been changing Tom at the molecular level and now Tom has to renew those cells."

"Right. I understand," Rebecca said, though she did not understand.

"I'll give him Reiki healing and aromatherapy, but mostly he needs rest."

Rebecca shivered. She was beginning to understand Sedona talk. "What can I do?"

"Send him strength. My meditation group was one level up on Bell Rock celebrating the Equinox as a time of change. I saw it all. My group helped me hold positive energy, but you and Tom did the hard work. The outcome could have gone either way. You remembered the diary.

Now hold his right hand." George took a green candle from her bag and lit it.

"That's what I did all night."

"Good. That's exactly what he needed." George laid her hand on Tom's forehead. He twitched. She closed her eyes and spoke so low Rebecca had to lean forward to hear her words. "Remember who you are. You are Tom. Rebecca is here. Sleep peacefully for as long as you need."

At her words Tom seemed to relax and sink deeper into the soft bed. "Rebecca," he whispered and fell asleep.

There was a quiet knock on the door and Aries tiptoed in. "Can I stay for a while?"

"Sure, honey. He's resting. Here, take his right hand. Talk to him." Rebecca patted Aries' head.

George led Rebecca outside. "You need rest, too. The battle was a rough experience for you."

"Crazed entities don't try to throw me off cliffs every day. The whole night is a blur." She shook her head. "Actually, I remember a lot that I wish were a blur."

On the porch Rebecca's father, mother, Cora, and Steve sat waiting for news. She told them, "He's fine. George says he's processing." They all nodded as if they understood.

Her father stood and hugged her. "Baby, this has been tough on you. Come out to my ranch and rest?"

"I want to stay close to Tom."

"We'll take him out there too."

"But what about everyone else?"

John looked at the group on the porch. "Bring 'em all. I have the room."

Rebecca looked at her mother. "Mom?"

"I'm staying at the ranch." Charlotte looked down, then raised her chin high. "John has asked me to move here from New York, ah, permanently," she added with a wink, "after a big romantic re-wedding, of course."

Rebecca grinned. She heard Aries call from inside and she and George went back in.

Tom was sitting on the side of the bed looking a little shaky but less pale and much more himself.

Rebecca sat next to him and hugged him. "I am so happy you are OK."

"I'm so happy you are safe. That bastard almost

killed you. I would never have forgiven myself. Damn him." Tom looked at George. "Please tell me there is only me in this body."

Rebecca looked anxiously at George. "Tom, I only want Tom."

George smiled. "Tom did damn him. That's exactly what happened. My guides tell me Max has finally gone over. He won't be back to bother you two." George smiled at their relieved expressions. "Tom, how do you feel?"

"I'm just me." Tom stood and walked to the table where a tray held the coffee. He seemed a little weak but very much himself. He poured himself a cup, then looked around.

"What do you want?" Rebecca rushed to his side. "Can I get you something?"

"A touch of rum for my coffee. Rebecca, my love."

Rebecca, George, and Aries looked shocked.

Tom laughed. "Only kidding." He took a long gulp of coffee, walked to Rebecca and put his arms around her. "But I have changed some. I feel very possessive."

She giggled.

"Very possessive. I don't want to let you go."

Epilogue: Summer Solstice

"I've quit Bankhead," Rebecca told her new sister-in-law, Arianna Paxton, on the perfect spring day she and Tom had chosen for their wedding on her father's Sedona ranch.

Arianna, Aries, and Rebecca's sister Scarlet wore bridesmaid dresses in pastels the colors of a western sunrise. Rebecca's creamy silk lace dress was topped with a matching mantilla that floated upon upswept blonde curls. Heather had commented that it was quite unsuitable for the least romantic woman in the world.

Tom was exuberant and relaxed in matching cream-colored silk. There were no rules in the bridal books for when the groom happened to be a guru. "And we're building a house and a channeling school here on John's land. I'll be at home writing, teaching, and spending time with Aries." He looked over at his daughter and Josch playing a computer game.

"What about your practice?" Rebecca's mother, offering a plate of tamales to George and Officer O'Hara, asked Rebecca.

"I'm opening a Sedona office." She indicated her clients drinking champagne on the patio. "I expect the wonderful three will sign with Dumaurier & Associates. Steve and Cora don't have a choice, especially now that they're starting their own movie company. And Babs really does love me. I'll bring in a couple of young attorneys and let them handle the New York and L.A. scenes. And, as soon as Heather finishes law school, she'll do most of the work."

Heather, sitting very close to Rebecca's brother Heathcliff, preened. "As if I haven't been doing all the work."

"Then what will you do?" Charlotte asked her daughter.

Rebecca took Tom's hand. "I'm going to write a romance novel."

## A word about the author...

Amber Polo has lived in more places than many people have visited. From careers as a librarian to a yoga teacher with a few stops in between, she most recently moved from Key Largo, Florida to Arizona near Sedona.

A recovering English major and librarian (two ways to make sure writing fiction is the last thing you'll ever do!), Amber turned to stories because she had no choice.

Her first novel, *Romancing Rebecca,* is a contemporary-comic-paranormal romance offering a lighthearted spicy look at romance authors and the business of the New Age.

*Relaxation One Breath at a Time*, her guided relaxation CD available through CDBaby.com and iTunes, is a twenty-minute listen guaranteed to solve plotting dilemmas or help you fall asleep.

Amber is working on a romantic suspense set in her neighborhood, an airpark on a mesa, and a sequel to *Romancing Rebecca* set in the Caribbean. Member of RWA and NARWA.

Visit Amber at www.amberpolo.com

Printed in the United States
116274LV00001B/31-54/P